IFRIT

An Element of Nostalgia

TELLUS IGNIS VENTUS AQUA

A Fantasy Fiction By: B. A. COOPER

First published in Great Britain in 2015
Published by: Benjamin A Cooper

Copyright © 2015 Benjamin A. Cooper
Cover Illustration copyright © Benjamin A. Cooper 2015

The moral right of the author has been asserted
a CIP catalogue record of this book is available from the
British Library

Paperback ISBN 978-0-9933186-0-3

Printed and Bound in Great Britain by Amazon UK
Distributed by Amazon UK

Cover Design by Benjamin A. Cooper and Laura Woolley

To David
For making me believe.

With Special Thanks to the Proof Readers
David Featonby, Aaron Henderson, Joanna Hayes & Rachael Haltam.

- Chapter I -
The Legend of Ifrit

"I thought everyone knew the story of Ifrit" Quin's expression portrayed his surprise at the lack of knowledge the wise Historian seemed to have. "In fact, more so now than ever" he added, as if to emphasis his point.

Smiling smugly and shaking his head gently in a patronising manner, Historian Nicolas looked directly into Quin's eyes and explained,

"You are a long way from home now my boy, and every story told holds one key element." Quin stared curiously at the Historian, waiting in anticipation for his next words "Experience! You cannot generalise History. You are Quin; tell me his story and how he came to be so far from home!"

"Well…" He said, knowing that his story began long before his life began, "The Legion of the Sky conquered all the continents of Gaia. It was respected, admired and feared by any and all who heard its name. A vast Kingdom was crafted and forged in the name of Duke Bartok the Heir to the Legion. The construction of such a Kingdom was entrusted to Bartok's most loyal subjects, Constan the Brave and his older brother, Ifrit the Humane. Within one-hundred and fifty days the Kingdom was complete." He continued "Only the noblest of men were granted the honour of living within the citadel that lay in the centre of the kingdom, surrounded by the fortified walls, which stood taller than five grown men. All the other citizens and allies to the Kingdom were given sanctuary within the commons outside the walls of the citadel. In the early days of Bartok's rule, and in his absence, Ifrit the Humane took it upon himself to take leadership of the Kingdom with the protection of Constan the Brave, who commanded the greatest army the lands of Gaia had ever seen.

After leaving the Kingdom for the final battle that ended 'The War of the Three Legions', Constan the Brave returned home to the Kingdom, joined with Lady Sophia the Wise in union and bore his heritage, his son Dion the Courageous and daughter Alexandria the Fated.

Meanwhile, Duke Bartok endured a many hundred days of careful negotiations with the leaders of the other Legions at the newly constructed Legion Halls that lay on the outskirts of the Kingdom borders. Eventually, cutting their losses, the leaders gave in to Duke Bartok's demands to surrender and he was finally able to return home to claim the crown, the throne, and more importantly to give the Kingdom a name. However, during the crowning ceremony Ifrit spoke out against Duke Bartok and declared that Constan should be crowned King. He claimed that it was Constan who had won the war against the Legions and, while Duke Bartok idly sat by discussing relations with their conquered enemies, Constan protected the Kingdom from the many attacks that took place in the Dukes absence, ensuring the construction of the Kingdom by fending off those who would seek to crush it. The citizens of the Kingdom would be given a vote on who would be crowned their King.

Enraged by his loss, Bartok vowed that he would have his revenge on the newly crowned 'King Constan' and abandoned the Kingdom to travel north into the Magus Lands taking his few devoted followers with him."

Quin paused for a moment, suddenly becoming very aware of his surroundings as his story progressed towards the shocking truth. Surveying the area he watched the citizens going about their daily lives, and eyeballed the Historian, who stood in draped woollen robes, cradled in the wings of the gigantic monument of a golden phoenix, which marked the centre of the garrison. Feeling a little out of place he realised that his thick, black leather armour and accompanying sword, which was holstered on his belt, made him look suspicious. Catching a glimpse of shimmering armour out the corner of his eye, he noticed that the few guards that patrolled the Garrison were now stood with him in their sights, glaring at him as if waiting for him to make the slightest wrong move. To make sure the Historian was still listening, and to curb any further suspicion, he invited Historian Nicolas to sit with him on the small bench that lay beneath the Phoenix' gaze. Convinced that all was well, he lowered his voice slightly as he continued with his account.

"Countless days passed and all was peaceful. The lands around the Kingdom were stunningly beautiful. Constan would spend much of his time with his children, running through the meadows and exploring the cool waters of the many streams that ran through the countryside.

And then one day, without warning, an army of Bartok's followers made siege to the Kingdom. King Constan, who was returning with Ifrit from his deliberations at the Legion Hall's, ordered Ifrit to run ahead and protect his family at all costs and to escort them to safety inside the palace. True to his word, Ifrit valiantly fought his way through the multitude of men in his path. Upon reaching the citadel, he had to find Queen Sophia the

Wise and her children and escort them to the Throne room within the fortified Palace walls.

After a long and rigorous search, Ifrit eventually found the family guarded by a handful of noble Knights inside The Hall of Feasts. He ordered the Knights to take up arms and aid Constan in the fight against the invaders. The Queen joined Ifrit and fled towards the palace with her children, and as they dashed through the citadel Ifrit used himself as a human shield against any attackers; standing in harm's way whilst the Queen and her children made an escape into the palace.

However, as they reached the Palace doors and Ifrit thought all was safe, he let his guard down. Little did he know one of the invading archers stood watching at a safe distance, concealed on top of the citadels fortified wall! Firing a single arrow, it struck Princess Alexandria in the chest. In panic, Ifrit immediately ran into the palace with the Queen and Dion, leaving Alexandria outside, alone and dying.

Inside the throne room the Queen was overwrought with hysterics that Ifrit did not even attempt to save Alexandria and ruthlessly branded him a coward and swore that he would never be forgiven as he blocked her from leaving the throne room to return to Alexandria's side.

A new day dawned in the Kingdom and, praise be to the heavens, the battle for the Kingdom was won. But it was at a great price. Constan burst into the palace aggrieved, carrying the body of Alexandria in his arms. Delicately laying her down on the floor, beside himself with grief, he mourned her death with his wife and son. Taking only a single moment to speak to his finest Knight, he ordered that the Kingdom henceforth shall be known as 'the Kingdom of Alexandria', so that his daughter may never be forgotten.

Later, hearing of Ifrit's apparent cowardice from the Queen, Constan shunned his brother and banished him to a lifetime in the dungeons, claiming that death was too good for him. Instead he would serve a lifetime of guilt for his betrayal to his brother, the Kingdom, and most of all, his beloved daughter, Alexandria.

Seven hundred and thirty two days passed, as Ifrit stared at the ever decaying walls of his cell with a single score marking each day spent within the walls, watching prisoner after prisoner come and go, each one sent to die, be it for treason, theft, or, most severely of all, for the possession of magic. With each passing day Ifrit's anger and hatred for his brother grew, until it consumed his very soul. Soon

Ifrit's only thoughts dwelled, not on guilt for Alexandria's death, but with an overwhelming, burning desire to see Constan and his family suffer for their betrayal, just as he had, and ultimately their slow and agonising deaths.

On one fateful day a celebration disturbed Ifrit's thoughts, as the townspeople cheered and paraded through the citadel above the dungeons. It was not long before Ifrit realised that someone of great importance had been captured and sentenced to death, or had already been killed by Constan and his men. Soon after Ifrit discovered that it was Bartok himself that had been captured and, by some stroke of fate, had been thrown into the cell next to him.

Battered and bruised, Bartok could barely speak. Knowing that his time was short he strained himself to inform Ifrit of his scheme. He explained how he had allowed himself to be captured for a very important purpose. During his adventures in the Magus Lands, Bartok had discovered a powerful Seer, a human with magical powers that gave him the ability to see many versions of the future. This seer foretold that Ifrit's journey had just begun and the lands of Gaia would one day be under his rule as a 'Mighty Overlord'. The seer warned that there would be a great cost for this victory, and told Bartok that he must allow Constan to kill him for the chance to set Ifrit free from his prison.

Bartok handed Ifrit the Lost Jewel of Martialis telling him that it was forged by a single tear of remorse from a mighty warlord. Only Ifrit had the power to harness the full potential of the jewel's special power that would guide him to his destiny. Ifrit cautiously took the jewel and Bartok used the last ounce of his strength to blast open Ifrit's cell door. He left Ifrit with one more instruction. He must travel to the furthest corner of the Northern Magus Lands and find the entrance to what would become his new Kingdom, Agartha. There, his fate awaited him. With that Bartok died and Ifrit fled the Kingdom of Alexandria.

It was not long before King Constan discovered his brother's escape. Without hesitation, The Knights of Alexandria were despatched to find Ifrit and return him to the Kingdom for the harshest of punishments, followed by slow execution.

Not long after Ifrit had begun his fated journey he was greeted by a wolf and a woodpecker. The Jewel of Martialis gave Ifrit the ability to communicate with these creatures; the Wolf introduced himself as 'Fenrir' and the Woodpecker as 'Picus'.

Fenrir was a ferocious beast, twice the size of any wolf and thrice as ugly, with thick black fur that could withstand the sharpest blades edges, teeth as large as your hand that could easily tear the meat off your bones and breath that reeked of death. Picus on the other hand was agile and wise and, unlike Fenrir, elegantly beautiful with shimmering feathers that gleamed in the sun, striking warmth into the coldest hearts of the hardest brutes. An elegant red stripe flowed from his beak and down his back, separating the black feathers that made up the primary colour of this seemingly sweet bird. Ifrit's new companions explained to him that the Jewel of Martialis was both a gift and curse. The jewel had already bound their souls together in a most mysterious way, and only death could separate them.

Picus and Fenrir accompanied Ifrit through the Northern Magus Lands; travelling both day and night through rough and inhospitable terrain, seemingly endless deserts and the most incredible storms any of them had ever experienced, until they finally reached the cave of Agartha. Ifrit was quick to enter the cave to see his future Kingdom with his own eyes. Travelling deeper and deeper into the earth, Ifrit could clearly see a rise in temperature as the walls progressively glowed and flamed the further they went. Yet, to his amazement Ifrit, Fenrir and Picus could not feel the heat, not even when they touched the flames. Ifrit could only conclude that this was the magic of The Jewel of Martialis.

Upon successfully reaching the very centre of the planet Ifrit stared in utter amazement as a Seer stood before him. This Seer did not speak, but simply pointed at the Jewel of Martialis and then pointed to where the centre of gravity itself was. Without hesitation Ifrit thrust the Jewel into the centre of gravity and stepped back in anticipation. The jewel began to glow with a blinding white light that consumed the shadows, striking deeply into the soul of Ifrit. An immense pain no mortal man could ever hope to withstand flooded through him and his companions. As their souls merged further into Ifrit's they joined mentally and physically too, causing Ifrit to transform into what would be a new race that would rise to power against the Kingdom of Alexandria. His jaw and nose protruded to form a snout while masses of thick black fur began to grow all over his body. His hands and feet turned to claws, and wings began to sprout from his spine. Each part of the transformation cracked his bones and reshaped his physical being while Ifrit screamed out in pain and begged the seer to kill him, rather than let him continue with the torture. But it was too late, the transformation was nearly complete and his eyes tinted yellow and the black of his eyes reshaped to vertical slits. Finally the pain was over, as Ifrit panted and shuddered all over from the shock. Slowly standing he looked at his clawed hands in disgust, realising he had transformed into some kind of freakish monster. Taking a deep breath Ifrit released a mighty roar that shook the cave violently as the final part of his transformation flowed from his snout and down his spine and his fur changed to a flowing stripe of red.

Ifrit stood alone; no longer human but the result of an unquestionable magic. In an instant, Fenrir and Picus were banished by the power of the Jewel of Martialis. His soul companions were now cursed to roam the lands of Gaia alone forever. Although this was just the beginning of the price Ifrit would pay for such a power, for while the immortal Ifrit lives none shall ever find eternal rest.

As immortal ruler of Agartha, Ifrit now possessed the power to create his own kin, by feeding his followers with a single drop of his blood. Gradually, group by group, Bartok's scattered followers began to come together after hearing the divine call from the Jewel of Martialis. Without question they answered the call, mindlessly wandering into Agartha to drink the blood of Ifrit, transforming them into

Ifrit's kin, naming themselves 'The Ifryte'. Within Thirty days Ifrit had raised a powerfully magical army of Ifryte and began his assault on the Kingdom of Alexandria.

Upon his arrival at the Kingdom, Ifrit called out to Constan and challenged him to the Knights Duel; which was simply a more elegant way of saying 'a fight to the death'. However, it was Dion who answered Ifrit's challenge by informing him that King Constan and Queen Sophia had unexpectedly died together shortly after Ifrit's escape from the dungeon. It was no coincidence that Ifrit's mortal enemies, and the only reason for him becoming such a beast, had died around the same time as he became immortal. It was at that moment that Ifrit realised the price he would pay for his 'gift' of immortality would see no end. Angered that he could never truly have the chance to exact his revenge, Ifrit commanded his army to destroy Alexandria leaving no survivors; to hunt them down and slaughter every last one of them. Ifrit then returned to Agartha, never to be seen again. Just as quickly as each Ifryte was slain, another one arrived to take its place and continue the assault. That war waged on for seven thousand long days and then one day it just suddenly ended…"

There was a moment of silence as Quin's expression turned to one of great sadness

"I have heard the story many times" said Historian Nicolas, attempting to break the silence and interrupt the thoughts going through Quin's mind that were clearly upsetting him, "But others have never told it as well as you, perhaps you are a scribe or scholar?" Yet Quin's expression persisted as he gazed into the distance and confessed.

"No, I am a Blacksmith. Well - I was, before my life was thrown into disarray."

"No less than three thousands days had passed since the last wave of Ifryte attacked, without so much as a hint of Ifrit or his army returning. As a young boy I saw only one Ifryte, who wandered into Alexandrian territory alone and unarmed, even though it posed no immediate threat it was still quickly slain before the citizens of Alexandria. Congregating around the guillotine they watched as the beasts head was separated from its body. I was very young and my mother discouraged me from watching, but regardless of her warning I still joined the congregation and found it to be utterly terrifying. The beast truly did fit the descriptions told in the old Ifrit legend, a mix of human, wolf and bird. Truly beastly looking, I still recall the fear I saw in its eyes during its last few moments, a sense of sympathy washed over me as its life was abruptly ended. Although I could not understand it then, I now know that it was for the safety of all Alexandria.

Since that day, the proud Kingdom of Alexandria lived in peace. Ruled over by King Dion and his only child Prince Reaven, who now commanded the noble Knights of Alexandria; however there was not much commanding to be done, after all, we had not seen any such war or battle in our lands since the days of Ifrit's invasions abruptly ended. Because of Bartok's actions magic was now completely outlawed, since Dion blamed magic for the loss of his parents and also his late wife, Queen Thea, who is rumoured to have been killed by magic. No-one knows the true story of how she actually died beyond mere speculations and wives tales.

King Dion was relentless in his fight against magic. Naturally, if you cannot understand it then it is to be feared, or at least that is the outlook Dion had, not that he would have ever admitted being afraid. Merely having this opinion would have been treason against the Kingdom. But I cannot help feeling that way because I am one with magic and I have a fuller understanding of it, I know it is nothing to be afraid of. I always had the ability to harness the power of the elements and I have always wondered, 'What is there to fear?' Whenever I use my magic I feel at peace. The wind flows through me, fire warms my heart, water sustains me and the earth binds it all together and strengthens my resolve. A truly wonderful feeling that gives my life meaning! How anything like that could be feared by the ruler of a mighty Kingdom such as Alexandria, I shall never understand…"

Historian Nicolas brashly hushed Quin,

"Are you stricken with madness boy? You should not speak so openly about-" Lowering his voice and leaning closer to him, Nicolas took a moment to check for anyone who might be listening. Satisfied that no-one was, he continued,

"...Magic!"

Quin suddenly became extremely aware of his surroundings, paranoid that the passing citizens were glaring at him in fear of him and his magic. Even though he was a great distance away from the Alexandrian border and the oppressive rules enforced by King Dion, it appeared that the human intolerance of magic spanned much further than he had previously thought.

"Come with me boy," Historian Nicolas whispered as he began to walk away, "You should continue your story somewhere a little more - private!"

The Historian invited Quin into his tattered old hovel, sitting him down at the rickety old table in the centre of the room and pouring him a tankard of water, he could see that the life of an Historian was a poor one and felt comforted in the knowledge that someone as poor as this would never be taken seriously if he was to tell anyone that he had magic. Confident in his assumption, he felt comfortable openly confiding in the Historian and even if Nicolas was to eventually turn-coat on him, his obligation to pass on his story so that Alexandria would live on forever in the minds of a mankind was all that mattered to him. Furthermore, should he perish before he made it back to Alexandria, King Dion would inevitably discover the news that he was reporting.

Settling down at the table, Historian Nicolas placed a plate of bread in front of Quin.

"Eat. You must be hungry."

Quin gratefully grabbed a slice of bread and ate it with an air of elegance, even though he was clearly starving from days without sustenance.

"I think I have been asking the wrong questions of you young man," Nicolas exclaimed, while looking into Quin's ethereal green eyes as he shamefully lowered his head and focused on the plate in front of him. A feeling of embarrassment came over Quin as he knew his dirty little secret was out and realised that he was now totally alone in the world, surrounded by those who would condemn him for possessing magic. He almost felt as if he stood naked in the middle of the town, completely vulnerable and shamed. Nicolas carefully reached out his hand and pushed Quin's chin up, almost forcing their eyes to meet.

"I think the question I should be asking is probably the most simple. Who are you?" Quin took a moment to collect his thoughts while slumping back into his chair, and attempted to find a suitable place from where to continue his story.

"My name is Quin. I am the son of Verrier, the most prestigious Blacksmith in Alexandria. My elder brother Origen and I had been trained in the art of crafting weapons and armour since the day we were born, but it saddens me to speak of such times. My father was a hard man, stern and almost without love for us, a largely built masculine man who always acted with logic and reason, never emotion. As a result of his stubbornness, he felt it was his duty to fight for Constan during the time of Ifrit's assault. Regretfully, he died fighting for his Kingdom during the fifth wave of the second siege, which is why both Origen and I took it upon ourselves to ensure we never spoke of nor used our powers, but instead kept it a secret to maintain our father's honour, for he too feared us. Unfortunately, I can only speak for myself when I state that we both hid our powers. You see, Origen had different ideas and would use his powers quite freely. It was little wonder that he was never caught and hanged as a result of his carelessness. Origen strongly believed that the King could not capture him, let alone execute him, because his powers were too strong for a mere human he used to say. I sometimes questioned that word - 'human'. Are we really more than ordinary people or are we cursed or sick? Am I really all that different, or are we just connected to Gaia in different ways?

As a child I would often sit in the courtyard watching other people and perceived their professions and knowledge as different forms of magic. Take the physician for example: I used to think that he was blessed with a power too; the power of knowledge, wisdom and healing. Then there were the farmers; blessed with the power of creating new life through nature's spirit. Perhaps I was so desperate to fit in that I wanted them to have magic, so I did not feel so alone and secluded from everyone else."

Fascinated by Quin's words, Nicolas had an expression of pure joy on his face as he excitedly chirped "So you and your brother were born with these powers? You did not inherit them from relics or some other form of magical objects?" He paused for a moment, "And your father and mother were not one with magic either - fascinating." Without giving Quin the chance to reply, Nicolas went on "Continue your story, please". Before he continued he watched Nicolas as his eyes scoured the building, flicking from pillar to post. Something was clearly going through his mind and he hoped that in time his story would encourage Nicolas to share this knowledge.

"Since the passing of my father and my coming of age, the King was given the task of selecting a new Blacksmith to serve as the royal forge man. Fortunately, thanks to my father our family home was the closest forge to the Citadel and therefore most likely to be selected, which left only two possible candidates – Origen or me.

When Origen refused his candidacy it fell to me, and it was my privilege to have been selected to succeed my father in becoming the Blacksmith for the Royal Household. I had heard many great things about Prince Reaven and although I had never had the honour of meeting him in person. He was said to be kind and caring, but strong and willing too. I was looking forward to meeting such a man and it was my hope that one day I would have a good enough relationship with the Prince to tell him of my magic and then, with his blessing, I might join his ranks as one of the noble Knights of Alexandria, as a powerful sorcerer. Then I would complete that which my father started; to become a noble family.

I spent an entire day and most of the night working on the perfect swords for both the King and the Prince.

Forged from Adamantine ore and a drop of my own blood, I imbued each sword with elemental power. The power of these swords would be controlled by my will alone, so that in battle I would be able to command the swords to release incredible magic to assist in thwarting our common enemies, whilst maintaining the secrecy of my magic. I could not tell anyone of the swords powers as it would raise concerns about sorcery and I may have been discovered. So I merely forged them a generous gift - with a hidden meaning."

Historian Nicolas leapt to his feet and rushed over to a small shelf full of books that barely gripped the wall. Slowly reading the titles, he located a book called 'The Origins of Magic'. Pulling it out he brought down the shelf with it. It was evident that Nicolas had something perplexing on his mind as his book collection fell to the floor and some were even damaged, yet he did not seem to care. Slamming his book down on the table, Historian Nicolas began to frantically flick through the pages as if searching for an antidote after being bitten by a deadly Amphista serpent. Muttering a few words from various pages, he almost acted as if he had forgotten Quin was even there. Curiously, Quin peered over at the book and attempted to see what Nicolas was so engrossed in.

However it was not long before he remembered that he was never taught the art of calligraphy and therefore couldn't read.

"What are you reading?" He asked, somewhat frustrated that he could not find out for himself. But Nicolas appeared to ignore his question and continued to read. Quin began to feel somewhat uncomfortable sitting in the Historian's home, like he had become an unwelcomed guest.

"Ah-ha!" Nicolas suddenly shouted, breaking the awkward silence and startling Quin all at once. Turning the book around and sliding it under Quin's nose, Nicolas went on. "So it is possible. You can be born with magic!" looking down at the book, Quin could only see a piece of parchment with a picture of some kind of crystal and lots of words that he knew he had no hope of understanding.

"I- I cannot," Quin mumbled, lowering his head in shame yet again. Laughing out loud, Nicolas unintentionally patronised him.

"You have all this magic, yet you lack the basic understanding of standard calligraphy?" Quin's expression turned to a stern and disapproving glare. Realising that he was being condescending, Nicolas attempted to apologise and justify his reaction. "Now I understand why you sought me out. Without the ability to record the story yourself, you had to find someone that could. Am I correct?"

Quin's expression changed to one of guilt, feeling he had embarrassed Nicolas. For his benefit Nicolas read, "The book states:

Beyond the tale of Gaia and Tartaros, the Telchines were the only beings born of magic. They were the original creators of all enchanted relics and crystals. Magic is something that can only be acquired by one with the foolishness to seek it. A Magical relic cannot be created by any other being and the magic will not be passed on to offspring by the acquisitioned. Magic will not only result in a blessing for all Magic comes at a cost. Such costs vary and will never consist of mere possession. To obtain magic through acquisition has been described as more of a curse than a blessing".

Horrified by the words that Quin was hearing, a gutting realisation struck him; the swords he made for the King and Prince were cursed!

"Are you telling me that I cursed the King and Prince by giving them those swords?" he exclaimed, completely mortified with himself.

"I cannot say for certain. As you stated, you had complete control over the swords' powers and therefore you did not actually give magic to the King and Prince. Although what effect the swords may have on them long term, I would not dare guess."

Quin jumped to his feet, concerned for the safety of the Kings life and any who would wield the cursed weapons.

"I must return to Alexandria at once! If what you say is true, then many lives could be in danger and their blood will be on my hands."

Attempting to calm Quin down, Nicolas tried to reason with him. "Quin, you walked into the Phoenix Garrison a few days after a handful of half dead refugees from Alexandria arrived. I watched as you searched the Garrison for something, or perhaps someone. You stood and listened to me telling my tales for three days before you eventually spoke to me. Perhaps you were waiting for my audience to disperse before you could tell me your tale? You have placed your life at great risk by telling me that you are one with magic." Sighing deeply, Nicolas felt that his words would not change Quin's mind, however he had one last thing to say before he gave up. "If you must leave, then please return here and finish your story. I feel that it is extremely important otherwise you would not have sought me out. I only fear that you may not make it back to your Kingdom and the story that you wanted to tell me will die with you!"

Quin paused as his thoughts shifted to a sense of duty, conflicted by his duty to protect the people of Alexandria and his duty to the importance of his story, and furthermore knowing that the news of the Prince would die with him if he was to perish on his return to Alexandria. He realised that he had no choice but to finish his story before he could return to Alexandria.

- Chapter III -
A Royal Ass!

"Morning had arrived, after a long and searing night of forging two swords to present to the King and Prince. I was on my way to meet the nobles of Alexandria. It was an overwhelming honour to be walking through the gates from the lower town into the grounds of the citadel for the very first time.

Taking in every detail of its glory, it was hard to believe that on the other side of a single gate could be an entirely different world. The noblemen and their ladies dressed with such elegance. Impressive Knights with their gleaming armour, some still wielded weapons forged by my father possibly more than a thousand days past, perfectly shining and sharp as the day they were forged. If there was one thing that was certain, these people took great pride in the way they looked and presented themselves within the grounds of the grand citadel although it was no surprise; always being under the watchful eyes of the King.

I eventually arrived at the grand doors of the palace, which stood tall, beaming the brightest white you could ever hope to see. The sun reflected off these portals with such magnificence, as if touched with divinity. It was almost as if I had died and was walking through the doors of the heavens into Gaia's embrace and what felt like a lifetime standing at the doors, was soon ended as the sound of laughter and taunts caught my attention as a group of noblemen mockingly pushed a lower town civilian around. The guards stood by and watched, and they too laughed at the 'peasant's' expense. If I was to become a nobleman, I felt that it was my duty to put a stop to such actions. Without another thought I soon found myself face to face with these thugs.

Attempting to sound mature and noble myself, I stood firmly and asked the men politely to let the citizen go. It was almost as if they had just heard an expletive as they bitterly snapped their heads round to glare at me. Suddenly I felt rather foolish! The ring leader of the group looked at me, as if I were a piece of excrement on his boot. I became very aware of my clothing and the way I looked compared to these nobles, I was nothing in comparison to anyone in the citadel and I stood out like black crow among snowy white doves. Answering back, the leader of the group spoke out and told me to move along as it 'does not concern peasants'. I was embarrassed, and a little shocked that he would use such a word. It seemed that the honour of being a nobleman also came with an abundance of arrogance. It was difficult to control my temper and not simply set this man ablaze with my magic, although I knew I could not. Instead I attempted to regain my pride by telling him who I was and the importance of my skills of crafting the finest weapons and armour. Before I could finish my sentence, the pig headed leader interrupted me and exclaimed that he did not care who I was, quickly following up with the threat of smashing my teeth in with a dull hilt, if I did not move on.

It was blatantly obvious that this man was the most arrogant of them all, if only he knew who he was dealing with. For a moment, I actually stopped to thank the heavens that I was chosen for this task and not Origen. For if Origen was in my position, I know for a fact he would have used his magic to shred them into tiny pieces, merely for looking down on him.

With that in mind, I felt it only wise to warn this arrogant ass that he should be careful with whom he threatens and that he had no idea of what I could do to him. My attempts to calm the situation seemed to have had the opposite effect; however the guards just laughed and the other noblemen around encouraged the leader to teach me some manners, the leader moved towards me and gave me the chance of the first hit before he put me down. Naturally without thinking of the consequences I was only too pleased to throw a punch with all the rage I had in me. Landing my fist directly in his face, he dropped straight to the floor. All the guards laughed and I felt a sense of accomplishment and pride. Little did I know they were actually laughing at me, not with me! As the leader rose to his feet he brushed himself down and called the guards over ordering them to arrest me. Of course I laughed in return and taunted the idiot, as I knew only the royal family had the authority to so order the guards. I mocked 'Who do you think you are, the King?' Of course you could almost predict that he would now identify himself 'No, I am the Prince, Reaven!' I quickly reflected on the events that should have happened. I was to simply go into the palace, present the swords and leave. Instead I assaulted the Prince and earned myself a place in the dungeon, I could not have planned it any worse!

I was thrown into the cell face first onto the floor. Fearing that I was going to be hanged. While I sat alone I thought about what I was going to say to the Prince when he came to gloat of his victory. Although it was not long before my attention was drawn to the wall of my cell. It was covered in carvings: four vertical lines with a single horizontal line through them, the same carving over and over again. There were hundreds of them covering the wall from top to bottom. I had to wonder to myself where they had come from. Glancing over at the cell door as a guard sauntered by, whistling an old death tune, I noticed there were scorch marks around the lock as if it had been blasted, probably with magic. A cold chill flowed through me and down my spine as I realised that the cell I was sat in was almost certainly the same cell that Ifrit was placed in so very long ago. I could only assume that the carvings on the wall were some sort of depiction of how long he had been languishing in the cell. I began to fear that this cell was reserved for the most severe punishments. I was afraid I was about to be tortured or would simply be left to rot. I remember the distant sound of gates opening and footsteps growing ever closer to my cell. I hoped it would be my family, come to free me. With each step that echoed through the dungeon, like a beating drum, my heart began to thump. The footsteps stopped outside my cell, I gazed upon the gloriously presented man stood before me. He wore black leather boots, shiny as polished metal, trousers sewn with expert tailoring and a vestment fit for the King. Seeing the red cape draped over the man's shoulders - It was the King!

I immediately stood to attention and dusting myself down. Then bowed my head to honour the Kings' presence. In a very bland and uninterested way, the King asked for my name. Naturally I was terrified and stuttered my words and practically belched my name at the King. Unimpressed, the King went on to ask me why I had entered the citadel armed with two blades and assaulted the Prince. Once again in a complete babble, I attempted to explain that the swords were a gift and that I was to be my father's successor as the royal Blacksmith. I felt I had no other choice but to go on to explain that I was only trying to do the right thing by putting a stop to the group of men tormenting other citizen; which resulted in me, albeit unknowingly, punching the Prince. Oddly, the King smiled and ordered the guards to release me. I grovelled pathetically thanking the King while bowing repeatedly like a moron, before swiftly walking towards the exit of the dungeon. However, before I could escape this most uncomfortable situation, the King called out to me to seal his stamp of authority and put me back in my place. He told me that I was nothing more than a peasant and while within the citadel I held no authority. I was shocked to hear him continue that should I see a person being murdered in the street, I am to go about my own business. 'That is the duty of a peasant,' he commanded of me. I felt that his pig headed words did not deserve dignifying with a response. So I simply bowed my head, retrieved my swords, and left.

As I emerged from the dark dungeon, back out into the light of the citadel, I bumped into a familiar face, which immediately calmed my nerves. It was Asha, in my opinion the most beautiful girl in the whole Kingdom. Calling out to me, she looked pleased as she walked over to greet me. We stood and spoke for a while about how my day had been; sadly it was not a pleasant story on my part. But as always, Asha would listen, laughing at my misfortune, all the while telling me that everything would be ok. She always looked on the brighter side of life. Asha was a servant of the royal family and would spend her days in the kitchen with the chef, assisting in any way she could. Her main duty was to deliver the dishes to the royal banquet hall where the noble Knights would sit alongside the royal family and tell war stories while scoffing down their food and drink. They would always leave as much mess as they liked for Asha to then go and clean up after they were done. I used to think that it was a crime for a lady such as Asha to have to clean up after those royal asses; but she always seemed so happy to do it.

I often imagined running away and finding a magical abandoned castle in the northern magus lands where I would be crowned King and Asha my Queen. Her beautiful deep brown eyes shone like the crown jewels that sat upon her flowing black hair and would have been complimented by a royal adaptation of that sky blue dress she always wore whilst in the palace. As a boy I would listen to Asha's music while she sat outside the castle gates under her special tree playing her flute. She never knew I was listening, as I would sit high in the tree branches where she sat in the cool shade of the summer days. I would watch the birds swooping and soaring in the sky above her, as if dancing to her magical songs. I used to think she was an angel sent from the heavens, with the power to bring happiness and harmony to any heart worthy of hearing her music.

Before I knew it, the day was getting on and still I had not given my gifts to the Prince or the King. Reluctantly, I had to bid Asha farewell and headed to the training grounds where I would find the Prince, humbly extend an apology and present him with the sword I had especially crafted for him.

Arriving at the training grounds I was impressed with the skills of the Prince's swordsmanship. I stood and watched him tackle three armed men all at once; however I noticed that he was not quite getting the correct use out of the balance of his sword, although I knew it would not be wise to mention it. The Prince finished training with the noble Knights, walking over to the weapon racks to set his sword down; he spotted me and with a grin began to walk towards me. I hoped he was coming over to apologise, but then I realised that was just wishful thinking.

As the Prince got within speaking distance he began by taunting me about being let out of the cells by the King. Of course I was not in any rush to go back to the cells and so I felt the obvious thing to do was to apologise for my earlier actions in the hope that the Prince would be as noble as people say and return the favour of the apology. Oddly; it felt easy to say sorry, because in the back of my mind I knew I did not really mean it. Naturally being the arrogant ass I suspected he was, he simply laughed in my face and claimed that he had felt girls hit harder. Knowing I probably was not going to get any kind of apology from this man, I felt I should just present him with his sword and beg my leave.

Pulling the sword from its scabbard, I described the skill and intricacy of the crafting process. To my surprise, the Prince seemed interested and getting down on one knee I held the blade out with both hands, bowed my head and presented the sword to him. Clearly mesmerised by the weapon, the Prince slowly grasped the hilt and took it from me, not taking his eyes away for one moment. I felt this was as good a time as any to leave. Rising to my feet, I bowed my head once again and turned to walk away. I should have known it would not have been that easy.

The Prince stopped me and claimed he needed to test the blade to see if it really was as good as I claimed. Being a peasant he would naturally have assumed that my skills as a Blacksmith would be as crude as was my lowly class. The Prince invited me to grab myself a sword and shield, and train with him. My initial thought was to take up arms and put him to shame, but I knew that would result in being thrown back into the cells. However after the Kings warning, I was quite confident that I would be adding more carvings to the walls of that cell as I would spend the rest of my life in custody. I humbly declined the Prince's offer and with a sarcastic tone, added that I would not wish to be thrown back into the dungeon for harming the Prince yet again.

I bowed my head and once again turned to walk away from a situation that could potentially get out of hand, however it seemed the Prince had not yet finished with me. Cruelly taunting me he claimed I would not be up to the challenge just as my father was not. Insulting my father's memory hit the rawest nerve and in a blind rage at his lack of respect for my father, I turned and walked towards the weapon racks grabbing myself a sword. Taking up the fight, I quickly had to raise my sword as the Prince had already started his assault. Fighting back without any thought of tactics, but merely a rage to see the Prince fail, I swung the blade randomly, as the Prince dodged and blocked each attempt I made, a tactic which only served to feed my anger even more. As the wrath inside me grew, I felt a burning rage flowing through my veins and the Prince's sword began to glow with the power of fire. For the first time in my life I feared I was losing control over my feelings and emotions and above all, my powers. Stepping back, I knew I had to calm myself quickly to regain control. The sudden flow of adrenaline of battle against my inner self resulted in my whole body shaking. My throat constricted and I found it hard to breathe while tears welled up and fell from my eyes. In a final attempt to control myself I lowered my sword to forfeit the fight. However, the Prince continued darting towards me and slammed his fist into my chest, knocking me brutally to the ground. The guards and Knights cheered their Prince, as I lay on the floor, gasping for air while still trying to calm myself down.

I did not have time to get myself up before the guards grabbed me and started dragging me away to the dungeons. The only thought going through my mind was 'what a complete royal ass'. But before the guards had a chance to lead me out of the grounds, the Prince stopped them in their tracks and commanded them to release me. Without any hesitation, the guards loosened their grip and threw me back to the ground. I felt dishonoured; and more than that, I felt I had shamed my father's memory and honour.

The Prince came over to me and offered a helping hand. Reaching out and grabbing it he quickly pulled me to my feet. Still angry, I bit my tongue, so that I did not say anything that would get me into further trouble. The Prince looked directly into tear stained eyes and explained that, in truth, he thought my father was a brave and honourable man and a great loss to the Kingdom of Alexandria. He advised me to learn to control my emotions, as they serve no purpose in battle and would as likely get me killed. I wondered if he was trying to taunt me or if he had a hidden agenda; either way, I simply thanked the Prince and waited for him to say something else. A few moments passed as the Prince gazed at me and patted my shoulder to comfort me. Raising his voice so that all the other Knights could hear him, he finished our encounter. 'What are you waiting for, a medal? Go on, go and make weapons or do whatever it is Blacksmiths do in their lives'. I wanted to think he was a noble and kind man, but at that moment I had just one opinion of him. He was indeed a complete royal ass!

As each of the many days passed, I was called back to the training grounds to meet with the Prince and his Knights. After each session I was ordered to replace any damaged weapons and repair any that could be mended or re-forged. Although I did not have much of a chance to interact with these noblemen, I learnt much about the art of war by watching all their different tactics; The appropriately named Sir Benjamin the 'Right-Hand' refused to wield anything in his left hand and used brute strength to conquer his opponents, whereas Prince Reaven and Sir Leander the Brave-Heart used speed and cunning to outwit theirs. Taking all this into consideration, I crafted customised weapons for each of the Knights based on their fighting style. When presenting these weapons I gave the Knight an explanation about how I crafted it because of the way they fought. At first the Knights saw this as patronising, but as they used them they came to understand that the weapons I was forging for them were truly outstanding and worked just as I had told them. Within a few days the Knights skills had increased to the same level as Prince Reaven, as they became challenging opponents in the training grounds. This pleased the Prince, and as time went on, he began to treat me with a little less arrogance and more like one of his noblemen, and I dare say, as a trusted friend. Even though he still claimed I was an idiot and his compliments were always very back-handed. Over time I came to understand that it was just the Prince's way of being kind, but without treating me as anyone above my class.

I truly felt that soon I would be seen as a nobleman and would have my family honoured with a grant from King Dion himself. I was well aware that the King was not in the habit of giving out such grants without very serious consideration but I held hope in my heart that the Prince would help him with the decision thus giving the King the reasons he needed to be benevolent.

Sadly, I could not foresee the most terrible events about to descend upon the Kingdom. Had I known what was coming in just a few more days, I dare say I would have enchanted all the weapons of the Knights of Alexandria. Furthermore I would have revealed myself as a sorcerer to the Prince, in the hope that we could have stopped the Kingdoms demise. I cannot help but feel responsible for the Kingdom falling… I know I could have done more to prevent it. I could have joined Origen and used my magic in public for the greater good. It saddens me to think of what I did, what I sacrificed, and lost!"

"Roughly Twenty days ago the attack on Alexandria began. Ifrit's army had returned, but this time it seemed they had no intention of leaving without control of Alexandria. They would take it, or they would destroy it!

The morning began much like any other. The sun was shining down on the fields which were as lush and beautiful as ever. The citizens of the lower town were bustling about earning their daily bread from their various trades as always, and I was on my way to the training ground within the citadel, after having a wonderful night's sleep. For the first time in around eighty days I was given the night off from forging and was blessed with the great honour of joining the noblemen for a feast in the royal banquet hall, in celebration of Prince Reaven's name day. It was a truly wonderful night, we drank ales and wines, overindulging on the finest hog roast and drunkenly sang the songs of old; almost as if camping out around a fire in the deep forests of Alexandria. I must confess I did not feel completely relaxed as I was not a nobleman myself, although I was being treated like one by Asha. She kept my tankard full of ale and my plate piled with meat, fruit and bread, and each time she came over to me I was greeted with her beautiful smile. I stayed up until all of the noblemen and the royal family had retired to their chambers, for when they were all gone I knew that Asha would return to clean up. I spied as she left the Hall to get her broom and whilst all was quiet I used my magic. With a gust of air I created a small tornado, which sucked up all of the mess and scraps from the floor and tables and pushed it all in to a pile in the middle of the floor. Then using my earth magic, I opened a fissure in the ground, beneath the pile of slop and watched triumphantly as it disappeared into the earth. Releasing my magic, the hole sealed up, leaving the tiles of the great hall just as they were before. I had never seen the hall so spotless and wondered if perhaps I had gone a little overboard. But I was intoxicated and at the time felt that it was a good enough excuse as any.

As Asha entered the hall, I stood and watched her gazing around the room as if searching for the hidden mess, in astonishment at how clean it was. The look of confusion on her face made me want to laugh as if I were still a child playing tricks on her. I slowly walked towards her and reached out my hands to take hers and pulled her closer, gazing deeply into her eyes, I informed her that her services would not be required that night. Looking back into my eyes she nervously bit her bottom lip, yet with a joyous smile and surprised expression, she exclaimed 'You did this?' At the time I was not interested in gloating, for it seemed the excessive amount of ale I had consumed had gone to my head and given me the confidence to finally speak with Asha the way I had always wanted to. Smiling, I requested that she dance with me. She sweetly reciprocating and rested her head gently onto my chest, listening to my heart beating, each beat a dedication of my love for her, as we gently moved around the floor. After a while, she looked up and gazed into my eyes as if looking straight through to my soul and leaned in to kiss me. Sharing a kiss with this woman filled me with a joy and excitement that I had never felt before. Momentarily losing control of myself, my magic lit up every single candle in the hall, followed by blazing flames from within the fireplace. Shocked by this Asha quickly looked around the room, clearly trying to make sense of what was happening. After a moment she gazed back at me, and her expression spoke a thousand words. I could almost read her like a book, even though I cannot actually read! Her expression said 'You have magic? I am glad!' as she shied her blushing cheeks away, yet still smiling sweetly. After a few moments we stopped dancing and she stepped back. Thanking me for a wonderful night, she presented her hand,

and I respectfully held and kissed it. Releasing her, I watched as she turned and left the hall to return to her home. Perhaps it was the ale or perhaps it was love flowing through me, but whatever it was it knocked me out cold and I fell unconscious on to the cold, hard floor of the hall. I am still not sure how I got home to my own bed, but when I awoke I was indeed at home. I remember thinking, 'was it all just a dream or did it really happen?', however my throbbing headache was confirmation enough that it actually did.

After pulling myself together I set off for yet another day of training within the citadel. I remember feeling apprehensive as I walked towards the gates, knowing that the combination of clanging metal blades and my pounding head were going to make the day rather long and painful. As I reached the gates of the citadel I greeted the guards with the usual, pleasant 'good morning'. The irony of that statement could not have been planned any better, as the siege on the Kingdom began with a huge ball of fire crashing down from the skies and landing in the middle of the street behind me. The brutal force of the blast threw me off the ground, and for the first time in my life I felt the power of the element turning against me. Crashing into the gates in front of me, I landed violently on the ground, my ears started ringing and the sound all around me became muffled. Through the dizziness that now rang in my mind, I could just make out the faint screams of the citizens and the calls of the war horns being blown from atop the citadel towers. Attempting to make sense of what was happening, as the dark shroud of war came crashing down around me, it was all too much for my mind to fathom as I lost consciousness.

I cannot say how long I was unconscious for, although it seemed like mere moments, but when I awoke there was no longer daylight. Disorientated, I glanced around at what remained, as the forefront of the town was now almost unrecognisable and there was little more than a blaze of rubble and ash where the lower town, my home, once stood. Straining, to pick myself up, I turned to see that the gates of the citadel were still standing tall in front of me. However, it transpired that the guards had not been as fortunate as I was as they now lay lifeless on the ground before me.

Pushing the gates open and entering the citadel, I witnessed how noblemen and women were now no better off than the rest of the citizens of Alexandria, as they ran around helping each other with their wounds and locating their families. When looked upon in a different light, the madness and anarchy seemed to be what Alexandria needed to realise that one's class is irrelevant when it comes to a matter of life and death. As I scanned the area in a desperate attempt to see a familiar face, I began to wonder about those I cared about most. Struck with a fearful shock in my gut, I saw many dead citizens littering the ground as their loved ones mourned their losses, seemingly giving up hope with nothing left in their lives to fight for. Realising that I too could soon be mourning my losses, I feared for the lives of my Mother, Origen, Asha and Prince Reaven.

Over the screams and shouts of the citizens I could hear the Knights of Alexandria mounting up and riding through the great northern gates, roaring as they entered onto the plains of the northern lands. Standing tall and watching over the battle outside the city walls from the safety of his balcony was King Dion. I soon noticed he was holding the sword I had forged for him. Knowing this, I hoped in my heart that the Prince was also using the blade I gave him. Yet, at the moment, there was no point in worrying about that. My first priority was to find and reunite myself with Origen and my mother.

Searching for my family seemed impossible, as I struggled to push my way through the panicked citizens. While they were all rushing around either shouting out for loved ones or crying over their lifeless bodies, more were killed by the endless balls of fire that rained into the Kingdom one-by-one. If ever there was a moment that I yearned to use my magic to clear my path, it was then. I was angry, scared and frustrated that the simple task of locating my family seemed like such hard work. I was practically ready to lie down, give up and wait for the end.

My depressive thoughts were soon interrupted by the sudden cry from a citizen next to me. Grabbing my shoulder and pointing up at a tower that stood above the northern gates, he shouted out 'Sorcerer!' Quickly turning to look, in the direction he pointed, I hoped it would not be – But, alas, there he was!

Origen stood high on the wall above the Gatehouse, overlooking the battle that was now clashing in the Northern lands. Holding his favoured sceptre high in the air, obviously using his magic within the battle field below, it glowed with an eerie purple haze. He stood with his eyes closed, not moving a muscle, I had seen Origen using this magic before. He was making minions of the fallen soldiers and controlling them like puppets to do his bidding, though lifeless and without soul he could control their bodies with his magic to create a formidable foe, which were almost indestructible. Although I could not see exactly what he was doing, there was only one other time that he was able to perform such a spell, as keeping such a creature under ones control requires life force, slowly sapping them of their strength. A particularly dangerous spell, if unmastered it had the potentially to drain all life from the caster, leaving them as nothing more than a pile of bones. At that moment I was less concerned for Origen's life as I was for Prince Reaven's and the Knights who were fighting on the other side of the wall. The last time Origen performed this magic he lost control and was unable to release his magic. The drain on him eventually became so great it rendered him unconscious, but by then the creature had gained enough life force to sustain itself. It could then feast on the life force of others around it. These creatures no longer had any sense of allegiance and merely acted upon its master's wishes. Once the master was no longer able to control it, they would seek to sustain themselves by feeding on the life of anyone around it, he called them 'his minions'. Knowing this, I had to stop Origen before he killed himself, or worse, the Prince and his Knights.

Everything seemed to slow down ten-fold as I watched the King, turning his sight towards Origen. Without regard for my own safety, I quickly conjured a gust of air and enveloped my brother in a shroud of dust. Using the power of winds I cast a quickening spell upon myself and rushed towards Origen, breaking away from the citizen who was holding my arm. In the blink of an eye I reached Origen and grabbed him, throwing us both from the wall and onto the path below out of sight of the King, landing behind the Great Northern Gates.

Picking myself up, I felt an anger swell inside me at my brothers stupidity. Being older than me surely he was wiser, but I feared his powers had only made him arrogant. Stopping only to glare at him with discontent, I walked away to find my mother. Origen, however, had different plans for me.

Scorning me as I walked away, he asking me what I thought I was doing. Most unfortunately, I had still not calmed myself down from my anger at his stupidity, for he had placed our family in danger. Furthermore had he been seen by the King we would all have been executed for the crime of practicing magic! Even our mother would have been punished, regardless of her obvious lack of power. I was enraged that he would destroy all that our father had worked so hard for and paid for with his life. I had gained the Royal Family's trust and in a single act he could have destroyed it all and branded our whole family with dishonour. So when he asked me what I was thinking when I disrupted his spell and potentially just saved all our lives, I could no longer turn the other cheek. I was not willing to pretend that Origen's actions were a simple cry for help or an act of immaturity. This time he had gone too far and I was enraged to the point of wanting to put an end to Origen's blatant lack of respect. One way or another I would make him yield and he would never use his magic again!

In the blindness of my rage, I turned with hostility and scolded him with every ounce of fury within me. I reminded him that I had repeatedly warned him about it before, and now he dared use magic in plain sight, worse than that he did it right under the Kings' nose. His stupidity never ceased to amaze me. The anger I felt inside brought tears of rage to my eyes and I remembered back to the day when Prince Reaven angered me so, that I almost lost control of my magic. The frustration at my brother's disregard for our family's safety served only to rattle my nerves to the point of utter detestation."

Quin broke down in tears, as he recalled the anger he felt at the time of Alexandria's demise and, moreover, the deaths he witnessed. Historian Nicolas looked at him with great sympathy as he understood the pain he must have been feeling. "To recall such a devastating time in one's mind can be just as painful as the moment it happened." Nicolas explained "Are you sure you wish to go on, young sorcerer?"

Filled with a rage and resentment at his powers he snapped at Nicolas "Do not call me that! Do not try to justify what I am by giving me a title. I am nothing more than an abomination and a traitor to my Kingdom and my family" flashes of events coursed through his mind and Quin finally came to terms with his former actions, accepting himself for what he truly believed he was. "I am not a sorcerer, I am a murderer!" Unsure how to respond to the horrifying words that just left his lips, Historian Nicolas sat back and pondered for a moment. Both remained in silence as Nicolas gazed off in to space, imagining what it must have been like for the people of the city as the siege went on. Quin sat and stared blankly at the empty plate in front of him baring his reflection, haunted with various thoughts and feelings, trying to make sense of his tragic past. After a short interlude of silence, Quin knew that he could not escape his past, he thought for a moment about bending the truth of what had truly happened that day, but remembered the lesson his father once taught him as a child; 'a small lie started, ends with a web of falseness.' Knowing the story had to be told he broke the silence and continued.

"I wish that the next moments of my life had never come to pass, as I now live in shame and regret at the outcome, and fear that I will feel that regret for the rest of my days.

Origen rebuked my rage with reason of his own perverse logic, even though his words were treasonous. He explained that our powers were a gift and that we should embrace that gift by crushing those who would dare to deny us our birth right. Royal blood or not, we still had the power to crush them with a single flick of magic. It was at that moment that I finally understood the true beliefs that my brother held. He practised his powers so carelessly because he wanted to be caught. He would then have an excuse to use his powers in defence against the King. I dare say he would have attempted to claim the throne for himself and our family. It made sense that he wanted this, he too wanted us to become a noble family just as I did, but I feared he would take it too far. As arrogant as the Prince was, I had grown to admire him and dared to believe he was my friend. I had a good enough relationship with him to know that I would lay down my life to protect him and the King for the good of Alexandria, even if that meant fighting my own brother.

In a desperate attempt to make my brother recognise the error of his ways, I reminded him that he was plotting against the King, against all that Alexandria stood for, and how a Kingdom built on mutiny would be a Kingdom that lives by mutiny. 'Live by the sword, die by the sword'. I hoped my brother would just accepted my words and walk away. I only wish I had seen what was coming next. Origen glared at me with anger and stated that if I was not with him then I was against him. The Royal Family would die, just as soon as he saved the Kingdom from Ifrit and anyone that would stand in his way.

Immediately, Origen began to attack me with his magic. Flinging his sceptre, he cast a spell of enfeeblement on me. I instantly felt drained of all my energy and began to fear that Origen's resolve was so great that he would use his powers to consume mine and claim them for his own. Such is the way of a Necromancer; his powers come from the souls of those he consumes. It is such a dangerous power that always lusts for more and more.

Falling to the floor I could feel my powers being sucked out of me, leaving me with a chill as cold as ice. The coldness began to stab my body all over as if my blood was shattering into shards of ice, ripping me apart from the inside out. As I began to weaken, I was saved by the cry of my mother as she ran towards us and cried out to Origen to make him stop, but it was too late. Origen had finally come to understand the greatness of my powers and now wanted it for himself and so did not listen to my mother's hysterical cries to save me. With all the energy I could muster I had only one final wish, to see my mother one last time. Attempting to turn my head in order to see her, as I lay flat on my back with every muscle stiff as wood, I was physically unable to do so; instead I was greeted with the dark clouds in the skies above, burning, as they suddenly parted releasing a fireball that headed straight toward us. I prayed that it would strike me and destroy me before I finally slipped away to Origen's magic, thus denying him the pleasure of obtaining my power. Holding on to life for as long as I could I felt compelled to give in, as I could hear Origen's voice in my mind calmly telling me to let go. It seemed like days passed as the fire ball progressed closer and closer, and I almost wished for it to move faster so as to end my suffering quickly.

As Origen noticed the fire ball descending upon us, his gaze was interrupted and his magical hold on me was released for a few moments. Holding my hand out to the fireball I attempted to use my magic to destroy it, but I was too weakened by Origen to do anything. Following the fireball with my eyes, it came crashing down on my mother. Origen's face dropped as he watched her life end before us. Dashing over to the crater where she previously stood begging for my life, Origen fell to his knees and cried out for her. It was only a matter of moments before my own powers flowed back to me and the pain of Origen's magic ceased. Climbing to my feet my rage and hatred began to boil inside of me while the mixed tears of anger and sorrow fell from my eyes. The hatred I felt for my brother now consumed me, because his selfish actions had ultimately led to our mother's death. I was filled with a deep grievance that felt as if it had shattered my heart. But as I watched my brother fall to his knees at the crater, regardless of how much I hated him, I could not bear to see him cry. My mind now in a complete whirl, I tried to make sense of what had just happened. Because I was not thinking straight, my only conclusion was that it was all Origen's fault. With every ounce of energy I had I cast an almighty wind spell that struck him unyielding, throwing him like a child's ragdoll into the debris of the now shattered buildings that surrounded us. As he landed, his body disturbed an internal pillar and the rest of the building collapsed on top of him. Full of anger and hatred that I could not control, I set my sights on getting revenge for my mother. Raising my hand slowly I tried to talk myself out of my rage, but it was as if I was trapped inside my own mind and my thoughts of reasoning and compassion were simply futile. I summoned the blazing element of fire and cast it over the debris where my brother was concealed, I stood watching for a moment as the remains blazed with scorching heat and created masses of thick black smoke that seemingly danced in celebration of my actions. A weight was suddenly lifted as my powers gave into me and I regained control of myself and my thoughts. Everything became clear. My thoughts immediately turned to my mother's death being all Origen's fault, however, she would not have wanted us to fight, let alone kill each other. As I walked away from the blazing debris of my brother's final resting place I felt no guilt or remorse for his death... That came later!

I was confused and alone in the world my mind wondered around aimlessly searching for resolution, but fortunately my body took over and I made my way through the palace to the Kings chambers. Walking over to the King as he watched over the battle below, it was as if I was not even there. Looking down I could see the Prince fighting. It was apparent he was carrying the blade I gifted to him and as I closed my eyes to focus my energy, I activated the Princes' swords hidden power. Glowing with a yellow aura it dispersed a fiery mist around the blade, and without noticing the glow the Prince continued to battle. Striking an Ifryte, the beast burst into flames and fell to the ground, squirming and flailing. For a moment the Prince dropped his gaze and witnessed the magic surrounding the weapon in disbelief. Knowing that the Prince would shun such a weapon, I cast a spell that bound the blade to him, until death, at which time the weapon would find its way back to me. The Prince's grip tightened around the hilt as he attempted to drop it. My spell was simple, but effective; while the Prince did not want the sword, it would cling tightly too him. Only when he comes to accept the magic of the sword, would he have the ability to release its hold. I knew that the Prince had to learn to accept magic and use it in his battles if Alexandria was to stand any chance of survival. Realising that he could not rid himself of the weapon, Prince Reaven had no choice but to continue his battle against the Ifryte that swarmed all over the Northern lands. Looking around I could see large monuments ablaze, as shots of fire flew up into the air as if fired from a trebuchet, raining down fire balls upon the city. The King's expression suddenly turned to a look of confusion as he spotted the power his son had suddenly acquired. He turned his attention away from the battle below and gazed at me with a blank and defeated expression. I knew I had already lost everything that was important to me in my life and I had nothing more to lose. I explained to the King that his son did not have magic; instead it was I who had blessed both blades with magic that had always been under my control. Expecting the King to strike me down on the spot, I was surprised that he simply turned back towards the battle below and asked me to join the fight and protect his son. But he warned, if Reaven were ever to find out that I had magic, he would surely kill me and the King could not do anything to prevent it. Understanding, I bowed my head and smiled slightly at the pleasure of knowing that although my magic would be outlawed in these lands, the King had all but accepted it.

As I walked away, I pondered the possibility that the King had become a broken man. I surmised that the many days of assaults on the Kingdom had taken their toll on the King and he had finally given up all hope of ever permanently defeating the forces of Ifrit. However, I had no time to worry about that as I dashed toward the Great Northern Gates to assist Prince Reaven and the Knights in battle. Stopping off at the armoury, I grabbed myself some armour and put it on as quickly as I could. Seizing a sword and scabbard belt, I was ready to join the battle, for it had now become personal. Before I knew it, the Great Northern Gates opened up in front of me, and I stepped through into the battle ahead."

"On the other side of the gates I was greeted by searing flames in every direction. Once again, in my life I was experiencing the searing element of fire with fear as it turned against me. The blistering heat dried my eyes, which began to sting due to the toxic smoke that arose from the flames. Attempting to control the element, I discovered that there was far too much for me to control as it overwhelmed me and pushed me back, taunting my every attempt. Knowing that I was unable to subdue a powerful element such as this, I could not help doubting myself and my ability to control the elements and felt weak. I realised that Origen was possibly correct in some aspects of his beliefs. Although his actions were reckless and had put my family in grave danger, he at least had practised the use of his powers and had grown to understand them, and with that knowledge and experience he had become more powerful. I began to regret not having practised my magic with him as he had suggested so often. Perhaps if I had not been so stubborn and resolute against using magic in Alexandria, then perhaps I would have been able to control the Flames that now danced menacingly around me. As they took hold of the noble Knights and incinerated them, whilst I stood powerless to help them.

Knowing I could not control the fire, I turned my efforts instead to destroying it. I focused on the clouds above and summoned forth the power of water. The clouds began to gather above; heavy and dark as night. Ordering these clouds to bow to my will and send forth their magic, the rain began to fall and doused the flames that blocked my way through to the battlefield ahead. I could hear them hissing as if they screamed out in agony like were water was slicing through them, dealing a deadly blow with every drop. A sense of guilt washed over me as the fires began to extinguish, knowing that I had turned my allies, the elements, against each other, which, in my heart, felt as though I was betraying my own children. Having enough control to command what remained of the flames, I put them to rest. I could now see the battle ahead, where Prince Reaven stood alone fighting off hoards of the Ifryte beasts. Rushing over to him with haste, I commanded the few remaining flames around me to hurry to his aid.

Holding out my hand and focusing on his sword, the flames and embers flew through the air, rushing to the Prince's aid. Enveloping the weapon, the flames and embers then circled round the Prince scorching any Ifryte within spitting distance. The fire circle gradually extended further and forced the Ifryte to retreat backwards away from the flames, although I knew that the larger I made it, the weaker it would become. Jumping unharmed through the field of fire, I called out to the Prince and drew my sword. But the Prince simply stood and stared in astonishment at the field of fire and the power that had just unravelled around him; I could see in his face that he was beginning to wonder if it was he himself who had the magic. Knowing that he would now be a lot safer with me at his side to subtly use my magic to aid him in battle, I extinguished the fire.

Turning to me, the Prince asked me what had just happened. Fearing for my safety, I had to come up with an answer quickly to elude his wrath. Looking around I attempted to find someone, or something, to pin the blame on. The first person I saw was King Dion, who was standing high on the balcony of the throne room, overlooking the battle. I quickly realised that it was foolish, but I passed the blame onto him. Without hesitation the Prince snapped back at me, cursing at me angrily for daring to accuse his father of being a 'demon of magic'. Thankfully any punishment for the treasonous accusation was placed on hold as the Ifryte continued to charge towards us. Using the healing element of water, I blessed the rain that still fell from the sky, giving each droplet the ability to heal the wounds of the injured soldiers. Although unable to resurrect the dead, my magic was effective in healing minor wounds it touched. One-by-one the injured knights and soldiers rose to their feet and joined behind us in arms against the endless waves of Ifryte.

Aggravatingly my efforts were in vain, as the shriek of a mighty horn in the distance of the Ifryte hoards filled the air. The attacking Ifryte halted their progression towards us, paying close attention to the sound, and, without turning their backs on us, they began to retreat. Arrogant as the Prince was, he felt it was his chance to prove his bravery under his father's watchful gaze, and charge after the scattering Ifryte, however I sensed that something was amiss, like a discomforting stirring in my gut after eating a plate of stale meat. Standing still, frozen to the spot, I could feel a great magic in the air flowing through me which warned of the danger that was about to unravel. In a desperate attempt to warn my comrades, I called to the Prince pleading him to stop his advance, however he was too far away from me to hear my call over the roaring of the knights that charged behind him. Suddenly in the distance, a huge beam of white light shot into the skies. Looking down on the events unfolding before him, the King could see that the Ifryte had brought a magical Relic with them and were using their powers to activate its magic. Screaming to his son, the King ordered the retreat, as the Prince and Knights halted and gazed upon the magical light that stood before them. Astonished and curious, none of them moved, but simply stood their ground staring into the sky, mesmerised by its wonder. The light began to pulse and the sky above turned a fiery red. In mere moments the heavens had opened and cast forth masses of flaming boulders. Seeing the first of the countless flames falling from the sky, the Prince and Knights began to fall back towards Alexandria's Northern Gates for safety. But I was unable to focus as the incredible magnitude of different magic hit me like a swinging punch and called to me in a garble of a thousand voices spoken all at once, as both enemy and ally. I was frozen to the spot in a daze as each Knight rushed past me screaming 'Retreat!', yet I was physically incapable of acting while this magic toyed with my mind, almost forcing me to gawp at the falling flames.

The Prince reached out and grabbed me. Screaming in my face 'move!' he promptly rushed through the gates. Having been snapped out of my daze, I too began the sprint towards the gates as the falling flames drew closer and closer. Reaching the other side of the gate all I could do was stand watching the citizens run from the Citadel into the lower town and out onto the Southern fields of Alexandria.

That was the last time I lay eyes on the Great Kingdom of Alexandria in its former glory, as the Fire fell around me and collided with the ground just outside the gate causing a blast that threw me to the cobbled stone floor. The Great Northern Gate crumbled around me, burying me under rubble and dust. A single piece of debris bashed my head with such force, it rendered me unconscious.

I still have no idea how long I was lying under the rubble, it could have been days, but as I regained consciousness and gradually freed myself I was greeted with an unfamiliar scene. I eventually started to piece together the view that lay before my eyes to realise where I was.

Much to my despair Alexandria had been destroyed and reduced to nothing more than a pile of rock. The castle no longer stood proud, the training grounds left as nothing more than a graveyard and all that remained of this once mighty Kingdom was a tattered wall that separated the

Northern and Southern lands. As I wandered through the ruins I noticed there were no sounds; no cries or shouts nor the horns of war. Not even the Ifryte were to be seen. The thick black fog that now cloaked the sky made it difficult to see where I was heading, for even the stars seemed to have given up the fight and surrendered to the Ifryte magic. As I wandered through the town aimlessly, searching for any form of life, I soon found myself in the southern fields.

The once beautiful meadows were now nothing more than mounds of dirt and ash. The rivers and lakes that once flowed with crystal clear water were now a filthy, bubbling slush, like black swamp water, the shores stained with blood and the fish rotting on the surface created a foul stench which spread throughout the lands of Alexandria. Forlorn in the hope that I would find Asha, I walked to the tree where she used to sit playing her flute. However, when I arrived the tree was but a shadow of its former beauty. The leaves that remained were brown and dead. Most of the branches had been burnt and snapped and my once peaceful hiding spot lay to waste in the middle of this barren scene. Leaning against the tree's trunk, I finally realised that I was entirely alone. Already heartbroken and devastated, I thought there was nothing more that could worsen my hopeless situation. But a small glimmer of light drew my eye to the ground and as I brushed away the ashes and dead leaves I discovered an even deeper sorrow.

Asha's Flute lay there snapped in half, silent and lifeless as the land around it. Turning my head away as the sight became unbearable, my heart felt as if it had been torn open as I was then confronted with a piece of blue cloth hanging from a branch of the fallen tree. Tormented by my own mind, I imagined the scene that had unfolded here. Aggrieved, I fell to my knees. My life had seemingly lost all meaning, for a life without Asha was not a life at all.

I slumped back against the tree and sat gazing out at the distant lands, now burnt to ashes and coated in blood. I tortured myself by sitting there imagining the horrors that must have been happening whilst I lay unconscious as the kingdom fell, and of all those terrors my deepest regret was killing my brother. I knew he would have been the only person with the power to bring Asha back from her untimely grave, but, because of me, his body lay under the ruins serving as a constant reminder of my recklessness.

In this time of need, I screamed from the very depths of my soul as tears of utter devastation streamed from my eyes. My only hope, was to be found.

Disturbed by a growl from behind me, I looked round to find myself face to face with four Ifryte, each of them staring at me greedily with drool dripping from their fangs, like I was no more than a roast hog. Without fear, I stood and waited for deaths embrace as these disgusting creatures drew their weapons to put me down. However, they foolish felt the need to taunt me first, laughing at my expense and to my surprise one of them spoke. 'We will not get much of a meal from this little rat'. His words reminded me of Origen's taunts. Throughout my entire life Origen would always play tricks on me with his magic and because I would not retaliate he would call me 'the little rat boy'.

I was filled with a huge mix of thoughts and emotions, which lead to a blind, uncontrollable rage as I unleashed my magic upon the Ifryte before me. A power that I had never seen before came from me, as bolts of thunder shot from my hands and entangled themselves around the Ifryte, causing them to spasm and twitch while my magic destroyed them. As they fell to the ground I began to calm and my magic ceased. Drawing my sword, I stood over the last remaining Ifryte and glared at it with tears of rage in my eyes as it looked back at me with fear in its eyes as I aggressively it stated, 'You disgusting creatures will all die, by my hand'. I pushed my sword into the beast's chest and listened to its gargled final breaths with great pleasure.

Gazing up at the sky awaiting salvation it felt like I was losing my mind. I lay with the broken flute in my hand and hummed the tunes that once filled this place with such tranquillity, as a tear rolled down my face for Asha's death. Even though it was torturing me I could not help but wonder how it happened; was it quick? Did she suffer? Did she think of me before she died? Did she blame me for not being there to save her? Why her?"

Breaking down in tears, his recollection of the past events were becoming more and more difficult as he revisited them, forcing himself to come to terms with the harsh reality of his past. Realising he had no way to hide from it or ignore it, he simply took a moment to compose himself. Sympathetically, Nicolas reach over and placed his hand on top of Quin's,

"I know what it is to lose someone you love so dearly, Quin." Nicolas went on to explain "I lost my dear soulmate precisely one thousand and eighty three days ago. I have been counting. As a young man I spent my days on fishing boats, away from home most of the time, then one day while I was away she became ill. When I arrived home, she had already gone. I wish I had taken a moment to consider that life is so fragile and each day counts. That is why I became an Historian, to tell the tales of those who have spent each day leading a great life. My mate's death made me change my lifestyle and reshape my future. Asha's death should serve the same purpose for you. If you do not take a lesson from it, then her death will have been in vain".

Feeling somewhat patronised, Quin looked up at Nicolas and wiped the tears from his eyes.

"What do you think I am doing here? Because of Asha's death I now seek a greater purpose. I want revenge!" Before Nicolas could respond to Quin's blatant lack of understanding of the meaning of life and death, he continued his story.

"I had long enough to think about what I should do next while lying on the ground staring at the sky above, for what seemed like an eternity. However, with every trail of thought it always ended the same - getting revenge and finding death to join Asha and my family in the Heavens, or underworld. But as cruel as Fate had been to me, it appeared that my lack of motivation to do anything thereafter got its attention and it finally threw me a lifeline as a familiar voice called out to me. At first I thought I was imagining things. Wishing the Prince was alive and coming to find me seemed too much like a fantasy and so each time I heard the Prince's voice calling out I simply closed my eyes and told myself that it was nothing more than an echoing memory within my mind. After a while the calls stopped and opening my eyes I was greeted with a vision of the Prince standing over me. Smiling with a look of joy on his face, he offered out his hand to me and exclaimed 'You are not as soft as you appear Quin.' Reaching out to the vision I expected my hand to flow straight through the Prince's, to confirm that I was imagining it all. But our fingers locked and I realised that I was not going crazy after all. Pulling me to my feet and looking me up and down, the Prince laughed with such glee that I was alive. It seemed he truly was overjoyed to see me as he pulled me close to hug me while all of the time patting me on the back. Taking out a horn, the Prince blew into the mouthpiece emitting a loud siren that further snapped me out of my former dreary, sorrowful state. In the distance, another horn could be heard in response to the Prince. Glancing down at the four dead Ifryte with a disgruntled expression, he looked back at me and smiled, again laughing he said 'you are with me now!' and with those simple words he gave me the will to carry on. With great joy he flung his arm around my shoulders and nodded his head approvingly leading off toward his sanctuary where the remaining Knights of Alexandria awaited the return of their Prince.

- Chapter VI -
A Royal Reunion

"Prince Reaven and I travelled for miles through the night until the sun came up. Leading the way, the Prince escorted me down a small chasm between two towering mountains. Ahead of us I could see a small entrance into a cave where the gentle flickering flame of a lantern could be seen. Calling out towards the mouth of the cave, the Prince assured the occupants that all was safe and he had one other with him. I was surprised he did not say exactly who I was, but I figured he wanted it to be as joyous a moment for them as it were for him; to discover for themselves that I had survived the siege.

Gradually, one by one, the remaining survivors emerged and stood watching us as we walked closer to the safety of the cave. I was expecting to see all of the Knights come to greet us, however only five stood before us. I hoped others may be inside, resting or perhaps eating, and I would see them upon entering the sanctuary. The Prince held out his arm and greeted each of his Knights with a hand shake and reminded me of their names with a formal introduction; Sir Daniel the Judged, Sir Leander the Brave-Heart, Sir Shimri the Guardian, Sir Benjamin the Right-Hand and lastly Sir David the Admired. Turning to me, the Prince stared with an expression as if to say, 'Well… Say something!', but I could not find the words to express my relief, and at the same time my misery and heart-ache. The flood of emotions in my heart began to make my bottom lip tremble and my eyes welled up, as all these noble Knights gazed upon me. I had an overwhelming urge to hold back my emotions so as not to appear weak in front of such strong men, until Sir Leander spoke up and said that he was not ashamed to admit he too had shed his share of tears. Knowing that the even Sir Leander, who was quite clearly the strongest, bravest and easily the most obvious person to disconnect heart and mind from the day he was born, indicated there was no shame in letting my emotions get the better of me, I lowered my head and began to weep. Stepping forward Sir Daniel wrapped his arms around me and held me close so that no-one would see my shame as I allowed my emotions to overwhelm me. In turn, the other Knights stepped forward and wrapped their arms around me too, until we were just a mass of embraced bodies. The Prince just smiled and walked off into the cave, shaking his head. After a few moments the Knights released me, each one giving a physical gesture of encouragement; patting my back, grabbing my shoulder, ruffling my hair or just simply a smile and a nod, then leading the way into what I thought would be my new home for the rest of my life, as we retired into the cave.

As I looked around inside the flickering lanterns revealed roughly twenty citizens scattered around the large open area, the vast majority were either injured or dying, while others catered to their needs. Over in one corner I noticed an elderly woman grasping a man's hand, crying quietly over him as his cold, battered, and lifeless body lay before her. She rocked back and forth as if she had no idea what to do next, knowing there were no words I could offer, I turned my attention to the campfire in the centre of the cave where Prince Reaven and his Knights now sat planning their next move.

Standing on my own I felt as if I did not really have a place within this community. I did not want to disturb those who were mourning their losses and as I had no knowledge of alchemy, nor was I a physician - I could not help the wounded without the use of my magic, which was seemingly impossible to do without being discovered. I had no place alongside the Knights and the Prince as I was definitely not a hero or nobleman. It was then I realised that no matter what situation I was in, I would always be an outsider. I had bumbled through my entire life foolishly thinking that my magic was the only thing that made me different to everyone else, which was why I never seemed to fit in. But looking around that cave made me understand, magic was simply a cover for the reality of my life. I had never truly fitted into any society and knew I probably never would.

Releasing a sigh, I knew that my friends were safe and that was all I could have hoped for. Comforted in that knowledge, I turned to the entrance of the cave and decided I would find my own path. I left quietly with no idea where I was going, and quite honestly I did not care, but what I did know was that I would keep walking until fate's cruel hand either struck me down or showed me the way. A life fit for an outcast.

I left the cave as the sun was highest in the sky, and as I looked up to see what I hoped to be a beautiful day, I was reminded of the horror that had befallen the lands. The sun was mostly obscured by thick black clouds and the once blue sky now ran a bloody red. I began to hope that this was all just a terrible nightmare and that I was actually lying on the floor of the Royal Banquet Hall, still drunk and waiting to be woken up with a bucket of freezing cold water being poured over my face by the disgruntled Prince.

Snapping out of my thoughts for a moment, I looked around to find I had mindlessly wandered out of the chasm. Glancing back down the path I had walked from, I pondered for a moment and asked myself if I was doing the right thing. Was leaving really the best thing to do? In all honesty, my mind had become such a scramble I could not make sense of anything anymore. So I simply decided to follow the elements wherever they would lead me. Closing my eyes, I connected, body and mind, with the elements around me, listening to them. But only to my horror as they all cried out in pain; the poison all around polluted the water turning it to a thick sludge, the air wrought with fumes of noxious smoke and gasses. While the clash of fire and earth battling on against each other for their very survival. I tried to calm them and regain control to help them heal, but it was all too much, and I soon discovered that the land was dying.

Just then I was startled as I heard the Prince calling out to me. Opening my eyes and attempting to catch my breath as the trauma of my failed efforts to protect the elements had built up and stuck deep to my heart, I turned to find the Prince staring at me with a look of concern on his face, and rightly so, I can only imagine how strange my actions must have looked to him. He asked me what I was doing, but quite honestly I had no idea and it scared me to think that I had completely lost control of my powers. I felt stranded, like a lost child without his mother, powerless to do anything about it. It was only then that I realised how dependant I was on my powers just being there for me to use as I saw fit. Having them but not using them was fine, for I knew I could use them if I needed to. Without them, I had not only lost my inner sense of security, I had also lost my way, and I felt more alone now than ever before. All I could do was open my heart and tell the Prince what I was thinking. Blurting out my thoughts without any care of the possible consequences, I explained that Alexandria was dying and I could not stop it. I told him I was weak and even my closest allies were now fighting amongst each other for survival. The Prince's confusion was clear to see as he attempted to make sense of my babbling. Sitting down on a nearby rock, he looked at me and explained 'We argue amongst ourselves because survival is everything, and while one person relies on another, they both have a duty to make the right choices. Some do not agree with others, but a choice made in disagreement is better than no choice at all.' I have to admit that I was humbled by the Prince and his attempt to sound wise, even though I knew he had completely misunderstood the truth I was trying to surrender to him. The Prince went on to explain that after the Kingdom fell they found the cave and took shelter there from the rain of fire that fell from the skies. The cave opening collapsed while they were inside and they spent every waking moment digging it out. As we stood there together, side by side, the Prince looked into the distance of the tarnished lands that were once his home and continued to explain that he had no idea how long they were trapped inside the cave, as there was no sunlight and the air inside the cave was running out making everyone grow sleepy, giddy and confused. Eventually they managed to break through the blockage and the air returned. However, hunger and thirst had set in long before and some of the weaker refugees were by now starving, exhausted, and on the brink of death.

Five people died in that cave and the Prince laid claim to their deaths as his fault. Having no idea how long it had been since the Kingdom was destroyed, the Prince pointed out that he did not know if his father was still alive, however he could not afford to focus on such a thought. Honourably, he told me that his primary concern was to find any remaining survivors and keep them safe until such a time that they could fight back against the Ifryte, to reclaim the fallen Kingdom of Alexandria and begin to rebuild their lives. As the prince spoke I realised that the 'Royal Ass' I once knew now stood before me as an honourable, humbled man. A strange feeling of pride came over me as I heard him speaking in this manner, as if he was Origen turning over a new leaf. The Prince went on to inform me that he was glad I had been on the battleground before the Kingdom fell. He then turned away and walked back towards the cave, but before leaving he took a moment to present me with a revelation that changed my life forever. 'I am the Prince' he said 'it is, therefore, my sworn duty to protect all the people of Alexandria. I cannot help but wonder, whose duty is it to protect me?' I thought the answer was obvious; it would surely be the noble Knights that protected the Prince. Yet, turning to give my assumed answer to the Prince, I was faced with another expression that spoke one simple word 'You'. Knowing that I had understood, he bowed his head, turned and walked away, leaving me with a choice; I could leave if I wanted to, or I could stay and find my place beside the Prince as his guardian. With that, I believed I had finally found my place in the world. Perhaps the reason I had felt so alone for all this time was simply because there was only one true place for me to be; by the Prince's side, secretly using my magic to protect him. Perhaps one day he would learn of my powers and would grant me the title of nobleman. How ironic that I would only receive such a title after Alexandria was no more. It seemed Fate plays a distasteful game. It can guide you to the top one day and cast you back to the bottom the next. Although for all that I have learnt, Fate sometimes throws itself directly in your path to ensure you make the right choices set out for you. To ignore such a calling filled me with a deep foreboding that something terrible would happen if I were to leave, so I knew then what I had to do. The events that had led me to that moment already had me declaring Fate as my darkest enemy, and yet, there I was about to enter into its embrace and play its vulgar games.

Arriving back at the cave, the Prince called me over to the campfire and sat me down with the other Knight's. Strangely they all seemed welcoming and passed me a battered old tankard filled with murky water. Wondering how they managed to acquire any water that was not the thick black sludge I had seen out in the lands, I looked around and noticed an old ale barrel on one side of the cave that was catching drips of water running down a small stalagmite that protruded from the ceiling of the cave. Realising this was all we had to drink, I felt selfish for taking it. So while the Knights discussed their tactics and argued amongst themselves, I focused my magic on the caves ceiling to create a larger crack that gushed with fresh water, splashing into the barrel below filling it to the rim. Startled by the sound of the gushing water the Knights jumped up and drew their weapons. Astonished at the sudden abundance of water, they holstered their swords and began to laugh and cheer joyously. Sir Shimri proclaimed 'It is a miracle! The heavens have truly blessed us this day!' Calling everyone over he generously handed out full tankards of water to quench the thirsts of everyone in the cave, without any concern for rationing. Discretely flicking my hand, I blessed the water with powerful healing magic that would cure the ailments and wounds of the injured, quenching any thirst for days to come. Watching the joy around me I questioned myself as I was not quite sure if some of Prince Reaven's arrogance had rubbed off on me. However I began to think that the survivors were under my protection, and although the Prince was their leader I would be their saviour.

After a few moments of bustle and celebration, the cave's inhabitants settled down. As each citizen drank their water the Knights excitedly continued their discussion of what the next move for the people of Alexandria would be, with a rekindled enthusiasm thanks to the gift of water I had provided. I listened to the conversations and it appeared there was still a difference of opinions. Sir Benjamin firmly believed there was no more time to sit around and wait for rescue or reinforcements and they simply had to evacuate and spread out across the lands and find shelter wherever they could. Sir Shimri, on the other hand, argued that separation would simply lead to extinction as they would be hunted down and killed one-by-one. It seemed that Sir David was intent on finding the King, be it dead or alive, so that they could at least obtain some closure on the unknown. Naturally Sir Leander wanted to take off with a small group of Knights and any who were strong enough to fight, and form a counter attack on the Ifryte and of course Sir Daniel claimed that they all had a valid point. Despite all the suggestions put forward, it seemed as if Prince Reaven's mind was elsewhere as he stared into the campfire, snapping off small segments of the twigs that lay on the ground around him, tossing them into the flames, fixated on the embers. I looked at the Prince and asked him what he thought we should do. Coming around from his day dream, the Prince raised his head, and without saying a word looked directly into the eyes of each of his men, and at that moment I saw the true feelings of the Prince as plain as day. He was defeated! He simply muttered, 'Fight or run

- either way Ifrit has won.' the Prince let out a small sigh and resignedly walked out of the cave. The Knights sat around and looked at each other waiting for an answer to the question they were all thinking 'What just happened?' Without another word they all looked at me. I did not need the powers of a seer to 'hear' their thoughts saying, 'Fix this Quin.' Feeling somewhat uncomfortable with the situation, I muttered 'I assume I am going to speak to him then?' and promptly left the Knights to sit in silence and await the outcome of my conversation with the Prince.

I walked out and found Prince Reaven sitting on a rock, again in his own little world. However this time, he was staring at his sword as he tilted it from side to side, all the while watching his reflection in the perfectly buffed metal. Abruptly interrupting his thoughts, I respectfully asked him what was going through his mind. He rose to his feet and began to walk away, claiming that I could never hope to understand. Angered by his blatant disregard for what I too had been through, I scolded him harshly as I lost control of my temper. I reminded him that he was not the only one who had lost someone close; my home, friends, family and loved ones. But the most disrespectful thing of all was that he had neglected to see that there was a cave full of people who would follow him through Agartha and the depths of the Underworld, and back again, he would only have to say the word! Biting back at me the Prince asked if I had any idea what it was like to be a leader. The people in that cave relied on him, and each death was blood on his hands. Should he fail, it would not simply be his own life he would lose, but the lives of everyone that would place their trust in his leadership, and to be the one who would lead them to safety, in an unsafe world.

For all that he had said to belittle me, on his part, he was right. I had no idea of the strain it could be, having people relying on your every word. The burden that the Prince had to bear was too much for one person alone, although that is the price of being a Prince. After all, a leader is expected to make choices and those choices may not always be the right ones. But without those choices it was all too clear that nothing would be done at all. Calming myself down, I gently reached out with compassion and suggested that all he had to do was say the word and we would march with him, we were all ready to die for our Prince in the name of Alexandria, because that was our choice!

Suddenly the Prince's gaze looked straight past me and his expression turned to utter amazement. As I turned to look, I saw the citizens leaving the cave and joining us in the open, the once severely injured men and women walking out into the daylight with nothing to show for their wounds but small scars. Shedding their bandages and makeshift crutches they stood ready for the Prince's orders. I watched closely as Sir Shimri stepped forward and quietly spoke into the Prince's ear. I overheard him explain to the Prince how the wounded had suddenly started to rise up with their injuries fully healed. Remaining speechless he gazed at the sight, the formerly wounded citizens stepped forward and dedicated their lives to him.

Unsure of what else to do, the Prince spoke out as a leader, and ordered the people to arm themselves 'We move for the Legion Halls to the west. If there is to be any hope of Alexandria's survival, we will find it there!'

Later that day we marched for the Legion Halls, a place further south than the Great Wall itself, where the legion leaders used to congregate. Prince Reaven was right, if there was but one place left in the Kingdom that was unharmed, it would be the Legion Halls as they lay just outside the border of Alexandria. Travelling by foot, it was difficult for our large group to remain discrete and undetected by any predators. Fortunately, we did not encounter any resistance from the Ifryte. At the time I wondered where they all were and why they had not come to claim the lands to the south, but I was equally as glad they had not, as our group would have been spotted and slain many times over had the Ifryte been close by. As we wandered through the once beautiful meadows and small settlements that surrounded Alexandria, it was hard to take in the devastating sights of death and destruction that lay before us. We passed through crumbled hovels and were forced to step over the bodies of the dead. It felt disrespectful to leave them just lying there on the ground but we knew that we had to move on quickly or we too would join them in death. For my part, all I felt I was able to do was beseech Gaia to care for their souls, and beg the element of fire to sweep through the area and cremate the bodies, at least that would provide them with a slightly more dignified death.

As we reached the top of a hill overlooking the Legion Halls, the morale of our group sank to an all new low as we witnessed the crumbled buildings that lay before us. Some of the women cried out, as their family and friends comforted them, for we now had to accept that Alexandria was completely lost. Like the weight of the world itself had just been placed on Prince Reaven's shoulders, his head flopped forward and he fell to his knees. It was obvious that we had lost all hope and given up completely. Slowly raising his head, as if being forced to look upon the ruins, he glared at the Legion Halls with such a rage, as if he blamed the buildings themselves for falling. Just then the Prince spotted a figure dashing across an opening where a window once stood. Unable to make out what it was and, furthermore, if he had actually seen anything at all, the Prince focused his sights on the opening and stared for another sign. Just then another figure moved past the opening causing Prince Reaven to spring to his feet and charge towards the Halls, blade unleashed. Without hesitation the entire group willingly charged after the Prince, also drawing our weapons as we followed, although no-one knew why, or what we were charging for. Nearing the open gates into the Legion Halls, Prince Reaven called out, 'Die you Ifryte bastards!' Now realising what we were running towards, and furthermore what we would be facing if we continued, a few of the citizens stopped and held their position, afraid to face any Ifryte that had sought sanctuary within the remains of the Legion Halls. Rushing as fast as my legs could carry me without the use of magic, I bravely followed the Prince through the crumbling gateway and into the first hall, just in time to see a sword appear from behind a pillar, swinging towards Prince Reaven as his back was turned. Holding out my hands, I screamed, 'Stop' and my magical reflexes took over and engulfed the sword forcing it into submission. Turning sharply, Prince Reaven gazed at the sword in amazement as its tip lay but an eyelash away from his face, and then looked along the blade towards me, as I continued to hold out my hands using my magic on the sword between us, holding it in mid-air. Concentrating on the sword, I quickly recognised it as that which I had forged for King Dion, the sister of Prince Reaven's sword. While my thoughts were pre-occupied on the identification of the blade, I had foolishly forgotten that I was using magic to suspend it, as the Prince gazed in astonishment. Dropping my hands suddenly, I released my magical hold on the sword, hoping that the Prince had not seen it; however as it fell to the floor with a mighty clang, it was blatantly obvious to everyone what had just happened.

The Prince did not take his eyes off me while his expression of astonishment slowly turned to one of extreme anger as he had now become aware of my power, the forbidden magic, and I can only assume he looked upon me as a traitor and an enemy of Alexandria. Glaring at me he proclaimed 'You have magic?' An almighty fear sank deep into my stomach and through every muscle in my body. I stood looking back at the Prince completely petrified, as if under a Basilisk's eye, causing me to feel, literally, sick to my stomach, so much so I felt like I was going to vomit. It was as if I had been standing there under the Princes glare for days, until a familiar voice called out and broke the tension that one could have cut through with a knife. Revealing himself from behind the pillar, King Dion stepped forward, 'Reaven? My son! Thank the heavens you are alive.'

Gradually, the Kings surviving party revealed themselves as they stepped out of their hiding places, the majority of them being simple maids and workers from the Royal Palace. Looking around I hoped that Asha would emerge too, but sadly my hopes were quickly dashed as there was no sign of her amongst the survivors. The King and his son hugged and shared a joyful moment of reunion, while I shamefully slipped out of the building unnoticed and returned to the Knights and survivors outside, informing them that it was safe to proceed. As each one of them entered the Hall, I forced a false smile onto my face, because I knew that my magic had been discovered, a charge usually resulting in exile or more commonly execution. A sweep of melancholy came over me as I reflected upon my actions and the irony of either outcome.

Had I not acted as I did, the Prince would have assuredly been slain by his father's hand, although as a result of my actions I would most certainly lose Prince Reaven anyway, along with my life.

Sitting outside on a large piece of debris that had fallen from the highest tower of the Hall, I sat and awaited my punishment from the Prince and the King. There was a clear sense of happiness in the air, as the two groups of survivors came together to be reunited with their friends and family, who they previously had thought were dead. For my part, all I could do was sit and wait, secluding myself from the celebrations taking place inside the hall. Each passing moment filled me with an even greater dread knowing that sooner or later the Prince would come for me and would either banish me from Alexandria, or ironically, strike me down with the sword I had forged for him to destroy his enemies with. Although fearful that the Prince would kill me, strangely I was more afraid of the question that repeatedly ran through my mind. Had I now suddenly become the enemy he so hated?

When night was upon us I still sat waiting for the Prince to make his move, as the celebration still lingered on. Sir David Burst out of the Hall with a woman in hand and kissed her neck seductively as they embraced.

Discomforted by this, I turned away and stared out into the meadows, however Sir David had already noticed me. Shooing the lady away, he came over and sat by my side, asking me why I had been sitting in the same spot from the moment we had arrived. I felt compelled to ask him what he knew, however I did not want to prompt him to start asking awkward questions if he had not been informed, and so I subtly lied and told him that being trapped under debris made me appreciate being outside in the large open spaces. Taking a bite out of the warm meat he held, that had been cooking inside the Halls since our arrival, he passed the rest onto me. Having not eaten anything since the feast in the Banquet Hall the night before the siege began on Alexandria, I was, by now, starving. I thanked David for his kindness and promptly gorged it down my gullet. Tired and weary from the days past, I lay myself down to sleep for the night. Resting his head next to me David offered to keep me company for the night, which I was extremely grateful for.

At early sunrise the next morning, I was sharply awoken by a sudden thump to my chest as the Prince took hold of my clothing, lifting me up and then throwing me to the ground. In a terrible rage he bellowed at me in such a way that I felt his words alone could have killed me, 'You would dare to seek a life in Alexandria knowing you are plagued with magic? Your kind has no purpose or place among us. What is worse, you would dare to insult my family by pretending to be our friend and ally.' Grovelling in fear and begging for my life, I attempted to explain to the enraged Prince that I was born this way 'I never wanted nor asked for this, I only wish to help.' Grabbing me by my chest once again the Prince threw his fist in my face and cast me away, back onto the ground. He continued to bellow at me, 'The fire from my sword, the water in the cave, the miracle healing of my people. Was it all your doing?' He asked, without giving me a chance to respond 'Do you have any idea what you have done by spreading your plague amongst my people?' Drawing forth his sword, the Prince places the tip of the blade on my chest. The worst part of all this was the knowledge that I could have killed him with a single flick of my wrist, and that cast even more fear into my heart, as it now appeared I had to make a choice, his life or mine? I could not choose.

At that precise moment the King emerged hastily from the Hall and, to my relief, called out and ordered his son to stop and surrender his weapon. Turning to his father the Prince asked him if he knew what I really was. Thankfully, King

Dion revealed to his son that he did know and had, in fact, known for some days. Enraged and disgusted, the Prince scolded the King and claimed he had betrayed him for allowing me to go untried, knowing that I had magic. By now the raised voices had awoken everyone else and they all stood around watching and taking in every last detail, including me lying on the ground, ashamed of myself and what I was. Beside himself with anger, the Prince aggressively darted towards me, raising his sword to strike me down, the King cried out dominantly and ordered the Prince to stand down. Halting his progress the Prince refused to obey his father's orders, which angered the King tremendously. 'You dare to defy your King!?' he growled. To which the Prince retorted 'My King is an old fool if he believes that this abomination deserves to live!' At that moment, what was supposed to be a wonderful reunion was torn apart because of my magic, as the King struck out at the Prince, slapping him with the back of his hand directly round the face. The King leaned in close towards Prince Reaven, and nose-to-nose he spoke soft and calmly, yet menacingly, with words that still haunt me to this day. 'Then you are no longer our Prince and you are no longer a son of mine. You are hereby banished from Alexandria.' Backing away in shock the Prince called out to the people and proclaimed that his father was a fool to believe that Alexandria would ever stand again. He went on to inform the crowd that he would be travelling south-west, to the Phoenix Garrison, where he would start a new life and form a new home for the defeated people of Alexandria, free from Ifrit and his army of magical beings. His one request was for those who wished to survive, to follow him. As the Prince walked away the Knights gathered their weapons and rations and dutifully followed along with around twenty-five refugees. Passing me, the Prince stopped, towering over me, he looked down and warned that should I follow him, he would hunt me down and have me killed, just like the rat I was! Slamming his sword into the dirt beside me, he went on to say with a bitter taste in his mouth that he did not want my cursed artefacts, as he took possession of another sword passed to him by Sir Leander. Of course I knew that the sword was still enchanted and would inevitably return to the Prince, one way or another."

Interrupting Quin's story, Historian Nicolas couldn't help but express candid his opinion.

"Your Prince Reaven sounds like an imbecile. You are not cursed or plagued, you are blessed with a gift. Albeit using your magic on a human, would certainly curse them. You must take great care when using your gifts for the benefit of others."

Quin now understood the danger of using his powers, having discovered that magical possession by humans was a curse, apparently regardless of where it comes from, be it a relic or directly from someone, such as himself.

"I thought it was only blessed relics that cursed people!" he stated, hoping that Nicolas would confirm his assumption and put his mind at ease,

"Magic is not biased, Quin. It does not care how others come to possess it. Those who were born without magic are not meant to possess it at all. Imagine if fire possessed the power to control water, the fire would thrive and spread causing devastation to the planet; however the power it possessed would ultimately lead to its destruction. The principal is the same for humans!" explained Historian Nicolas. Quin took a moment and began to wonder how any magical being could live with the knowledge that using their magic to help others would curse them. On the other hand if he did not use his powers to help others, they would die. He couldn't help but wonder; which was the lesser of the two evils?

Quin began to feel his way of life and beliefs had taking a mighty blow, and had become trapped in a paradoxical situation. Either way, no matter what course of action he took, those he cared for would inevitably die around him. It was a hard concept for him to swallow, he knew he was quite possibly the most selfless person to walk Gaia, but was now forced to recognise that, from that moment onwards, he could only use his magic for himself and his own benefits. Quin began to feel a dark shroud consuming him as the reality of his situation came to light, and it explained why those with magic had been branded as evil. It now made sense that those with magic were selfish because any good deed they enacted for others would ultimately be punished.

Lost within his thoughts and feelings. Slowly looking up at Nicolas, Quin's eyes began to glow an eerie shade of red. He frowned angrily at Nicolas, as a sinister entity appeared to be coming forward from the darkest depths of his heart, taking over his thoughts and turning them to hatred for the world and those that dared to condemned him for having magic. Quin perceiving all his past actions as acts of good, yet each step he took ultimately resulted in an act of evil. Nicolas began to feel discomforted as Quin's gaze lingered upon him and his body language changed before his eyes. Fearful of Quin's current state, Nicolas felt he had to remind him of whom he was,

"Do you believe Origen felt this way Quin?" Pausing for a moment to think carefully about the question, Quin's mind started spinning. Trembling and breathing heavily he attempted to calm himself down, and as he did so, his eyes slowly returned back to their natural green tone. He allowed himself a few moments to regained control of his thoughts and feelings and then went on to whisper a single word "Reaven…"

Historian Nicolas gave Quin a little more time for him to clear his head of the conflict and then politely asked him to continue his story.

"Rather than walking away, I stayed with the King and the remaining people of Alexandria for another day. The King kept a close eye on me at all times, claiming he would protect me and I was to be his new advisor. I often wondered why the King would keep me so close to him, when I was a living embodiment of everything he detested. Perhaps he thought that in keeping me close he could ensure I did not use my magic. I had to wonder if he suspected I was a spy for Ifrit and he was staying true to his word 'keep one's allies close and one's enemies, even closer!' But if I had known what he was about to ask me, I never would have thought such a thing.

At early sunrise the following morning, the King came to me while I slept on my rock outside the Halls, waking me from my slumber. I could see from the look on his face, he was deeply troubled, and as I sat up, he began to babble and reminisce with stories of his past, which, if I was to be brutally honest, I did not really care to hear about. His sentimentally nostalgic stories explained the history of his soulmate, and Prince Reaven's childhood. It is only now that I wish I had listened and taken in every small detail of what he was telling me. While he revealed his life's stories to me, I began to wonder if he was drunk because, at that moment, I wanted to tell him to 'stop bumbling and get to the point'. When he finally got around to telling me why he had come to speak with me, the sun had risen and the people were starting to wake up. The King looked at me and I could see a deep sadness in his eyes as he came to realise how completely powerless he was to help his son during his dangerous journey across the open lands and snowy Centaur Mountains. To be honest, I believed it was more to do with the Kings stubbornness than his inability to help his son, and would rather let him die than accept that Prince Reaven may have been correct about Alexandria and should have followed him to the Phoenix Garrison. Thus the King handed me Prince Reaven's sword and charged me with a single task, 'Find my son. Protect him and ensure that he succeeds in rebuilding a new home for Alexandria'.

I do not know if I was scared or excited at the prospect of seeing Prince Reaven again, knowing that he would probably kill me if he saw me. Regardless, I wanted to be by his side; for I finally understood the meaning of a true friendship, one really does not know what they have until it is gone. I had accepted that Reaven was my best, and possibly only, friend. I would gladly sacrifice my life for him, even if it was to die by his own hand due to his hatred of me. Without so much as another thought, I snatched the sword from the King, saluted him and left immediately to catch up with the Prince.

As I walking away, I felt it was inappropriate to use my magic in front of the King as he sat watching me leave, although at the same time I wanted him to see with his own eyes that I would use whatever means necessary to catch up to Reaven and protect him. Furthermore, and more importantly, I wanted him to know that I was not ashamed of my magic anymore, and I had come too far to keep on pretending to be something other than myself. Thrusting my chest forward as I focused on the element of air, I briefly levitated before I transformed myself into, what I can only describe as, 'the winds', allowing me to move freely through the breeze. Flying away at an almighty speed, I left the Legion Halls and the King's side to I set off on a journey across dangerous lands in pursuit of the Prince and the Knights of Alexandria.

Sweeping through the lands, it gradually became evident that I was leaving the desolation of the lands around Alexandria, as the plant life began to thrive, the further I moved away from the capital. The blood red fog in the sky cleared back into a glorious blue sky, revealing the beaming sun that I had almost forgotten existed. The birds chirping songs filled the area and the rivers ran with pure, crystal clear, water once again. Although I wanted to stop and take a moment to relish in the beautiful landscape and reacquainted myself with the elements, I had to keep in mind that the Prince had already progressed an entire day ahead. Although at my current enhanced speed, I presumed it would only take me half a day to catch up.

I pressed onwards until I came across a large forest. Knowing it would be difficult to safely manoeuvre through the trees at my current speed, I changed direction to go around the forest. At that moment an unexplained feeling of deep grief shot through my heart and interrupted my focus which instantly broke my spell, transforming me back into my solid form. Unfortunately I was still travelling at a great speed when my body reformed that the shear force tossed me along the ground, which painfully slowed my progress. Covered in grazes and bumps, I groaned at the pain, whilst aggravated at myself for not being able to control my powers as well as I should. Rolling over to push myself up off the ground, I discovered what had caught my attention.

A White Galanthus Flower! They were exceptionally rare in Alexandria, but equally as beautiful. Of course, it was not the fact that I had stumbled upon one that broke my concentration; it was the memory of Asha and her adoration of these flowers. I cast my mind back to the days when we were both children and Asha would say that the White Galanthus was her most loved flower. She used to keep a single Galanthus inside her diary, which was pressed and preserved perfectly as if it was picked that very morning. Of course, Asha was quite happy to show me her diary, for she knew I could not read. Many a time I would wonder if there was anything in it about me and although I often asked her to read it to me, she always laughed and made up some ridiculous story about what she had written. I knew she was not telling me the truth about the writings in that small leather-bound book with a silky blue ribbon flowing freely down the spine, but I was always happy to sit and listen to the stories about her adventures to faraway lands. There, she would tell me, were fields with masses of White Galanthus Flowers, as far as the eye could see and she would run through them, laughing and playing her flute as the flowers sang her songs.

Reaching forward I plucked the flower from the ground and used my magic to merge it within my very soul, so that it would live as long as I did, I knew that using my powers in this way could be dangerous, for if I was to use this magic on anything bigger it would probably kill me, however the flower was the only thing that I now possessed, which represented the everlasting love I have for Asha. Placing the Galanthus into my belt pouch I attempted to transform back into the winds, however, before I could my attention was drawn by a ghostly whisper coming from within the forest. Drawing my sword to protect myself from any dangers that may befall me, I cautiously walked towards the forest.

As I entered the forest and walked past the first few trees, the whispers became louder and louder. I soon discovered that each of the trees was sounding out a different section of a story, and as I progressed through the forest, each tree was emitting its own sound based on what it had heard. I had never experienced such a truly bizarre power before and quite honestly it scared me, the sounds of the trees echoing memories seemingly merged with the sounds that were happening at that precise moment, which soon became rather disjointed. The deeper into the forest I progressed, the harder it became to distinguish between the sounds of the past and present, however I continued to follow deeper into the forest and allowed the trees to guide me forward. Stopping periodically to listen, I realised the sounds were actually voices. Of those voices I recognised Prince Reaven and the Knights. The Prince was telling old tales of the forest;

'It is said that this forest holds great dangers, and the trees possess strange magical properties once bestowed upon them by a legion goddess names Dexithea, so watch your back and mind your step. My father used to tell me

that these forests hold giant spiders, ferocious basilisks and even chimera; a vicious fire-breathing beast with the body of a lion, a venomous snake for a tail and the head of a goat on its back. They are afraid of nothing but the Cerberus; which just so happens to be a ferocious fire breathing, three headed hound. It is said that one could press the Cerberus with a branding iron and it would have no effect. However you should not worry; these creatures are said to be nocturnal and have rarely been seen by humans.'

Another voice began to speak. Listening intently, I attempted to identify the voice. I can only assume it was Sir David as the words seemed to fit his personality; kind and gentle, but most of all courteous.

'My lord, night is almost upon us and I fear your stories will only serve to strike fear into the civilians. Perhaps we should seek refuge for the night and progress further at sunrise!'

As I listened to the end of the echo, the entire forest suddenly fell deathly silent. Looking around, I found myself in the middle of the large forest, without a clue of which way to go, or even which way I had come from. Luckily, as I gazed around I noticed something shining on the ground near the opening of a small cave. Walking over and picking it up, I recognised it as an Alexandrian coin, which lead me to believe that the Prince and his followers had stayed the night inside the cave. Placing the coin into my pocket, I called into the cave. There was no reply beyond my echo, bouncing down the deep caverns and passages. I progressed, to investigate.

Inside the cave I attempted to look around, although it was too dark to make anything out. Trampling over the unsteady ground, I thought the cave floor was covered in rocks that had fallen from above. Calling out again, I could hear my voice echoing through the passages, which lead deep into the ground. Listening carefully for any kind of response as the echoes died down, I could hear the sound of breathing close by, which sounded wheezy and deep. I feared that someone may be injured and so I created a flame in my hand to light the way. As the immediate area lit up, I found myself within touching distance of what I believe to have been a pack of Cerberus'. Frozen to the spot in fear of waking them, I slowly began pacing backwards holding my breath, so as not to make a sound. Placing my footing clumsily, I fell down and held back the yelp as best I could as the impact sent a painful shock down my leg. Looking down to see what I had tripped on I noticed the rocks were white and smooth and upon investigating closer I discovered it was, in fact, a human skull. In a frantic shock I gasped loudly and threw the skull away, having foolishly forgotten about the Cerberus'. The skull rolled along the ground knocking loudly over the sea of bones that covered the floor. With every muscle in my body tensed in fear as I willed the skull to stop rolling, I carefully got up and turned my back on the sleeping Cerberus to continue my escape. With but a single step forward, I trod on a bone that crunched loudly, forcing me to freeze again. Holding my position for a moment, I assumed that the Cerberus were still asleep. However, just as I was about to continue there was a deep and booming growl behind me. Fearfully turning around I could now see the white glow of the Cerberus' eyes as one-by-one they awoke and stared at me. Without another thought, I sprinted out of the cave as the Cerberus' barked manically and began their pursuit.

Exiting the cave into the bright sunlight, I threw my magical, behind me and watched over my shoulder as it hit a Cerberus in the snout. Without so much as flinching the Cerberus ran right through it as if it were air. Flitting in any direction I could, I ducked and dived through the trees and foliage of the forest, but the Cerberus were still closing in behind me, barking and growling and biting at each other in competition of which one would have the first taste of my blood. As I continued to run for my life, the smell of burning wood caught my attention. Looking around I could see a small wisp of smoke between two large trees. Hoping to find some allies or reinforcement, I sharply changed direction and ducked just as one of the Cerberus' dived overhead and snapped its jaws, barely missing me. Having a moment to look round I counted five in total although because I was so busy counting them, I had not noticed the gigantic spider-web in front of me which, as I ran through, caused me to trip, falling flat on my face. Fumbling back to my feet, I drew my sword and stumbled backwards to face the Cerberus', just in time to see one pouncing for me. Swinging my sword with all my strength I slashed the beast's throat and was splattered with its blood as it landed on me, forcing me back to the ground. Pushing the beast off, I clambered back to my feet. I was by now out of breath and exhausted, but was forced to run again as the remaining four persisted in their hunt. Arriving at the source of the smoke, I came across a small campfire which had been left unattended to burn out on its own. The campfire was still smoking due to a few remaining embers fighting to stay alive. Ironically I knew the feeling!" Quin said with a sarcastic tone, to which, Nicolas politely humoured his sarcasm as he listened attentively to his exciting, yet unnerving, story. Quin continued,

"Knowing that I could not outrun the Cerberus' for much longer, I turned to face them and the four of them spread out, tactfully surrounding me. Swinging my sword as they stepped towards me, I attempted to subdue them for as long as possible while I regained my energy, hoping to give myself the chance to use my powers. However, while I was so exhausted it made it near impossible for me to conjure even the smallest amount of magic. Then, there was a loud bark as the Cerberus I had previously injured appeared from behind a large tree, dragging its limp and lifeless middle head along the ground. It was only then that I realised they were not trying to kill me, but simply catch me in a trap to allow the victim of my attack to have its revenge. Quickly surveying the area I tried to find a way to escape, but there was nothing but spider webs overhead entangled around the tree tops. The campfire beside me had nothing but a few charred remains and the only means of escape were now guarded by each of the Cerberus'. My situation looked bleak. Pouncing into the air at me, the Cerberus made its move. At that moment, out of nowhere, something shot by my head and hit the Cerberus, sending it hurtling away towards a tree. Staring in amazement, I watched the Cerberus squirming and flailed to break free from the large shimmering web that now wrapped it up and kept it firmly in place, hanging from the tree trunk. Hearing a whimper from another Cerberus, I watched as they regrouped and slowly backed away from me as if afraid. Having gained enough distance, the Cerberus stopped and stood together in a tight group facing off in all directions. I can only assume they were unwilling to leave their meal or the other pack members behind. Suddenly there was a heavy thump behind me and I could hear the tapping of feet on the ground. Hoping to see a familiar face, I turned and bore witness to yet another creature and found myself face to face with a ginormous black arachnid which had a decoration on its back that looked like a pair of glowing red eyes. At the time, I could not quite work out why the pattern seemed so familiar to me. It almost felt like I was looking at some sort of memory, as the pattern seemingly drew closer and closer, mesmerising me while garbled words and unusual images flashed through my mind. In the few moments I stood staring at this behemoth spider, it had already started to entangle my feet in its web, which, I do not think the Cerberus were too pleased with, as their chance for revenge, and dinner, was about to be stolen away from them. Barking and howling loudly, they broke my fixation and began to charge in my direction.

Attempting to run I quickly realised my feet were tied together by the spiders web which caused me to fall flat on my face, yet again. Luckily I had fallen at the perfect moment as the Cerberus' pounced, missing me and landed on the spider, which delivered a blow that sent them all hurtling away. Still out of breath and tired, I worried that I still would not have the energy to summon any magic, and as I reached for my sword I found that in my tumble I had dropped it just out of reach. Frantically pulling and tugging at the web to break myself free, I discovered the web was as strong as iron wire, so much so that I concluded it would have been easier to hack off my own legs with the sword than cut through the web. I found it difficult to compose myself and keep calm, to allow myself the use of some magic, as the Cerberus' and Spider fumbled around attacking each other, although it was quite obvious that the spider was winning, as one by one the Cerberus' were shot with webs and stuck fast to trees. Soon only two remained, one of which continued to attack the spider, whilst the other stalked over to me, each of its mouths drooling and foaming as it growled viciously. Shutting my eyes and taking a deep cleansing breath, I let go of my fear and pleaded with the embers within the campfire to assist me. It was not a moment before they answered my call and agreed to help. I reached out my hand and exhaled sharply whilst snapping my eyes open to focus on the embers, the campfire roared as the flames bellowed out and reached up high into the air. Startled by the flames, the spider quickly scuttled away, leaving me alone with the two Cerberus'. Controlling the flames I thrust my hand down to my feet and drew them to the web, sundering it to ashes in the blink of an eye. Diving forwards, as the closest Cerberus charged at me, I grabbed my sword and thrust it through the beast's heart. Angrily summoning the power from within the blade to combust and destroy the creature from the inside, out, before I quickly scrambled to my feet and began to run, unknowing of the horrors that awaited me.

With only one Cerberus left hunting me, and without the energy to continue using my magic, all I could do was run. Looking back over my shoulder periodically I could see the beasts jumping along the tree stumps with incredible agility. As I witnessed it drawing closer once again, I had momentarily neglected to pay attention to where I was going. The ground suddenly disappeared from under my feet and it was not long before I realised I had just stepped off the side of an extremely steep slope. The last thing I remember is tumbling towards a rather large rock, set in my path.

When I eventually awoke I found myself at the bottom of the slope with a large cut on my forehead. However at the time I was more concerned of the whereabouts of the Cerberus. Gazing up the slope I attempted to focus my eyes from the double vision I had due to the impact of the fall. Covering one eye I was able to see straight and saw the Cerberus sitting atop the slope, glaring down at me. After a few moments, it howled, turned away and disappeared back into the forest. Pulling myself back to my feet I tried to determine where I was. Much to my relief, It appeared I was out of the woods and before me lay the continuation of the meadows that were separated by the ghastly forest I had just scarcely escaped.

As my vision returned I noticed a large rock formation in the distance with a figure sitting at the foot of it. As I approached and drew closer I recognised this person as Sir Benjamin the Right-Hand. Overjoyed at seeing a familiar face, I rushed over to him and called out his name. Slowly turning his head to see where the voice had come from, he caught sight of me and smiled. Without making any attempts to move from his spot, he just sat there and waited for me. It soon became obvious that he was wounded as blood dripped from a gash in his chainmail. Kneeling beside him I looked into his pale face and listened to him struggling to breathe, the veins in his neck were prominent and black and as I gazed into his eyes, I did not know what to say and so foolishly blurted out 'How are you?'. Thankfully Benjamin had a good sense of humour and laughed at my ridiculous question. 'I have been better Quin! Those spiders have a good bite on them!' he said. I wish there was something I could have done to cure him, but even with my healing powers I knew it was too late for this fine Knight and even if I had tried to heal him, it would have only prolonged his suffering before his inevitable end. I did not know what else to say; how can one look a dying man in the eyes and, even with all my powers, tell him that he was going to die? I thought of all things I could have said to him and wanted so much to tell him, 'everything will be ok', but I could not bear to fill him with a false hope. Benjamin smiled at me and gently said 'You realise Reaven is going to kill you for following us?', to which I laughed 'I know, but is that not what friends are for?' his head slowly began to fall to one side and his eyes lids grew heavy as he spoke with his final breath 'Only true friends Quin…' and with that his head fell forward and his soul seemingly left his physical form. As I looked upon his lifeless body, a single tear rolled down my cheek as I closed my eyes and placed my hand on his head to honour him and said my good-bye's to the noble Knight who had honourably given his life for his Kingdom; an honour that one day I hoped to have. Raising my hand gently over his restful head, I used the combined forces of fire and air to cremate his body into a fine ash which drifted away peacefully onto the beautiful meadows. I stood watching as the ashes floated away into the distance and bid a final farewell to Sir Benjamin, thanking him for all he had done for me. Perhaps it was my imagination, but as the wind whistled between the rocks where I stood, I was sure I heard the faint words 'thank you'.

Having to say good-bye to yet another person I considered my friend, I knew that I would have to hurry if I was to catch up with the Prince, for I could not bear to say good-bye to anyone else.

Swiftly transforming once more into the winds, I continued my journey toward the foot of the Snowy Mountains which marked the half-way point between Alexandria and the Phoenix Garrison. My only concern was that the Snowy Mountains belonged to the brutal Centaur tribe and was claimed as their homeland long before Alexandria was constructed. The stories told of the herds amassing in their hundreds, with large siege weapons of war placed all over the land, which they used to slaughter anyone who would dare to trespass. For me, it would be easy to simply wisp through in the form of the winds, but for one without magic, such as Prince Reaven and his followers, it would be nigh on impossible. I wanted to believe that he would find another way around the mountains, which admittedly would have added days to his journey, but it would keep him and his followers safe from harm. However I knew all too well that his arrogance would see him walk straight through the Centaur settlement. The only thing I knew for certain was that I had to get there quickly and would most probably be forced use my powers to protect him. Of course, I was well aware that I would have to remain in close concealment, as the Prince's rage at my presence alone would infuriate him and distract him from his objective of getting the refugee's to the Phoenix Garrison safely, preferably without killing me in the process."

- Chapter VIII -
An Icy End

"Flying freely through the land in my magical form, I held hope in my heart that I would not be too late, or that the Prince had simply taken the long detour around the Snowy Centaur Mountains. Unfortunately my hope was dashed when I finally arrived at the foot of the mountain, where the grass and ice met and a thick fog of snow fell from the sky. The air around me grew colder as I stood looking up at the footprints of a large group leading up the mountain, and it was only too clear to me that these were the tracks of the Prince and his followers, progressing towards the heart of the Centaur's Homeland. Scanning the tracks that led further into the distance, I spotted a small group ascending over the top of the mountain, which led them over to the perilous Centaur camp. I remember the relief I felt as I had caught up with the group and, for now, they were safe. Yet in truth, I was not sure how long they would remain that way up on the mountain's peak, where the air would be freezing cold and the lands vast and open, with little shelter in which to rest and conceal oneself, away from the ever vigilant, and preying Centaur. Having never been there before, I could only imagine what horrors awaited them, and myself for that matter, as we all stepped over the threshold, into unknown territory. I would like to say I knew what to expect, but I had never actually seen a Centaur and very few citizens within the Kingdom of Alexandria spoke of them; probably because they were never really much of a problem, as the Centaurs rarely ventured away from the Snowy Mountains and, generally, kept themselves to themselves, unless you ever came across one. I recalled once being told the story about the Knights of Alexandria's encounter with a single Centaur who had ventured away from the Snowy Mountains and into Alexandrian territory, while the Knights patrolled the lands between the Legion Halls and the Kingdom. It was said that the Centaur knew no fear as it charged at the Knights, even being outnumbered five to one. It was rumoured to have killed three of the Knights before it was finally slain, however that is just a tale I heard and it is a well-known fact that as the tales are passed on they are greatly exaggerated and twisted. For all my ignorance of these creatures, I felt more afraid of the unknown, rather than knowing what I was about to face.

I attempted to use my powers to re-form back into the winds, but I was confronted with an immense pain as the freezing temperature drained me of all warmth and replaced it with a pain like a thousand needles stinging my entire body. In this form I attempted to rush forward, but it became increasingly apparent that the force of the true elements, conjured by Gaia, were far more powerful than I could begin to comprehend. Bursting out of my magical form, I fell to my knees and quickly curled up into a tight ball, rubbing myself with haste to warm up and relieve myself of the stabbing pain from the shards of ice that turned my blood cold and jabbed my skin all over. Noticing a dead tree stump nearby I quickly cast a fire spell and dragged myself over to warm up by the flames, while taking a passing moment to see how far up the mountain I had come. What seemed to be a life of pain while travelling in my magical form, actually turned out to be no more than a few short steps! I sat for a moment and thought to myself that maybe my powers did not truly have a place in this world and this was simply the wisdom of Gaia trying to tell me that I do not belong in these mountains. Yet all the while my friends were still ahead of me, and their lives could be in very great danger, therefore not even Gaia could break my resolve. Recalling my reason for being there, I put aside my pain and reminded myself that it was my duty to protect Reaven or die for him if I had to. I needed to get to the top of that mountain as quickly as I could, but without the use of my magic. I had to stop feeling sorry for myself and find Reaven.

I stumbled and fell up the mountain as fast as my legs would carry me, while my feet sank into the soft snow that covered a hidden layer of ice beneath causing me to lose my footing every few steps.

After what seemed like days of struggle, I finally reached the top of the mountain, completely out of breath with a tremendous cramp in my side. Having reached this point I had planned to rest for a moment or two. However the horror that was suddenly before my eyes gave me no alternative but to press on through the coldness and pain, as I stood witness to the Centaur civilisation. I was confronted with the truth that these barbaric creatures I once imagined to be mere animals were, in fact, sophisticated builders and architects.

The astonishing view was of strong wooden bridges which stood over a large crevasse that led through the centre of the mountains, and a town surrounded by towering stone walls with a single gate for access. From within these walls, I could see smoke rising from the chimneys of the sturdy forges that churned out the masses of weapons which were scattered all over the mountain. Between the small manned outposts were all kinds of siege weapons and constructions, befitting of any human settlement.

For all my time studying the Centaur settlement, I saw no evidence of the Prince and his followers and no sign of a struggle, which lead me to believe that they had not been captured and had found a place to hide. I continued to search the immediate area for any signs of them. Then, spotting a set of human footsteps, I looked ahead and saw that they had found cover inside the crevasse itself, which spanned through the centre of the entire settlement and out the other side of the mountain, and into the lands outside the Phoenix Garrison. My concern grew for their safety while travelling along the bottom of the crevasse, as there was no overhead cover at any point while they travelled stealthily through. My immediate thought was, 'If any Centaur should notice the group below, they would be trapped and quickly slain.' I wanted to follow them through, however I knew it would be more beneficial to them if I stayed above and kept watch over the Centaur patrols and created diversions where necessary. Thankfully I arrived when I did, as it was at that very moment my assistance was required.

Three Centaurs trotted towards my location. Thankfully they had not noticed me as I dived behind a nearby rock mound to conceal myself. Now that I was safely out of sight I knew that I had to ensure that the Prince would not be discovered from the footprints in the snow that left a trail straight to him. Peering over the rock I focused my magic to create a small gust of wind that gently lifted a cloud of snow and covered the tracks over. Slipping back behind the rock I could hear the Centaur's hooves clattering closer until they eventually arrived and stood guard on the other side of the mound where I sat. My heart pounded in my chest as I sat trying not to breathe a sound, hoping they would not find me, knowing that I would be as good as dead if they did. As I sat and waited for them to pass I was shocked to hear them speak. Perhaps my ignorance was greater than I thought, of course they can talk, why would they not?

Overhearing their conversation, the Centaurs discussed the news of Alexandria's destruction and boasted as they shared their hatred for the 'idiotic' humans and bragged that they could never be so weak as to fall by Ifrit's hand, then went on to speak of the pride they felt for being such a mighty and unstoppable clan,

'We Centaur live on the highest height, which

makes us gods in comparison to the pathetic humans' they scoffed.

I stopped for a moment and wonder what he meant by 'gods'. It was not a word I was familiar with," Quin paused, gazing at Historian Nicolas in the hope that he would be wise enough to know the answer to his question. "God is a rather broad term, Quin. It is a word I have only recently come across myself, I believe it is used to describe a divine being, one with an omnipotent or omniscient power over the rest, by comparison. There is only one we could truly refer to as 'god'. We know her as 'Gaia - Mother of all life'. Although the tales of Gaia vary greatly, you should finish your story before I tell mine". Historian Nicolas said wisely, with a proud smile on his face for knowing so much.

"After a few moments the Centaurs walked away, then suddenly one of them shouted out 'Over there!' and another asked 'What is that?' The words struck a fear so deep within me, my every muscle tensed so incredibly I could not, and dared not move. A cold chill ran down my spine, I was truly petrified. 'It looks like cloth' the Centaur finished, at which point I realised they had not seen me but instead had found something that belonged to one of the

Prince's followers. This simply replaced one fear with another.

Peering over the rocks, I saw the Centaurs holding a green rag that looked as if it had torn off the bottom of a dress. I watched them and took in every detail as it was the first time I had ever seen a Centaur. It was confusing to witness their physiology; identical to a human from the waist up, but instead of two human legs they appeared to have the torso of a horse." Quin described "If one was acting as a 'god', as you so described. It would appear that they had cut off the horses head and put a human body in its place, a strange combination for any such divine being to create, which was almost perverse." Quin explained, making a point of his distaste for the Centaur race, before he pressed on with his account.

"Distinguishing the difference between them, I noted that one was pure black, another was brown with a white underbelly and the third was just grey. Their 'top halves' had no clothing covering them and so I could only assume that these creatures did not feel the cold as any normal human would. While watching them I guessed that the black coloured Centaur was their leader. He was much larger than the other two and bore a scar on his left arm that was in the shape of some kind of emblem which looked like the shape of three hooves stacked one on top of the other, progressively getting bigger. I can only assume these marks were purposefully put there by means of a branding iron. The other two had no such marking, and nothing to distinguish them apart, other than their obvious difference in colour. All three had a healthy head of long black hair drooping down to their extremely muscular shoulders and torsos. I swallowed hard as I imagined how each of them could crush my comparatively puny build with ease. As the leader held the rag, he raised it to his human like face and sniffed at it as if trying to identify what it was. Dropping the rag to the ground with a look of disgust on his face, the Centaur looked at the others and spat out the word 'Humans!' Scanning the area the Centaurs seemed somewhat confused as there were no visible tracks for them to follow and much like a child playing a trick on his parents I could not help but smile and taunt these creatures in my mind, silently jeering at how stupid they looked, searched for any other traces of humans, that were probably half way through the Crevasse pathway by now.

The leader pulled out a war horn and blew into the mouthpiece creating a deep and booming cry that echoed through the mountains. With a look of pure anger and hatred on his face, he called out 'Human intruders! Centaurs to your posts! Find them!' As they all galloped away towards the settlement on the eastern side of the mountain, within the walls of the town I could hear the Centaur troops taking up arms for the hunt, their armour clashing loudly, and the commanders barked out their orders to the tribe. I knew that if I was going to save the Prince, I would have to move quickly and probably put my own life in danger to distract the masses of Centaur that now spilled through the town gate. I had already come to terms with the fact I was going to die, but what filled me with fear most of all was the suffering I would be forced to endure at the hands of the Centaur if they managed to capture me alive.

Keeping myself as low as possible, I rushed over to a tall stack of wooden timber, which lay on the edge of the crevasse, and slipped myself between some nearby wooden barrels. Successfully concealing myself without being spotted, I began crawling on my hands and knees in an attempt to sneak over to the edge and look down to see if I could catch a glimpse of the Prince. However as I placed my hands down on the ground, I noticed that the contents of one of the barrels had seeped out onto the ground, and as I rubbing the strange yellowy powdered mixture between my fingers to see what it was, I was surprised to see the gritty texture of the powder slightly spark, leaving behind a smell of flint and sulphur, which were commonly found in these mountains.

It is said that before the Kingdom of Alexandria was constructed, miners were charged with obtaining these compounds from the mine on the western side of the Snowy Mountains, however they were heavily guarded by the Centaurs, and the miners that managed to return to Alexandria alive were only able to bring back small handfuls of either of the compounds.

Collecting a small amount of this powder, I placed it on the floor and carefully cast a fire spell over it, causing it to fizz and crackle as if angered by the heat. Within a few moments the powder consumed the flame and incinerated itself instantly. I thought if a small ember caused it to react this way, I wondered what would happen if I hit a larger amount it with a flame. Taking the pouch from my belt, I emptied it out onto the ground. However my focus was soon drawn to the White Galanthus that had fallen out of the pouch and lay on the snow before me. It was only then that began to question my dedication to the Prince, as I doubted my sincerity and willingness to die for him, believing that Asha could still be alive somewhere and if that were the case, I would die having never seen her again, furthermore if she was in danger, I would not be alive to protect her. I battled with the thought for a moment, but quickly came to the conclusion that, should I continue to sit by and argue with myself of the correct course of action, both Reaven and Asha could die. I knew that I had to keep my mind in the moment and do what I had to in order to save the Prince. Reluctantly I had to push Asha to the back of my mind and press on with my mission to save the Prince, Knights, and Refugees. I retrieved the flower and dropped it into my pocket.

Holding my hand over the snow beneath me and focused hard on the gritty earth below the thick layers of snow and ice. Summoning the power of earth I used a kind of magnetic aura, which pulled sharp stones and pebbles out of the snow and rested in my palm. My hand filled with the small shards of earth. I grasping them tightly and placed them into my pouch, filling the rest of it with the strange powder from the barrels. Attaching it back onto my belt for later use, I collected the White Galanthus and tied it securely to my vest over my heart and beseeched it to bless me.

Peering over the edge of the crevasse, I spotted the Prince directly below me. He looked pale and exhausted but pushed on regardless with his followers closely behind him, sandwiched between the Knights in front. The Prince was constantly watching for any signs of danger and all the while keeping deadly silent, even when stepping. Strangely, as if he had felt my presence, he turned and gazed over in my direction and I cowered backwards to hide from his sights. All I could do for now was to ensure I kept watch over him as he progressed through the crevasse, and out into the safety of the other side of the mountain. I had noticed that further along his path there was a three-way split. From my position I could see that one way led to a dead end, another led directly into a Centaur camp that was now buzzing with masses of beasts, all equipped with bows and arrows, and the third led out of the mountain. Somehow I had to ensure that they would not travel down the wrong route and so as the group passed my location, I grabbed a handful of snow, rolled it into a tight ball, and tossed it at Sir Shimri who had moved to the back of the group, ensuring no-one had fallen behind. Exploding as it collided with the back of his head, he quickly drew his sword and spun round to face his attacker. I was hoping he would spot me, however after glancing around for a moment he stowed his blade and turn to carry on without even having checked above him, which, obviously, would have been the first place one would check for attackers. Rolling my eyes and thinking to myself 'oh for crying out loud', I resorted to calling out to him as quietly as I could but in the hope that he would hear me. Spinning around Sir Shimri stared straight up at me and smiled joyfully as he whispered 'Quin? What are you doing here?' Naturally that was undoubtedly the most inconvenient time to be discussing such matters, however Sir Shimri always was the kind of person that found this sort of situation to be fun and games and was easily distracted from his goal, something, I am pleased to say, I did not share with him. I merely replied 'Now is not the time for idle discussion, the path ahead is split three ways, you need to take the path on your left', to which he nodded and then stood there as if he was expecting me to say something else, perhaps he wanted to continue with a bit of small talk. As if dealing with an infant I barked 'What are you waiting for? Get going!' He smiled then turned and ran to catch up with the rest of the group.

Comforted by the fact that they now at least knew which way they needed to go, all that remained was for me to find a way through the camps, which had become overrun with more Centaurs than I dared count. At that moment there was a cry from a Centaur sentry overlooking the Crevasse who had just spotted the Prince. Calling for backup from the nearby Centaur, he drew an arrow from his quiver and aimed down into the gulley below. Without any consideration for my continued concealment, I rose to my feet and watched as a heard progressed to the edge of the crevasse. Frantically searching for some sort of distraction I spotted a barrel next to the Centaur, without thought for the safety of those below, I raised my hand and conjured a ball of fire in my palm, which I quickly cast away, hurtling towards the barrel. The ball flew smoothly through the air and the moment seemed to slow as it sailed towards my target, I only hoped it would reach the barrel before the Centaur's arrow was released towards my friends.

My fire ball merely tapped the barrel and caused an incredible explosion that engulfed the entire area, setting fire to many of the Centaur in the vicinity, and a few which stood in closer proximity instantly dropped dead as shards of wood and debris penetrated deep into their bodies with a deadly force. Strangely there was no sign of the Centaur who was aiming his arrow into the gulley, I could only assume that the blast had instantly vaporised him, however I had never before experience such a power. Sadly the blast had weakened the edge of the crevasse and as a consequence snow began to fold inwards and collapse onto the path below. From where I stood I could see that the wall of snow had separated the Knights from the Prince and his group of refugees. The only chance they had now lay completely in the Prince's hands, and as I surveyed the area I bore witness to the hordes of Centaur alerted by the explosion, charging towards me and the crevasse opening.

What I can only describe as a mysterious power suddenly overwhelmed my body and mind, with a force more powerful than anything I had ever felt before. The fear inside me seemed to convert itself into pure energy and I found myself walking towards the crevasse edge preparing to unleash my new found powers. Magic far beyond my comprehension began to flow through me as the elements spoke to me making tactical suggestions to which I commanded them to use my body and fulfil their desires. As I continued forward to reveal my presence to Prince Reaven, the Centaur turned their attention to me and bombarded me with metal-headed arrows. The Element of fire surrounded me in a field, much the same as it did during the siege on Alexandria, and as each of the arrows entered the fires that surrounded me, they were instantly incinerated leaving only the arrow heads to fall to the ground and hiss loudly as the cold snow cooled the searing metal. In disbelief of what the Centaurs were seeing they soon stopped firing on me and stood gazing at the incredible power before them. I took a moment to identify where each Centaur stood and then with a mighty blast of a magnetic energy I attracted the arrow heads and sent them hurting away from me to return from whence they came at twice the force. In the blink of an eye the large group of Centaur that surrounded me simultaneously fell to the ground, dead... And I felt nothing!

On the other side of the crevasse a group of Centaur were lined up, aiming their arrows at the people below. Raising my hand up I called to the power of air and summoned forth a bolt of lightning that blasted down from the heavens and struck a single Centaur and continued to travel along the line. As each one absorbed the shock, their bodies jolted for a few moments, and then they simply fell down dead.

Having made my way to the crevasse I could now see the Prince holding up his shield for cover, with the cowering refugees behind him attempting to get cover under the protection of his inadequately sized sidearm. After a few moments the Prince slowly emerged from his defensive position, noticed a single Centaur's head drooped over the edge of the Ravine as it lay dead on the ground above him, and then spotted me looking down on him.

It seemed all too obvious that the Prince was unsure if he was angered by my presence, or thankful that I was there to give my support. From my vantage point all I could do was guide him 'Go! Take the left path in the fork ahead!' The refugee's quickly took off, leaving me and the Prince staring at each other with a conflict of words, if only in our minds. I did not know if I should have been pleasant or simply walked away to leave him to choose his own path, after all, I had done my part in saving him. I had used my magic to save him and the refugees and now all I had left to do was save the Knights. I had come to the conclusion that this was my sole purpose in life and it was only a matter of moments before the elements took complete control of my body and mind, to reclaim my powers and return me to Gaia's embrace.

Then, I saw a herd of Centaur galloping along the crevasse path bearing down upon the trapped Knights. Further in the distance there were even more Centaur heading along each side of the crevasse, chasing down the refugees and as I looked up toward the opposite side I could see the Centaur leader heading straight towards the Prince and myself. It seemed as if fate had put a metaphorical 'fork in the road' for me as well, I only wished there was someone looking down on me that could have told me which way to turn, but all I could do was react.

I could hear Sir Shimri calling for my assistance, while the Prince ordered me to save the refugees. However my own priority was to save the Prince, I just hoped that I would be quick enough to find a way to save them all. Rushing over to the Knights, I summoned a wall of flames between them and the Centaurs which blocked their progress, if only for a while, to allow me more time to save the others. Pulling the pouch full of powder from my belt I cast it into the fire and yelled to the Knights to take cover. Diving to the ground and raising their shields, the pouch hit the flames and promptly exploded, scattering fragments of stones which impaled the oncoming Centaur. After a moment of silence, the Knights peered over their shields and cheered at the sight of the dead Centaurs as Sir Leander roared 'For Alexandria!' and lead the Knights forward, climbing the walls of the crevasse, and rushing towards the Centaur stronghold.

As they all rushed off into the distance, I stood and watched holding onto the hope that, if they were to die, then it would be with honour in the name of Alexandria and everything they held dear. I almost envied them, for in the afterlife they would be reunited with their fallen comrades and loved ones, a place where I would one day hope to see them all once again.

I headed back towards the Prince, who was rushing off towards the refugees, with the Centaur leader still galloping in his direction. Running along the edge of the crevasse, it was not long before I caught up with the Prince, and looking up at me he exclaimed 'Save *them* Quin!' In accordance to his wishes, I pressed onwards, however there was a sudden explosion behind me and the crevasse began collapsing in the Prince's path. I stopped and turned to see the Centaur leader pulling out an arrow with a pouch on the end. I now realised what the Centaurs were using the explosive powder for. By attaching pouches of the powder to the end of their arrows it created an exploding shot that would ignite upon collision with its target. This being the case, I knew the Centaur would kill the Prince in a single shot unless I did something to intervene. The Centaur leader aimed his arrow as he continued to gallop towards the Prince. I quickly focused my sight on the arrow and allowed my fire magic to ignite it, causing it to explode in the Centaurs face. As the flames cleared and the echoes grew silent, the Centaur flopped to the ground and lay still as smoke rose from its scorched skin.

Somehow I felt that I had conquered fate's trial as it attempted to force me to choose who I would save, and although it seemed that fate had underestimated my power, I soon discovered that it had a larger plan, that I foolishly overlooked, perhaps due to my own stupid arrogance.

By now the refugees had reached the end of the crevasse path and were rushing down the other side of the mountain. Due to the sheer drop before them, the Centaurs were forced to stop and formed a group on the edge of the large cliff, aiming their bows into the air and prepared to rain a barrage down upon the fleeing refugees. Knowing I could not hope to get to them in time, I used all my strength to cast a tremendous gust of wind that burst along the mountains surface, forming mounds of snow into an avalanche that pushed the hopeless Centaurs from the mountain top to their deaths below. With some pride of our victory I stood and watched the refugees as they rushed onward towards the Phoenix Garrison, which stood tall and mighty in the near distance.

I truly felt relieved as I thought our journey was nearing its end and all that remained was to go back and get the Prince out of his pit. But as I turned back to the Prince, my relief was crushed by a gut wrenching horror as I watched the Centaur leader picking himself up off the ground, having somehow survived the explosion. Leaving his quiver and bow on the ground, the Centaur leader drew a sword and charged towards Prince Reaven.

In a race against the Centaur, I too began to run towards the Prince, however it was difficult to remain optimistic as the Centaur leader was already much closer to the Prince than I was, and without the ability to survive forming into the winds it became increasingly obvious that I would not win this race. I watched the Centaurs every step and cast spell after spell against him even though I knew he was too far out of the reach for my magic to have any effect. Having only made it half way to Reaven myself, I began to lose hope as I watched the Centaur jump down onto the path where the Prince waited.

Refusing to give up on him I pushed on with all my strength as fate laughed in my face and taunted me for being as naive as to believe I had outwitted it. The closer I got to the Prince, the louder the clashing of swords became and as I reached him and looked down I was greeted with the awful sight of the Centaur's sword penetrating deep into Prince Reaven's chest. My horrified scream caught the Centaur's eye, and as he gazed up at me he smiled sinisterly, proud of his victory, before dashing back along the path towards his settlement. I know that I should have chased him and seen to the end of that disgusting vermin, however I could not pass up the chance to speak to my friend one last time and to comfort him while he took his last breaths.

I rushed down to Reaven and gently lifting his head up, cradling it in my lap. Gasping for air and unable to focus his sight, I could see the Prince was quickly slipping away in front of me. I knew it was too late for my magic but still I tried with everything I had in me, yet - I could not heal him and, as much as I wanted to save him, all I could do was weep and tell him to hold on, all the while apologising because I did not have the power to save him. Helplessly, I looked Reaven in the eyes as he uttered with a fearful tone,

'Quin... f-forgive me...' And with that the Prince closed his eyes and passed away in my arms.

I sat with him for days, mourning the loss of my best friend and went through a multitude of emotions. Hysterics, anger, confusion... I did not know what to do, how to think, all the time wondering 'why!?' Until eventually, I was numb. My mind was completely blank and I just sat there in a daze, staring, into nothingness. I knew that he was at peace and had found solace in Gaia's embrace along with all the fallen citizens of Alexandria.

Eventually I had no other choice but to pick myself up and continue on with my life.

Laying my Prince down to rest I finally reunited him with his sword, placing it on his chest, grasped between both hands. I climbed out of the crevasse and stood overlooking the path where he lay. I summoned the power of water to flood the crevasse below and watched for a further day as the water gradually froze around him, preserving his body forever. Perhaps one day I will return to see his face once again. For what it was worth, I promised him I would complete his task and see the refugees safely across the border of the Phoenix Garrison and find a settlement for them so they could finally start a new life free from war, fear and the oppression that had befallen Alexandria.

I remember glaring over at the Centaur camp with such anger and hatred in my heart. Thinking back now, I am curious to know why the Centaur's continued on with their daily lives knowing of my presence, yet allowed me to remain for as long as I wanted. Even the Centaur Leader made no attempt to come for me and merely stood at his fort seemingly studying me.

Wiping away my tears I left the mountain, I kicked and beat a fallen Centaur in blind rage, blaming it and its disgusting race for the loss of my friend. Mindlessly, I walked over the lands exhausted and run down, until I finally reached the gates of the Phoenix Garrison. My only concern was to find someone I could tell my story to, in the hope that all those lost in the events that led up to that moment, would be remembered in the tales of heroes, forever."

- Chapter IX -
The Hooded Man

"It would appear your journey has been a traumatic and emotional one." Historian Nicolas said, extending his sympathy. Gratefully, Quin offered his hand to thank the Historian for listening to his story and gazed out of the tattered wooden shutters that formed a window in the side of the hovel. Nicolas noticed that night was now upon them and wondered what Quin was going to do next. For someone so physically, mentally, and above all emotionally exhausted, he knew he wouldn't get very far before he collapsed. Should that happen he would have to carry him back inside, so Nicolas thought it would only be prudent to invite Quin to extend his stay.

"Quin, you are far too weak to continue travelling, especially alone at night. Although the Phoenix Garrison is well guarded, it still has some dangerous cutthroats around who would not think twice about killing you for your possessions. Please rest here for the night; I have an additional bed upon which you can rest."

Glancing over to the other side of the room, Quin noted a curtain covering a small corner of the hovel, which must have concealed the bed. He paused for a moment and realised he wanted nothing more than to sleep, in the hope that he would wake up in the morning to find himself back in his own bed in Alexandria, and all the torment was merely a horrendous nightmare. Quin smiled and nodded gratefully at the kind gesture,

"Thank you Nicolas, I will stay." Without another word he walked towards the curtain and pulled it aside, revealing a small room with two beds on either side. Noticing that one was perfectly made and the other looked as if it had been slept in, he thought it best to lie in the tidy bed, as it was most likely the spare one.

Resting his weary head gently onto the pillow stuffed with crispy hay, Quin instantly felt his eyes growing heavy and allowed his body to rest, releasing the tension of his muscles that had built up over the days past. Shutting his eyes, his thoughts returned to memories of his journey,

"Nicolas - you will write my story?" Beyond the curtain Nicolas remained at the old table glancing over the texts within his book, reading through passages that referred to various documented magical relics. One relic in particular caught his eye,

"Yes Quin, it will be my honour to both write and tell your story for all those who would show an interest." But there was no response. Nicolas anxiously rose to his feet and pulled back the curtain to check on him. It was obvious that the journey had taken a lot out of him, as he had already fallen into a deep sleep. Lowering his head in shame, Nicolas whispered, "Sleep well Quin, and for what little my shame is worth, I am truly sorry." before grabbing his cloak from the clothing stand and covered his head over with the hood. Grabbing his walking stick, he then retrieved the book from the table and left the hovel, closing the door quietly behind him.

As he walked through the Garrison, Nicolas utilised his walking stick to give the impression he was nothing more than a feeble old man and the many cutthroats and pirates that passed him simply sauntered by without so much as sniffing in his direction.

He eventually reached the docks, the sound of the waves echoed all around. He searched from left to right for his, contact to arrive. After a while he grew impatient and decided that perhaps his contact would not show up that night. But as he turned to walk away he was startled by a hooded figure, who was standing almost nose to nose with him. Shocked by the sudden appearance of this person, Nicolas dropped his stick and book, and hastily backed away before recognising him as the one he was waiting to meet.

"You came." Nicolas said, somewhat surprised at

the presence of this person. For a moment the Hooded Man just stood in silence without any response. Then, with a deep and raspy voice, asked,

"The boy?"

Although Nicolas had only known Quin for a short while, a grieving guilt began to swell inside of him, and he carefully contemplated the repercussions of the next few moments of his life, which would either lead to a betraying Quin, or immediate death for defying The Hooded Man who now stood menacingly before him. Gritting his teeth, Nicolas accepted that he was not a brave enough man to withstand the horrors that would befall him should he protect Quin, and as such, felt that it would be less uncomfortable if he quickly got it all over with.

"It is as you foretold; the boy came to me and told me everything. The tale was *almost* identical, except-" He paused for moment as he considered finding a gentle way to break the unfortunate news "There was one difference to the tale" Displeased with his words, The Hooded Man lashed out and slapped Nicolas around the face,

"Out with it!" he growled. Intimidated by this man and now too scared to hold anything back, Nicolas went on,

"The Prince of Alexandria is dead and the King's whereabouts are unknown."

Frustrated by the news, The Hooded Man turned his head to one side and took a moment to contemplate the situation, while Nicolas cowered and waited anxiously to be dismissed.

"No matter, this is merely a setback that can be rectified. I shall find another bloodline. The boy is the key!" The Hooded Man said snapping his gaze back to Nicolas. Being too afraid to look directly into his eyes Nicolas lowered his head and fixed his sight on the wooden decking. The Hooded Man then revealed the next part of his plan "A man named 'Ragnar the Cause' will arrive in these docks at mid-day. Make certain that their paths cross".

Having heard Quin's story, Historian Nicolas knew that Quin was in no hurry to make new friends and therefore it may not be something to rely on,

"But how can you be certain he will go with this Ragnar the Cause?" Nicolas enquired. Clearly terrified that The Hooded Man would blame him if things did not transpire this way. Scoffing at Nicolas' lack of faith, The Hooded Man simply turned his back and began to walk away.

"We both know that he has already lost everything he ever cared for! Ragnar the Cause possesses the knowledge to bring it all back. He is vulnerable and will hang on Ragnar's every word."

Turning his head away in disgust, Nicolas began to feel a cold stab of guilt running through him, weighing heavily on his heart, for having just betrayed the boy of whom he had grown quite fond of.

"Wait! You did not tell me. What will become of him - in the end?" Nicolas pleaded.

Without caring enough to even turn around, The Hooded Man stopped and muttered greedily,

"The boy will die, and you will receive your reward, as promised."

Distraught by the effect of his own actions that night, Nicolas stared out at the sea, pondering the thought that in the morning Quin would leave the Garrison assisting Ragnar the Cause in his undisclosed quest. He felt a great sadness realising that this would be the last time he would ever see him. Attempting to extend a plea for some alternative solution, Nicolas turned back.

"But -" However The Hooded Man was already gone, leaving Nicolas cold and alone on the docks of the Phoenix Garrison plagued, shamed and dishonoured. With little more he could do, Nicolas felt lost, and gazing up at the stars in the night sky, illuminated by a silvery moon. He focused his sights on a single star and, falling to his knees, prayed to it.

"Forgive me, my darling. You were stolen away from me and now I have a chance, my only chance to be with you once again. You know I would give anything to touch your face just one more time and it transpires the price I must pay is the life of a boy who has already been through more suffering than anyone should ever have to endure. Why must it be he that is prophesised to save us all when everyone he knows has plotted, schemed and taken everything from him? A prophecy that was spoken of and recorded since the beginning of all life – and then for one man to come along and tell me that in order to save you, he must die. What am I to do?"

A single tear rolled down Nicolas' cheek as he struggled with a conflict of conscience, the return of his wife, or the life of an innocent boy. Awaiting a response from his wife's star, tear followed tear as he sobbed with nothing but the sound of the waves to answer his call. Wiping his eyes and rising to his feet, Nicolas spoke out into the silence;

"Very well, I will do my part and introduce Quin to this Ragnar the Cause. I only hope that he realises his true power and finds a way to change his fate and fulfil his true purpose. My darling, you must help to guide him, for if he dies, then I have single headedly condemned us all to death, and I greet it with open arms as a just reward for my treachery and dishonour".

Before returning to his hovel, Nicolas took one last look at the sea and cursed the very waves in anger. "You have taken everything from me and I have accepted it, but if you take him too, I will exact my revenge… old friend!"

- Chapter X -
The Mysterious Book

The fated morning dawned in the Phoenix Garrison and Historian Nicolas sat in his hovel, reading through pages of his books, hunched over his tattered old table while he waited for Quin to wake. Unable to think of anything but different scenarios of what the future may hold for them both, the sound of him groaning as he stretched and prepared to get up made Nicolas' stomach turn with fear. He now knew what he had to do to fulfil his promise to The Hooded Man and his heart began to race. The fear swelled inside him as Quin threw back the curtain, entering the room. Without a single word, Nicolas simply stared at him as he pacing over to the table. Petrified, Nicolas felt as though he was face to face with a prowling chimera, and realising that the moment had come to kill or be killed.

"Good Morning Nicolas" He chirped, smiling sweetly at him. "I feel much better, although I fear I may have overstayed my welcome. I will depart this very morning."

Nicolas felt it was only prudent to act casual thereby slowly introducing Quin into the conversation of meeting Ragnar, and his fate.

"Where will you go?" Nicolas asked. Quin's smile

dropped as his expression suddenly reflected his thoughts of the coming journey,

"I must return to Alexandria and find the King. It is my duty to inform him of Prince Reaven's death and to confiscate the sword that I foolishly crafted for him."

Nicolas took a moment to think, attempting to find a delicate way to sway Quin's decision. He knew that if he was to let him return back to the King, he would not meet Ragnar, and therefore he would lose the only chance he had of being reunited with his deceased mate. However he also realised that if he was to interfere, he would be condemning him to death. Swallowing his pride and attempting to allay his guilt, Nicolas felt he had no other choice, but to seal Quin's fate.

"Of course, however I have a friend I would like to introduce you to, before you go."

Quin felt somewhat inconvenienced with the suggestion and searched for the words to graciously decline.

"I cannot thank you enough for all you have done for me Nicolas, however I cannot afford to wait any longer, with each passing moment that he wields his magical sword the danger surrounding the King increases. I cannot stand by and see another person die as a result of my actions, or lack thereof. It is just one more thing I could not bear to live with!"

Quin offered out his hand and shook Nicolas', frowning in disappointment at himself for having made so many mistakes. Bowing his head, he moved towards the door. Nicolas wanted so much to let him go, but he needed to see his mate even more. Gritting his teeth and allowing his selfishness to come forward, he turned to Quin and shamelessly used his feelings against him, simply to force his hand.

"Ragnar the Cause, the man I wish you to meet, has a way to resurrect the dead." Hearing these words, Quin froze to the spot and gasped at what he had just heard.

"What did you say?" He replied having heard Nicolas but a little unsure if he should believe such a farfetched statement. Without even taking the time to breathe and give himself a moment to reconsider, Nicolas continued.

"Your Mother, Reaven, Benjamin and even Asha; he alone has the knowledge of a power to bring them all back."

Astonished by the revelation, Quin knew his heart desired the prospect of having these people back in his life more than anything, but he also knew that as there was no natural way to bring them back, magic was bound to be involved somewhere. Despite fearing the price he would have to pay to achieve such power, and concerned over what would become of the King if he did not return, he exclaimed

"Take me to him".

By the time Quin and Nicolas reached the docks the town was bustling with traders calling out to citizens to buy their goods. Children laughed and played, and seagulls squawked overhead, as the ship with the Phoenix emblem proudly emblazoned on the sails, gently cruised into the port. Quin felt his hopes rise as he saw the ship as the possibility of taking a step closer to being reunited with those he had lost. Nicolas however, stood and watched the ships arrival with an entirely different perspective, a sign of death, betrayal and great misery.

Just as the boat docked there was a loud scream for help from a woman at the front gates of the Garrison, disturbing the peaceful atmosphere amongst the townsfolk. Quin's attention was taken away from the boat and he turned to see what was happening as the screams felt like the echoes of Alexandria's fall, memories flashing back through his mind. Fearfully he raced towards where the cries were coming from, drawing his sword ready to strike down any Ifryte that he presumed had entered the Garrison.

A large group had gathered, all looking horrified at the ground, some women cried at the sight as their friends and family comforted them, and a physician barged his way through the crowd, yelling at people to let him pass. Patiently pushing his way through the crowd, Quin attempted to get a glimpse of what was happening and as he reached the forefront he was greeted with a familiar face that was covered in blood.

"Leander?" Quin cried out in horror, falling to his knees next to his friend. Leander opened his eyes and gazed over the faces that stood over him, noticing Quin he smiled and murmured,

"Quin, you made it? I knew you would! You did it, you saved the Refugees and the Prince."
Arriving at the scene, Nicolas assessed the situation and could only offer his sympathy to Quin as he placing his hand on his shoulder. Quin shut his eyes and attempted to use his healing magic.

"Quin, stop!" Nicolas barked.
"I have to, do you not understand? I cannot let him die!" Quin emotionally replied, holding his tears back. Nicolas placed both hands on his shoulders and whispered in his

ear,

"You cannot use your magic in front of all these people, they will hang you for it. Do not forget that your magic will curse him. Understand that you must stop using your magic so freely to help others. Magic is *your* gift Quin, but yours alone."

Pausing for a moment to think about his next course of actions, darkness descended over Quin once again as he realised that Nicolas was right. Looking down at Leander, Quin pleaded him for a single favour,

"Leander, please do not die, the King needs you. Find the King and take away his sword. Hide it, destroy it, I do not care, but it is too dangerous to remain in his hands." Leander smiled, bravely raising his broken arm to his chest to salute.

"Consider it done Quin, for Alexandria."

Leander's eyes closed and his breathing became shallow. In a panic Quin shook and called out to Leander as the physician placed his head to Leander's mouth to check for breath. Convinced that he was still breathing, the physician attempted to explain the situation.

"He lives, but I am unsure as to how long for. I must get him to my chambers immediately. I cannot help him here." A group of guards quickly grabbed Leander and gently lifted him up, hastily walking to the physician's home. Quin stood and watched, for at that time he knew their paths were fated to go their separate ways. Reassuringly, Nicolas knelt beside Quin and put his arm around him speaking softly.

"Do not worry Quin, he is in good hands. He will be fine." Shrugging off Nicolas' comforting embrace, Quin was visibly upset,

"He had better be, Nicolas!" was all he could say as he turned and walked back towards the docks to meet the ship that had now berthed. Before Quin's departure, Nicolas caught a quick glimpse at his eyes and noticed that they momentarily shimmered the same sinister red glow he had seen previously. Knowing the evil that was connected with it, Nicolas grew fearful of what Quin may soon become. He waited a moment before following behind Quin, aiming to keep a safe distance. His only thoughts went back to the scripts in his books:

"The Elementalist - Upon maturity, an Elementalist will become selfish and sinister. The earliest record of this power was discovered within 'Lycus', who was branded a tyrant as his attempts to conquer mankind were fed by his lust for more power. Such are the ways of the elements and all those who control them."

Nicolas quietly prayed for Quin and whispered in the hope that on some level he would hear;

"Please do not become this Quin, I know you are different. You are pure and righteous; I have seen that much in you. Do not lose yourself to your power." Watching as Quin walked away into the distance and beyond the crowds of the bustling townsfolk, Nicolas shed a tear for Quin's fate and the part he was forced to play in it.

Turning to face the citizens that now stood around Nicolas waiting to hear some new tales, a small boy gazed up at the Historian with his fair blue eyes and a smile from ear to ear, while holding his hand he innocently asked

"Historian Nicolas, why are you crying?" Wiping the tears from his eyes and attempting to compose himself, Nicolas sat down on the bench in front of the large Phoenix statue. Sitting the small boy on his knee, as the other children and parents gathered round, Historian Nicolas began a new story.

"I wish to share with you the tale of a boy who was plagued with the terrible curse of hiding who he truly was. For he was magical, but was forced to hide his magic, because those he held dear would fear the power that he possessed, and for the greater good of those around him, he never used his magic. Not even as he lost everything he loved and cared for. Powerless to save them, his twisted fate turned his world into corruption. Perhaps it is that very reason why his tale brings a tear to my weary old eyes. This is the tale of a boy from the recently fallen Kingdom of Alexandria. Listen and learn, for we will soon come to see the true value of those we love, what we would give to hold them forever, and, most importantly, what we would do to keep them from harm."

On the docks, Quin stood and watched each of the passengers on the boat greet their loved ones, somewhat envious by the happiness of the reunion that this boat brought to them, but not for him. It soon became apparent that he had no idea who he was looking for and if this so-called, Ragnar the Cause was even a passenger on this specific ship. At this time, ensuring the physician restored Sir Leander back to health was all he could think of and so he made the snap decision to stay by Leander's side until he was well again. However, Fate had a different agenda. As he turned away from the ship he was hindered by a collision with a man hastily making his way along the dock. Losing his footing Quin fell down followed by a book that was decorated with beautiful golden calligraphy on its cover. Before he had time to get a clearer look at the book, it was snatched up by a strangely dressed man wearing navy blue robes that were laced with a golden thread. The man did not leave nor did he say anything to Quin, but instead stood for a moment and dusted off the pages of his book, once satisfied that it had not sustained any damage he turned his attention to Quin, who still sat gazing curiously at him. Offering his hand to help him back to his feet the man still stood silently as he pulled him up.

"Be aware of where you are treading, you fool!" Quin snapped. A little taken aback by his abrupt rudeness he attempted to defuse the situation respectfully,

"I am very sorry for my clumsiness" he said, in a strange accent that Quin had never heard before. Scoffing arrogantly, Quin continued on his way. But not before the man said his piece,

"You appear to have much anger in your heart, I wonder what your mother would think of such bad manners." Enraged by his words, Quin turned and glared at him,

"If you speak of my mother again, I will strike you down where you stand."

"I meant no disrespect! Please accept my humble apologies, my name is Ragnar the Cause" he replied. Quin laughed and rolled his eyes,

"Yes, of course - You would be!" he said, unsurprised. Seemingly perplexed by Quin's reaction, Ragnar enquired,

"You know me? Well then perhaps I could buy you a drink in the tavern and you could tell me who you are!"

"Thank you, however I have somewhere to be…" Quin said, shrugging off the blatant call of fate as he began to walk away. Ragnar immediately dropped the facade as he realised that Quin was playing hard to get and now knew that he must reveal the truth,

"Oh Quin, I was trying to be casual!" Ragnar said, to Quin's surprise. Curious to know how he knew who he was, he honoured him with his undivided attention.

"You know my name! Do you know what I am?" He questioned. Scoffing at his simplistic stupidity Ragnar rapidly explained,

"You are Quin, you have magic, more specifically, control of the elements! You have come here from the fallen Kingdom of Alexandria and you came here because it is your fate. Just as it is my fate to meet you here this day to give you this." Ragnar pressed the book firmly into Quin's chest, winding him as he grabbed hold of it. Catching his breath Quin opened the book to a random page and gazed over the abundance of calligraphy, written in golden foil. Slamming the book shut he returned it to Ragnar, taunting him with the revelation,

"It would appear *fate* has a sense of humour, I cannot read!" to which Ragnar smiled and proclaimed,

"Fortunately, I can! Furthermore, I do not need you for your reading ability. I require your - other skills." Quin knew exactly what Ragnar was hinting at and felt the urge to put him in his place and explain to this mere human the harsh reality of possessing magic,

"I will not use my magic to help you nor anyone else! In case you were unaware, magic is a curse! Find someone else, I have enough blood on my hands." Quin explained before he began to walk away.

"Then it is, once again, fortunate for you that I already possess a kind of magic. Through this book I can chant the incantations that will cause certain events to unfold" Ragnar called to him. Curiously, Quin turned back to him and enquired,

"What events?" Knowing that he now had Quin's full attention, Ragnar went on to explain the matter at hand.

"This is the book of Necropoleis. It holds many incantations written by the ancient scribes of the lost island. However most of the incantations will only work whilst on the island itself. Sadly, this island has since sunk and now lies dormant on the ocean's floor, although its power still remains. The island is said to hold a portal to the underworld, which could be used to bring back certain fallen comrades."

Quin was amazed by what he was hearing, however he was concerned about what he would have to do to make such a mystical event unfold.

"But why do you need me?" Ragnar now knew he had him hooked and all that remained was to show him the way,

"The Lost Island was once inhabited by a magical civilisation. It was ruled over and protected by one of Gaia's own children, the Telchines'. It is said that during the war of the Legions, he went mad and used his magic to submerge the island, killing himself and all his kin and therefore erased himself from the world. Only one of his kin could ever bring the island back from the depths. That is why I need you, only you have the power to bring the island back so that together we can complete my quest!"

Quin was hanging on Ragnar's every word, until he mentioned 'his quest'. He wondered what Ragnar's quest was, and if it was worth getting himself mixed up with the stranger who he had only just met and knew nothing about, let alone trusting him,

"And what quest might that be?" Quin enquired.

"To complete my quest I require your powers to raise the island and then lead me to the ceremonial platform. There I will read the incantation to open the portal to the underworld and bring back those whose lives were ended unfairly. Among those could be your comrades. I estimate hundreds of lives could be saved and they would be indebted to us, a debt they will repay by following me to Agartha to destroy Ifrit, once and for all!" Supportive of the idea of seeing the end of Ifrit's reign and the revenge he would have for all of his suffering, Quin offered his hand and services to Ragnar,

"When do we leave?"

- Chapter XI -
Raising a Glass

The tavern was filled with laughter and general chatter, whilst the strongest men of the Phoenix Garrison came together to flex their massive muscles, arm wrestling to impress the maidens that watched and cheered on their favourite. As with any show of bravado, it would usually end with someone being smashed in the face with a tankard or fist. In the corner of the room there was a band playing and singing with great joy and enthusiasm about times gone past, while many a drunk sang along with their tankards raised in respect and admiration.

The door flung open banging loudly against a pillar that seemed to have the sole purpose of being pummelled by all who entered the tavern. Quin and Ragnar stood side-by-side in the doorway as the locals became silent and glared unwelcomingly at the two newcomers. All eyes were fixed on them as they sauntered over to the bar without any sign of feeling the slightest bit intimidated. Quin reached into his pocket and placed the highly valued Alexandrian coin on the bar and eye balled the obese Barmaid as she stood glaring at him while chewing loudly, without any elegance, on some mastic gum. She wore the expression of disgust on her face very well, as if Quin and Ragnar were nothing more than a large pile of dung stinking up the place.

Through an evil gaze, Quin made it known that he would not stand for any nonsense while he was there and, moreover, he feared no man. Turning his attention to the band, they quickly looked away and picked up their instruments and continued to play. He grinned arrogantly and turned his attention back to the Barmaid, confidently placing his order.

"Two Ales, if you would be so kind."

As if it were a chore, she grabbed a couple of tankards from behind the counter and slammed them down in front of him. The Barmaid looked him straight into his eyes and spat unceremoniously into the mug while pouring the ale on top of it. The room erupted in an uproar of taunting laughter as she continued by taking the other tankard while pushing her finger into her nose, pulling out a large glob of mucus, slowly wiping it around the inside of the mug and then poured the ale. Shoving both tankards along the bar and in the process spilling some over Quin's arm, she laughed and declared in a rough and somewhat masculine voice, "I appears this round is on you boy!" While all this had been happening Ragnar was completely unaware, as he had his eyes firmly fixated on his book leaving Quin to deal with the common barmaid. Without taking his eyes away, Ragnar felt around the bar to locate his tankard and upon finding it, he grabbed it and raised it towards his mouth. Quin subtly placed his hand on Ragnar's arm before he was able to take a sip. Only then did Ragnar stop reading and became aware that everyone was staring at him, he leant towards Quin and whispered "Do you get the feeling we are not welcome here?"

Without saying a word, nor breaking his glaring eye contact with the barmaid, Quin took the tankard from Ragnar and placed it back on the bar and pondered how he would best get his revenge on this pathetic woman. Having taken a moment to think about it, he decided that he would simply return the gesture,

"Thank you for your *kind* service. Please allow me to express my gratitude."

Raising his hand and holding it steadily over the tankards the liquid began to bubble mystically as he summoned his magic to separate the mucus and saliva from the ales. The barmaid stared in astonishment at the drinks as two putrid balls rose out of the tankards and combined, creating a disgusting glob of gunk. Folding his middle finger down to his palm, he magically flicked the ball of sloppy mucus straight into the barmaid's face, which rippled her skin as it slapped onto her chubby cheek and grotesquely dripped down her face. The barmaid flinched, grimaced and slowly wiped the spit from her face as Quin raised his tankard to her and taunted, "To good health!" before taking a mouthful of the amber nectar.

Of course by now, everyone in the tavern knew that Quin possessed extraordinary powers that could crush any man in the room with ease. With the excitement of the exchange over, everyone in the room turned a blind eye and returned to their business, whilst Quin looked around for a table to sit at. He noticed one in a corner, over by a filthy window once white but since browned with the stains of years of old ale and tobacco smoke. Quin invited Ragnar over to take a seat with him. Placing his book down, Ragnar drank his ale as Quin wondered about the journey ahead.

"How long will it take to reach the Lost Island?" he asked, while Ragnar quickly downed the tankard of ale all at once. Finishing his drink and slamming his tankard down, Ragnar wiped the froth from his lips and responded. "The supply ship we need to board should arrive here at midday. Once we set sail we should be at our destination within a day." Waiting for more, Quin wanted to know all the details and went on to ask more questions as it seemed

Ragnar was direct in his approach to answers.

"You said the island was submerged. How will we know where to find it?" Quin interrogated.

Ragnar smiled and began to realised that Quin would not be so easily fooled.

"There is an area in the middle of the Ocean known by a few as Diablos Delta. It is rumoured that many ships used to travel through the area and the passengers could see parts of the sunken ruins below the surface of the ocean. That is where we must travel to."

Satisfied that he now had enough information, Quin raised his empty tankard and waved it at the barmaid, who was still staring at him in amazement.

"Another ale - hold the spit!"

As the day gradually passed, and many tankards of ale later, Quin and Ragnar were heavily intoxicated as they merrily sang along with the band and were eventually accepted by the locals in the tavern. Quin confidently sat at the arm wrestling table, ready to face the local grand champion. The Champion took a hold of Quin's hand, almost covering it with his massive palms as the barmaid stood witness and bantered with them, "May the best magi-, oops, I mean *man,* win. Take your positions men, free drink to the winner, spit free!" She joked to the group as they all stood around and cheered. "3... 2... 1, Go!" she bellowed excitedly. Almost instantly Quin's arm buckled under the pressure, but using his magic he raised the temperature of his hand to a boiling heat and tightened his grip on the Champion until his hand set on fire and scolded him. Distracting him as he yelped out in pain Quin slammed his arm down onto the table, winning the match. Laughing and cheering for his victory the crowd watched with joyous glee as Quin released his hold on the *'former'* Champion and raised his flaming hand up for all to see, shouting out over the crowd,

"I do not know my own strength!" His victory, however, was short lived as the horn of the cargo ship filled the air with an almighty boom, quickly followed by a unified groan from the men in the tavern as they trudged off to collect their belongings and slowly began to leave the tavern. As the tavern emptied, Quin scoured around for Ragnar, who was, initially nowhere to be seen, but before long he found him, slumped in a corner, unconscious from an excessive consumption of ale. Quin kicked his foot lightly, yelling for him to wake up, however Ragnar was unresponsive and simply groaned then flopped over, slapping his face down on the floor, all the while mumbling and snoring loudly.

The barmaid laughed at Ragnar's misfortune and boomed, "If he does not usually get the sea sickness, I think he will today.", as she leant over the counter and unknowingly revealed her large bottom to Quin, which bore a inked pattern in the shape of a scroll with a few words written on it. Having collected a small vial and funnel from behind the bar she walked over to Ragnar and picked his head up off the floor, forcing his mouth open and slipping the funnel in, she pulled the cork from the vial with her teeth and spat it a great distance across the room and poured the liquid it into the funnel and down Ragnar's gullet. Having ensured the potion had gone down, the barmaid dropped Ragnar's head, leaving it to thump heavily on the hard wooden floor.

"Give it a moment to settle and he will be fine!" she said proudly, believing she was some sort of prestigious alchemist. Quin smiled, nodded and then looked down at his new found comrade. Ragnar let out a grunt of distain and screwed up his face while the potion churned in his stomach. As the barmaid walked away, Quin couldn't help but wonder what the mark on her back meant. Allowing his curiosity get the better of him he asked "What is that mark on your back?" abruptly poking his nose into the barmaids personal business. Halting instantly for a moment she froze and wondered if she should tell him. She slowly turned to meet his gaze as if she were turning to face an apparition.

"It… I mean…" she stumbled, trying to find the right words to explain, she was clearly upset by the tale she would tell "It says *Ligeia, Jewel of the ocean'*, she was my daughter, you know. Beautiful little creature she was. Slim and talented, adventurous, you would not think she came from me cos… Well look at me!"

Witnessing the sadness and sorrow in her eyes, Quin's heart melted as old feelings of nostalgia reminded him that he was a caring person who would give to those less fortunate than himself and would beat himself up if there was nothing he could do to help them. Now realising that he was no longer that person but instead forced to lead a selfish life as his magic so demanded, he attempted to swallow the lump in his throat softly asking, "What happened to her?"

Responding with a large sigh, as if the barmaid had lost all hope of ever seeing her daughter again, she replied, "She loved to swim. I used to say to her 'I think fish spend less time in the water than you do girl'. But she would just laugh at me while ringing the water out of her lovely blonde hair. She would say 'There is a whole world to explore under the waves, full of beautiful creatures'."

Attempting to hold back the tears, she took a moment to

compose herself, however it was in vain as she began to snivel. "If only she were not so bloomin' secretive, I could have stopped her." She blubbered, as if angered at herself for her daughter's actions. "How was I to know there was a boy down there? He used his magic and stole her heart! She swam out lookin' for him and never came back."

Somewhat confused, Quin began to think she had lost her mind due to the stresses of the current state of the lands and assumed she was simply spurting complete gibberish. But no sooner had he began to bid her farewell, than Ragnar regained consciousness and uttered a word that struck deep into the barmaid's heart,

"Sirens!"

"Yeah" she confirmed.

Now getting to his feet, Ragnar saw in Quin's expression that he was unaware of what the Sirens were and felt that perhaps he should elaborate on the topic for his benefit, oblivious to the emotional pain it was causing the barmaid, who was now wiping her tears on her apron.

"They are a vile breed of creatures that prey on the beautiful and strong. They use their handsome physique and charm to seduce anyone who would swim out into the deep sea. They are aquatic creatures that have the ability to breathe under the water; beings that are half human and half fish. The top half is that of any normal human being, however from the waist down they are fish like with scaly fins. Those who would dare encounter them will be judged. If you are deemed as beautiful or strong they will curse you and transform you into a Siren, forcing you to obey their master, Glaucus! Anyone else is dragged to the bottom of the ocean, to die in a most horrific way. Either the heavy ocean crushes your bones or you drown, either way it is most unpleasant and later they feast upon the bodies. The worst part is the way they lure you in. They appear to be harmless and kind, they sing to you, their songs mesmerise any who hear it and they lure you in closer and closer. Once you are close enough, they lead you into the deep sea to seal your fate. Few who encounter such creatures ever walk away!"

With a trembling voice and swallowing hard, the barmaid confirmed Ragnar's account, "Yes, that is right and my daughter is one of them. But I heard that those with magic are immune to the sirens, are they not? You have magic; you could find her and bring her back!" Quin wanted to accept the barmaid's request, but he had a conflict within himself. He knew he could not abandon his quest with Ragnar, but as he looked at the broken woman before him, he found it hard to decline and shatter the hopes of her ever seeing her daughter again. Quin knew that a lie would hurt much less than the truth ever would and a lie could only strengthen the hope she held in her heart. Hope being the one thing that he had slowly lost sight of since the day Alexandria fell.

"I will do what I can," he proposed "Although I will not make a promise that I cannot guarantee to fulfil. If fate has decided that you and your daughter are to be reunited, I will make it so."

As she sobbed uncontrollably, Ragnar folded his arms with a discontented expression on his face while looking impatiently towards the door. The barmaid then pulled from her pocket a lock of blonde hair that was bound with a piece old twine.

"This is a lock of her hair, it has got magic see. She left it to me the night she left with a letter that said I could visit her any time. I did not understand why at the time but she said it would let me breathe in the water." She explained as she became increasingly emotional, to the point she was finding it hard to speak. Regardless, she bravely continued, "But I cannot swim and I am not beautiful or strong and I know that they would kill me... I could not let my daughter..." Unable to contain herself any longer, the barmaid broke down. She pressed the lock of hair into his hand and promptly rushed off into a private room behind the bar.

Quin stood motionless with a heavy heart as the barmaid suddenly revealed the pain and anguish that had been consuming her for so long. In truth he knew there was very little he could do to help her, and as if to emphasise this point Ragnar snatched the lock of hair out of Quin's hand and looked at it with disdain.

"I think we have wasted enough time on her pathetic drivel!" Ragnar snapped, slamming the lock down on a table. He promptly walked across the tavern, flung the door open angrily and left, leaving Quin in no doubt that he was meant to follow.

Quin stood for a moment and listened to the barmaid blubbering behind the closed door of her private room, a foul taste of deception rose in his mouth, one that he quickly discovered was too foul to swallow. Secretly, he promised that he would attempt to find Ligeia while he was on his journey across the sea. Retrieving the lock of hair and put it into his pocket next to the enchanted White Galanthus Flower, he took one last glance around the tavern and held onto the memories of joy it had given him, if only for a short time. He now realised that he probably would never see the Phoenix Garrison again. Flicking his hood over his head, he took his leave and followed Ragnar to the awaiting cargo ship that would deliver him into the hands of his final destination, fate!

- Chapter XII -
Dark Clouds

Crowds of citizens from the Phoenix Garrison congregated to bid farewell to their loved ones as the ship moved out of the dock and set sail. Cheers from both citizens and sailors filled the air with excitement, except Quin, who sat alone on the steps that lead up to the helm, watching them wave, knowing that because of his coming actions this may well be the last time that many of the citizens would see their loved ones sail away from the Garrison.

As the deck hands and passengers began to withdraw to their posts. The band from the tavern, who were also on board, picked up their instruments and began to play gleefully while the deck hands worked and sang along with them in celebration of the coming journey.

Quin silently moved to the back of the ship and watched the bustle for a while before setting himself down on the banister and looked back at the Garrison just as the crowd rushed to congregate in the centre, as a blazing fire illuminated the town in celebration of the departed sailors. All but Historian Nicolas who stood watching the ship sail away. Having noticed that he had Quin's attention he coyly raised his hand and waved good-bye. Pleased that he was able to see Nicolas one last time, Quin raised his hand and cast an epic water spell that manipulated and created a huge geyser in front of Nicolas. Splashing over him each of the droplets of water created the sound "thank you", which made him smile and he embraced the water with open arms. Having said his good-byes Quin turned to the deck to look for Ragnar, but as he did so he caught a glimpse out the corner of his eye, noticing a strange yet eerily familiar figure standing over Historian Nicolas's shoulder. Whipping his head back for a double take, Historian Nicolas had by now begun to walk away, with no-one else in sight. Haunted by the vision that he thought he had just seen, sent a cold chill down his spine, he uttered "Origen?", and took a moment to wonder if it was even possible that it was real, before long he shrugged it off assuming that his eyes were playing tricks on him. He then moved on to join Ragnar who stood at the front of the ship comparing something from within his book, gazing up at the sea and then back to his book, with a compass in hand.

Quin crept up behind Ragnar with the intent of startling him, in an immature attempt to lighten his mood.

"What are you looking at?" he bellowed, to which Ragnar gave a slight jump, but otherwise did not react to his immaturity and ignored him as he continued to gaze at his compass.

"Quin, if you would care to make yourself useful you could use your magic on the ship and turn it forty-five degrees north. Currently we are travelling south-west and we need to be travelling west!"

Having never learnt how to read or write, Quin quickly realised that he had also never learnt to read a compass either.

"I cannot use my power to manipulate an entire ship." Ragnar, slammed the compass down on the open page of his book and placed it on the ships banister, turning to Quin with a patronising expression he went on to belittle his apparent stupidity.

"Not everything is about magic, you do not require the use of magic to spin that wheel around do you Quin!?" Ragnar barked as he pointed at the ships helm directly next to them. Feeling rather silly and belittled, Quin confidently walked over to the wheel which was currently unmanned, and span it around with a single pull, as Ragnar returned to his book. He turned back and smiled smugly at Ragnar before realising he was no longer the centre of attention.

"There. It is unfortunate that you lacked the ability to do that yourself. Just let me know if you need me to do it again for you - Captain" he joked as he turned his back on

Ragnar, watching the sailors hard at work on the deck as the Captain supervised and had obviously not noticed the helm being tampered with. However, it was not long before Ragnar rose to his sarcasm,

"Very good Quin, but how does one such as yourself explain to the Captain the reason that the ships compass is now reading west?" searching for a solution to this problem, Quin took a moment to examine the area and noticed a loose metal nail wedged in between two planks by his foot. Picking it up he gave it a magnetic charge with his magic and placed it down next to the ships compass which sat next to the helm wheel. The dial on the instrument immediately swung round to meet the nail. Ragnar's eyes lit up as he witnessed the novelty of Quin's magic, although he took great pleasure in moving the nail to make sure the compass dial was pointing south-west as he had placed it in the wrong location. Not at all embarrassed by Ragnar's obvious correction, Quin smugly asked "I realise not everything is about magic, but you would do well to respect it. Now, is there anything else?" Ragnar's face quickly lit up as he laughed and explained,

"I have been attempting to find a way to manipulate that compass since we got on board and you accomplished it in mere moments. I must admit, you are smarter than you appear!"

Still feeling somewhat patronised by Ragnar, yet knowing that he was quickly on his way to proving to him that he was not a complete dunce, Quin forced a smile and gave Ragnar a small scoff as he returned to the back of the ship to gaze upon the Phoenix Garrison, which was now just a small dot on the horizon. Quin stood solemnly and whispered to himself, "I am coming Asha, it will not be long now!"

He sat at the back of the ship gazing out at the ocean, watching the sun as it appeared to sink into the water, gradually revealing a starlit sky and the moon which glowed brighter with every passing moment. Through all of this, his only thoughts dwelled on Asha, as he imagined his glorious reunion with her. However he knew that he would have to explain himself, and so pondered; what would he say to her and how would she greet him after being risen, by his hands, from eternal rest? Following his trail of thoughts, he took a moment and contemplated the power that Ragnar may hold over her and all the people he would raise from the underworld.

He began to wonder what motivated Ragnar. With so many questions on his mind doubting his sincerity, he could not shake the feeling that Ragnar could not be trusted, but within himself he knew that he would have trouble trusting anyone again after all of the horrors he had seen. With all that in mind he couldn't help but question,

'Why is he so intent on destroying Ifrit? What has Ifrit done to him to constitute such drastic actions or retaliation? What will he do with the risen army once he is victorious?' But, the most pressing question of them all was 'What are his plans for me, once I have served my purpose? Commanding an army powerful enough to destroy Ifrit would be a dangerous thing to share with someone who you barely know and trust.'

Within his mind, Quin began to play out different scenarios for any and all eventualities, and with each one the ending was always the same. He knew that eventually he would have to kill Ragnar and take control of the risen army for himself. The very thought that he could easily crush Ragnar filled him with a confidence that he would not see the day when Ragnar conquered the lands of Gaia with his control over the souls of the resurrected. Quin was convinced that he would have to force him to give the resurrected an option to either go back to their lives, join in the fight against Ifrit, or return back to their eternal slumber, for if he refused to make such an offering it would mean the suffering of innocent souls. Quin could not let that happen and would have no choice but to destroy them all!

As night settled in the bustle of the ship grew silent, the sailors retiring to their bunks after lighting the lanterns that hung round the ship as the few night-watchmen began their patrol.

Still deep in thought, Quin seemed content with remaining outside all night, watching the waves breaking upon the bow of the ship. However his thoughts were interrupted as a glowing light lit up the immediate area and Ragnar drew ever closer, lantern in-hand.

"It will not be long now. At dawn we will be but a short distance away from the island. You should rest; you will need all of your strength to raise the lost island back to the surface." Ragnar reasoned.

Although Quin had heard Ragnar, he chose to ignore him and continued to gaze out at the ocean. Discomforted by Quin's ignorance, Ragnar placed the lantern down on the floor next to him and walked away without saying another word. As he reached the door that lead into the lower sections of the ship, Ragnar's suspicion began to peak, coming to suspect that Quin did not trust him. Although angered with a sense of betrayal, Ragnar simply left Quin to his thoughts and retired to the communal cabin deck.

On the other side of the ship at the helm, Quin could hear the Captain and his First Mate reminiscing over adventures they had shared together and laughing at each other's expense. After what felt to be half the night of hearty chatter, it had all become nothing more than background noise to Quin as he sat in a daze still consumed by his thoughts, but then he suddenly noticed that silence had descended on the deck. He paused and wondered if he had become so involved in his thoughts that he had not even noticed the Captain had retired. However as he looked over at the helm, he noticed the First Mate silently looking over the ocean with his lantern, cautiously reaching out over the edge of the ship as if he was searching for something.

Suddenly there was a loud bang that echoed through the ship, shaking it violently as if it has just hit something, causing the Captain to fall over. The First Mate dropped the lantern into the ocean and grabbed the ships rails to avoid falling overboard, meanwhile Quin jumped to his feet ready to secure the ship. There was complete silence as all three of them froze to the spot and looked around, curious to know what was transpiring. Without warning, there was a mighty 'whoosh' as a blurred figure appeared from the water and flew over the ship dragging the First Mate along with it, both vanishing off the other side of the ship, without having time to even react. There was nothing more that could have been done other than stand witness to a loud anguished scream, and with the following splash the First Mate was gone. For a moment, an uneasy silence befell the ship as both Quin and the Captain stared at each other with a vacant and shocked gaze, neither knowing what to do.

Quin quietly edged to the side of the ship and peered down at the water to see what had become of the First Mate, but there was nothing to be seen, save a few bubbles floating up to the surface. The Captain had by now picked himself up and crept over to join Quin, screaming to his First Mate "Jonah!" but then fearfully stepped away from the edge of the ship, tumbling over a coil of rope that lay on the deck. He dropped his lantern which smashed, setting fire to the rope. Quin stepped towards the Captain to help him to his feet and extinguish the fire with his water magic, but before he could do so the Captain scrambled to his feet and rushed off towards the helm, clumsily tripping over his own feet in his panic. With one arm on fire, it seemed he didn't care about the smouldering pain from the burning oil that had soaked his skin. Instead he grabbed the pull rope on the warning bell and thrust the clapper with all his force, wailing at the top of his lungs, "Siren! Man your stations, grab your swords!"

Quin slowly turned his head towards the sea and witnessed large waves creating an angry movement like a thick blanket of splashes and sprays, as the aquatic creatures he recently heard of in tales were approaching in their hundreds. He quickly realised that this wave was no mere warning, but instead an extermination, the stampede of Sirens all heading for the ship with one intention - mass slaughter.

Quin focused on the fire that was now ablaze in front of him and, using his magic, he raised his hand and took control of the fire, moving it over the water to illuminate the sea below. Gazing over the edge of the ship he could clearly see under the water and the masses of Sirens.

As the entire crew of the ship flooded out onto the deck, Quin turned and ran towards the weapon racks that were secured around the masts and attempted to arm himself, but by the time he got there, all that remained was a small chain, which he grabbed and wrapped around his fist in order to defend the ship.

Suddenly an icy cold shiver ran down Quin's spine and time seemed to dramatically slow down whilst all around him everything appeared to be moving in extreme slow motion. He sensed a dark yet strangely familiar power emerging, as he turned his head to look out the corner of his eye, terrified by the thought of what might be lurking. Beyond the Siren masses there lingered a dark entity in the form of a gigantic black cloud that enshrouded an incredible distance, and as Quin stood witness to this power a deeply mixed feeling of fear, guilt and sadness flowed through him, until a cry from the Captain broke him out of his fixated daze.

"Storm clouds are coming! Lower the sails and strike down any Siren that comes within spittin' distance!" He Commanded, as Quin stood staring at the cloud and muttered "That is no storm cloud -" unable to finish his sentence, the attack on the ship began.

Sirens began leaping from the water, soaring as high as the sails themselves and landing on the ship in small groups of three or four, drawing their rusted swords decorated with shells, pearls and coral, they made quick work of grabbing crew members and throwing them over the side of the ship. Quin attempted to defend the crew, but he could not react quickly enough to the sheer swiftness of the Sirens and soon found that they were losing the battle.

All of a sudden one of the Sirens landed right in front of Quin and, grabbed him by the throat, lifting him off the decking, and pinned him up against the mast. The hulking male Siren stared into his eyes, which felt like they were looking directly into his soul. The siren mystically spoke directly into his mind.

"You will all die for this!"

Quin reached out his hand and attempted to blast the Siren with fire magic. However, little more than a flickering ember appeared. He tried again to cast the spell but it became glaringly obvious that his power was somehow being blocked. With a sinister smile, the Siren tossed Quin across the ship with ease, crashing him into the mast and cracking his head as he collided with it. Quin slumped on the deck and held his head attempting to shake off the disorientation from the blow. The Siren male slithered up the stairs and regained eye contact with him and spoke into his mind again,

"A human with magic is just as feeble as any other. Your trickery cannot save you now."

The Siren progressed further upon Quin and grabbed him by the throat once more and lifted him to his feet as he drew a dagger intending to thrust it into his chest. Ragnar suddenly burst through a door onto the deck with a harpoon in hand. Taking a moment to dodge a spear that had been thrown by another Siren from the other side of the ship, then turning to see that it was stuck fast in the frame, Ragnar spotted Quin above him. His expression told a grim tale of defeat.

But Ragnar was not ready to accept such defeat, and threw his harpoon at the Siren that was holding Quin. The Siren dropped Quin and caught the harpoon in hand, and turned to glare back at Ragnar with malice. Having been released, Quin slumped backwards in disorientation and propped himself up on what remained of the helm as Ragnar shouted "Dive!"

Without another word, Ragnar rushed to the starboard side of the ship and leapt over the edge, and as Quin fumbled backwards and he too stumbled over to the starboard side and flopped over the railing and into the waiting sea.

With a mighty splash Quin submerged, however he was still weak and disorientated from his battering and couldn't muster the energy to slow his descent into deeper water. To his surprise he soon found himself surrounded by an aura of light that appeared to originate from his pocket, as the Siren's lock of hair blessed him with promised powers. Now able to see clearly and with the peculiar ability to breathe in the water, he had descended deep enough to see under the ship and witnessed the masses of Sirens dragging sailors down to the depths of the ocean, as they vainly flailed their arms around trying to break free. Greater numbers of Sirens appeared from the distance and behind them was the black cloud that he had seen in the distance, whilst on board the ship. He stared in amazement as the cloud he had previously thought to be an incredible power now proved to be even more powerful than he could have anticipated, as it stood before him spanning from the sky and down to the very depths of the ocean.

Startled by something grabbing his arm, he flipped around to defend himself against any attackers.

Ragnar clung to Quin's arm struggling for breath as the aura slowly extended over him too. Granting him the ability to breathe, and much to Quin's surprise, talk underwater, Ragnar shouted in a bubbled tone, "Swim!"

Within a few moments of swimming away Ragnar and Quin came face to face with another Siren, this one was female. She looked at them with an expression of curiosity as she floated in their path attempting to identify the magic that had surrounded them and blessed them with the power of the Sirens.

Glancing back anxiously, Ragnar curled himself up into a ball and, noticing his reaction, Quin turned to see what it was he was so afraid of, but all he could see was the ship. Ragnar garbled some undistinguishable words and not a moment later, Quin caught a glimpse of a blinding flash before he was blasted by an almighty wave as the ship exploded with an incredibly powerful force, rendering him unconscious. As the magic from the lock of hair dimmed along with Quin's consciousness, he began to sink further into the depths of the ocean. However, before he sank too deep the female Siren grabbed him and swam him to the surface allowing him to breathe. Ragnar, however, was nowhere to be seen. As the young Siren looked around, she found herself a short distance away from a small island and the glow from a beached campfire lit the way. Dragging Quin behind her, she swam for shore.

- Chapter XIII -
An Island to Remember

The sound of birds screeching filled the air of the sandy beach where Quin now found himself. Slowly beginning to open his eyes to see a bright sunlit sky with masses of seagulls circling above, he sat up and checked his surroundings, but all that could be seen for miles were endless dunes of sand littered with chunks of driftwood, the remains of the cargo ship. As he gazed out beyond the desolate beach and out to sea it became apparent that the cargo ship and its passengers had been destroyed and were now most likely lying at the bottom of the ocean as a monument to his failure, now home to the victorious creatures of the deep, the sirens.

While Quin took the time to reflect on his situation and, more importantly, his next move he suddenly heard a crackle from behind him and found he was sitting by an almost extinguished campfire. Neatly placed over the fire was a flat piece of slate with two cooked eggs on it, although it appeared there was no-one around to have put them there. Without another thought he grabbed the slate and scoffed them down. As he finished he was greeted by a pair of sand covered feet standing in front of him. His eyes slowly moved up the legs and torso of the stranger, and as his eyes fixated upon the face before him he suddenly felt quite ashamed of himself for scoffing the eggs that were probably not meant for him. A young and beautiful female stood before him, dressed in a rag that appeared to have been cut from old sails. Swallowing hard on the remnants of his stolen meal he greeted her,

"Hello. I- I am sorry, I was so very hungry and I -" he bumbled, before lowering his head in shame. She smiled sweetly and giggled, gracefully sitting down in front of him,

"Do not trouble yourself with guilt, they were meant for you!" she said softly tilting her head to one side to get a glimpse of Quin's face as he turned his head away to hide his blushing cheeks "How are you feeling?" She continued.

A little confused by the familiarity she was showing him, he turned his attention to her and began to examine her face, and wondered if he had met her somewhere before. Perhaps she was a passenger on the cargo ship too, or maybe hit his head so hard that he was experiencing amnesia and had forgotten who she was.

"Where am I?" he asked abruptly as he proceeded to scan the area confused at the given situation. The female also looked around and sarcastically replied,

"Well, we are on an island, a beach to be exact."
However Quin was not amused and scowled at her,
prompting her to stop playing games and tell him the facts.
"Your ship was destroyed, you must have washed up here;
you are very fortunate to be alive." Hearing her words, he
surmised that she was not a passenger of the cargo ship,
which caused him to wonder how he might have found his
way onto the island. Aiming to get answers, he began his
interrogation.

"*My* ship was destroyed?" He reiterated,
emphasising the point. "So you were not on board as a
passenger? If that is the case then perhaps you live on this
Island! So what it is called?" He grilled as she stood with
her jaw flapping in the wind. "Why are you acting familiar
towards me? Who are you!?" Her expression immediately
changed to an icy cold glare that stated "be cautious!"
which suddenly sparked a flash back in his mind, he
remembered being under water, looking at a female Siren
just before the cargo ship exploded. He recognised this
female as the Siren which swam before him in the water,
however to his confusion she now sat with him on the
beach as a human. He initially thought that he could be
mistaken, however having witnessed the power of the Siren
he realised that it was more than possible that she may be

using her powers on him, warping his mind. He jumped to his feet and stepped away while holding out his hands in an attempt to warn her not to come any closer "You are a Siren!" He proclaimed in fear.

She quickly dropped the façade knowing now that she would not be able to deny the accusation for long,

"And you are not! I have sensed your elemental magic. The ability to breathe under water is not something your kind is capable of. That magic is reserved for the Siren." She retorted while standing strong to show she was not afraid of him "So tell me, what kind of trickery was used to allow you to breathe in our ocean?" she asked, but he stood his ground.

"I will not justify myself to you, especially after you attacked us without provocation! Please do explain why I would even consider co-operating with your kind." he rebutted.

"How dare you!" She bellowed, shocked and insulted as if speaking to an ignorant child. "You struck first, attacking us with your dark magic!" Assuming for a moment that she may be telling the truth, he suspected that a third party could have been involved in the attack.

"Hold on! That cloud was *not* summoned by the Sirens?" he asked, as the Siren glared into his eyes searching for a glint of dishonesty. Although he appeared to be telling the truth the Siren was still unconvinced of his words but decided to play along with him in the hope he would eventually contradict himself, thus proving his guilt.

"Of course not, Sirens do not possess such power! We were fleeing from it. It appeared in our home and began devouring everything it touched, killing hundreds of my people. As we fled we discovered your ship!" She explained with a lump in her throat as she recalled the horror of the attack,

"So… That is why you attacked us? Because you assumed we summoned it?" he stated, but before another word could be exchanged the discussion was abruptly cut short by a sudden cry for help coming from the forest behind them. He did not waste any time and immediately rushed off to assist. However he couldn't resist a quick taunt before his departure.

"More of your fishy friends?"
Insulted by his comment, the Siren turned to him and retaliated,

"I am alone! It is probably more of your Dark Magic!" But it appeared her response had fallen upon deaf ears.

"Well wait for me then you uncultured brute". She bellowed and promptly huffing and stomping after him.

Quin dashed through small gaps in the trees, leaping over small ditches and roots all the while calling out, to locate the origin of the voice. However, he soon found himself lost and alone in the middle of the forest surrounded by an eerie silence. All around him were a masses of thick foliage lying deadly still,

"Where are you?" he called out as he stood searching the area for any evidence, but beyond the echo of his own voice there was only silence, until a few moments later when footsteps and snapping twigs could be heard drawing closer to him, although the echoes all around him made it impossible for him to pinpoint where the sound was coming from. Then appearing through a bush in front of him, he bore witness to a familiar face, albeit covered in cuts and scratches;

"Ragnar!?" He exclaimed as he let out a sigh of relief, now with a look of joy on his face as he was reunited with his comrade whom he had previously assumed to be dead. Although Ragnar did not react the way he would have expected as he paused only to identify Quin and then continued to run past him,

"Run you fool!" he yelled, vanishing further into

the forest. Quin paused for a moment and conjured a fire spell in his hand. Holding his ground to identify what it was that could have terrified Ragnar so much that he would run for his life. From the distance, there was an almighty roar that filled the forest with further echoes and then, to his concern, the following screams came from the female Siren. His heart sank to his stomach as he strangely and uncharacteristically, feared for the Siren's life. Pushing onwards into the forest he was filled with the hope he could find the Siren before it was too late, he began to panic as he realised the forest's acoustics could quite easily trick him into running the wrong way.

He skidded along the dirt floor after jumping through a bush and found himself balancing at the top of a small cliff, but much to his relief he had located the Siren who was sitting on the ground at the foot of the cliff below him. Quin stood silently, watching her as she scampered around on her hands and knees panicking while a thick sheet of dust settled around her as if it had mysterious fallen from the sky. Pushed her back up against a tree she appeared to be absolutely terrified. Gazing around frantically with tears in her eyes. After a moment she spotted him.

"Please call off your beast" she begged, holding out her hands to Quin in fear of his magic as if praying to an almighty god. Having no idea of what she was referring to he chose to ignore her drivel as he began his descent down the cliff.

Eventually making it to the bottom of the cliff he strolled over to the Siren, who was now cowering behind her arms and covering her face. Without speaking he simply grabbed the Siren, pulled her to her feet and gently took her by the hand and led her towards the sound of the ocean's waves in the distance. However, as he guided her along there was a huge explosion of soil between them that catapulted them both into the air with intense force. Following the blast was an almighty roar of a gushing black cloud which enshrouded the space between them. Staring in amazement, Quin now found himself within touching distance of the black cloud, possibly the same one that had attacked the Sirens and bought about the destruction of the cargo ship. Quin froze in terror and was bombarded with thoughts of possible actions which contradicted each other as he attempt to react, but resulting in no action at all as both Quin and the Siren stared at the cloud. Before long the cloud began to condense and form itself into the silhouetted shape of a human, with an eerie red eyed gaze as its only discerning feature. It glared angrily at Quin and took a single step towards him, and his thoughts silenced. Acting on instinct alone Quin flung out his hand in an attempt to blast fire at the Apparition, but nothing happened; a situation Quin had found himself in before. He knew that without his powers he could not hope to defeat this apparition, so conjured an alternative plan and yelled,

"Run!" They both jumped up and ran off in opposite directions. The Apparition roared angrily and turned to chase Quin.

Quin ducked and dodged between the trees and shrubbery, running in all possible directions in an attempt to elude the Apparition that continued in closing pursuit. He glanced back periodically only to see the Apparition catching up to him and then as if out of nowhere, he was faced with a sheer, rock faced, mountain wall providing him with no visible means of escape. He turned to run back out into the forest only to find the Apparition now standing in his path. Their gaze's connected and the Apparition slowly glided towards him, as if savouring this moment of victory.

Clenched his eyes shut, he prepared himself for whatever horrors this creature was about to unload on him. The moment was alarmingly interrupted as a loud *'crack'* startled Quin into opening his eyes. The ground beneath his feet unexpectedly collapsed and he fell with it, landing uncomfortably on his back inside a small concealed cavern below that had long since been buried and forgotten.

Quin sat up, but due to the wind being knocked out of him when he hit the floor, he struggled to catch his breath as he also choked on the dust still settling around him and groaned loudly from the pain that now throbbed in his spine,

"Can this day possibly get any worse!?" He grumbled while clambering back to his feet, shaking his head vigorously causing dust to fly out of his hair. Supporting himself against a sturdy wall, his curiosity peaked and he was somewhat surprised to find that the walls looked as though they had purposefully been constructed by someone. There seemed to be no way he could climb back out of the way he came in. Glancing around the immediate vicinity, he noticed a set of steps half buried inside a dirt wall, which he could only assume once provided a way in and out of the cavern. He couldn't help but wonder how and why they were put there in the first place as it was all too clear that the island was abandoned; bar the apparition. He realised that it was probably a blessing that the stairs were buried as he didn't want to go back out that way, what with the Apparition probably waiting for him to emerge. Continuing his search of the cavern he soon noticed a long passageway leading deeper into the darkness. As this path seemed to be his only way forward, he set off into unknown for one simple reason, which he explained to himself out loud, as if justifying his actions to another; "I would rather take my chances in the unknown than face the certainty of what remains awaits me!"

It was not long before he reached the end of the passage and found himself stood in a pitch black chamber. Each step echoed as he drew deeper and deeper into the darkness until he daren't go any further through fear of what could be laying ahead of him. He thought for a moment about heading back the way he came, when all of a sudden the room illuminated as huge bowl lanterns atop six-foot tall pillars lit up in each corner of the room with flames burning with a heavenly white glow. He shielded his eyes with his arm as the sudden change in light pained him. After a few moments passed he was able to lower his arm and began to examining the strange chamber he now found himself in.

In each corner of the room stood a single gold plated pillar with a similar marble. Acting as support structures but also with strange hieroglyphs upon them. Each one with different scripts written from top to bottom and each with a different emblem inset on the dusty, floor below it. He immediately recognised three of the emblems as those of the three legions, however one remained that he was unfamiliar with, yet a strange emotion flowed through him as he gazed upon it. As he continued to examine the pillars in more detail, he was suddenly faced with a baffling talent. He looked at each hieroglyph in turn and, for reasons beyond his understanding, he was able to read this strange forgotten language.

This new found ability was far too much for him to control as his eyes darted from glyph to glyph, with words echoing through his mind. Covering his ears and clenching his eyes shut tightly he turned away and walked forward blindly until he collided with a wall and sank to his knees until the voices in his head drew silent. He carefully began to open his eyes again and slowly stood up, ensuring he did not look at any of the pillars again, he soon noticed the wall he had been leaning against had an intricate painting upon it, Backing away from it to get a better look, he gazed in astonishment as he examined the image before him, one that immediately struck fear deep into his heart as he gazed upon the giant image of Ifrit, and there before Ifrit was a figure at least half the size of him, dressed in a dark hooded cloak and appearing to be attacking the fiend with some sort of fire magic, and floating behind Ifrit as a large swirling vortex of power was the black cloud Apparition. He now had no doubt in his mind that the Apparition had obviously been summoned by Ifrit. Now fearing for the safety of those who travelled with him, he realised that he must have caught Ifrit's attention and it seemed he was now using his power in an attempt to destroy Quin; however, he couldn't help but wonder why Ifrit saw him as such a threat. Although one thing was certain, in time, he would find out!

He took a step back and leaned against one of the pillars while staring at the image and began to reflect on everything that he had been through since Ifrit had come into his life, not least all of the people he had lost in that time. It seemed inevitable that he would lose many more before the world saw the end of his reign. He stared blankly at the picture for what seemed like days, studying every fine detail, although he wasn't sure if he was torturing himself or trying to make sense of the pandemonium of thoughts that circled in his mind.

"Why is Ifrit still attacking the land of Gaia? Who is the human in the picture? What is the Black Cloud and how can it be destroyed?" But above all else he asked "What do you want with me?"

The sudden clatter of bare footsteps from somewhere within the chamber startled him. He cautiously peered around the pillar and scanned the room, but it appeared he was alone. A little disturbed, his attention was quickly drawn to a strange stone doorway that he could have sworn was not there when he entered the chamber. He nervously walked over to the door, all the while peering around the room for anyone that may be watching him. He reached the door which towered twice his height and noticed four emblems neatly engraved into the stone's face. He took a moment to examine it and found it had no locks, no handle and seemingly no way of opening. He stood back from the door and cast a fireball in an attempt to blast his way through, however as the ball exploded he was astounded to see the magic was simply absorbed into the door. Although his best attempt at opening the door initially failed, it soon became apparent that there was much more to this chamber than he could have ever imagined.

The four emblems that were depicted around the room all began to glow with a white aura, except for one on the door which caught his eye. The fourth emblem lay before him pulsing with a red glow and as if enchanted and he felt compelled to touch it, instinctively reaching out he pressed his palm firmly against it. A flash of white light filled the room, burning his eyes, forcing him to shut them tight as he cried out in pain from the burning sensation that flowed from the emblem and through his body, shortly followed by a high pitch squealing in his ears that could still be heard clearly when he pushed his palms against them. After a few moments the overwhelming sensation dithered and he slowly opened his eyes to find himself stood in a strange land.

Unable to believe his eyes, Quin stared in disbelief at the people that were now standing right in front of him. A large circular stone platform lay in front of him, with hieroglyphs engraved upon its edge, but he was unable to see clearly enough to read. This minor detail seemed irrelevant as he watched a strange scenario playing before his eyes. A beautiful woman, dressed in a glowing white gown that swept the floor was standing in the centre of the stone circle with an expression of sadness as she looked at each of the four others stood in front of her. In an attempt to ask for help, walked over and spoke to the woman,

"Where am I?" He asked her, but with no acknowledgement to his existence, the woman simply continued to gaze sorrowfully at the four others one by one. Quin turned to the only other female and asked again,

"Can you help me?" But she showed no reaction to

his presence either. Somewhat insulted at their ignorance, he grew angry and reached out to grab the blonde haired man stood beside him. To his horror his hand simply passed through him as if waving his hand through thin air. Now extremely confused and quite afraid, he began to think that perhaps his actions within the chamber had set off some kind of magical power which had killed him and he now stood witnessing this scenario as nothing more than a spirit or perhaps they were the spirits. He had barely had time to examine his strange surroundings or come up with a logical explanation to this bizarre turn of events, before the five people began,

"My children; the time has come. I have summoned you here because we are all that is left in the land now, as you are all aware Tartaros has all but won the endless battle we have been fighting since the great birth, unless we act to counter his dark magic he will gain complete control and bring chaos to our world." Spoke the woman who stood firm and dominant in the centre of the circle as she glanced over her congregation "I understand that you four have had your fair share of rivalry between one and other, but now is the time that you must all come together and unite as one to protect our world".

The youngest of the four children stepped forward

from out of the shadow of a pillar and revealed himself, to Quin's absolute shock "Mother Gaia, I must protest, two acts of evil can never amount to prosperity and justice." He said firmly, unwavering of his words. Quin could only stare in disbelief as he was face to face with a young man identical to himself in every way. Frightened and unable to comprehend what was happening, he stumbled backwards and fell onto his back side as the scene continued.

Mother Gaia, looked upon Quin's double with a sweet smile of pride and she shook her head, and gently replied,

"My dear Lycus, you have selflessly sacrificed your powers and became mortal to protect us all from Tartaros' curse, despite the differences you have had with your siblings. We all bore witness to Tartaros' power. We all know he has imprisoned our kin and continues to hold them within his new realm 'The Underworld'. You must understand your kin are being tortured as we speak! His goal is to condemn their souls to evil so he may harvest them and gain enough power to destroy me. If we do not act he will gain complete control over everything, and we will die! My only hope is for you all to survive, my children." Gaia explained.

Taking a moment to look upon the saddened faces of each

of her children she then continued "You are the future now; the four Telchines: The Lands, The Seas, The Skies and The Elements."

Quin's eyes lit up as he heard Gaia's words and the revelation that the fourth legion was that of "The Legion of The Elements" although, strangely, he was not surprised and there was a sense of familiarity about it. He suddenly started to remember events from, what he could only understand to be another life, he rose to his feet and watched his double, *'Lycus'*.

Gaia held out her hands to Lycus in gratitude and commended him,

"Your sacrifice has saved our family from an unthinkable fate, but now it is my turn to make a sacrifice and return the power of the elements back unto you. With my sacrifice and your combined powers I will create 'The Heavens' to oppose The Underworld and restore balance to our world."

The other female, with long black hair and tight shining leather clothing, spoke abruptly

"You betray us with your words Mother!" She accused, commanding the attention of the others. As they all gazed at her in anticipation of her knowledge, she joined her mother on the stone platform and revealed the truth

"Granted, what Mother claims is the truth, creating a balance will free our kin, but what she has neglected to divulge is that once Gaia is gone her protective magic over our kin will end and as a result they will gain the ability to use our magic and when they die their power will be absorbed by their Telchine, making us strong, I shudder to think what my brothers would do to their kin knowing this! What is worse, if our kin should lead an impure and unjust life, their souls will be consumed by the Underworld and therefore Tartaros will eventually gain enough power to return to the lands and finish what he started! Without Mother Gaia to counter his return, we shall all perish. Can you not see that we are simply delaying the inevitable?" Another child stepped forward; however this one seemed very different to the others as he stood naked save a pair of rawhide trousers and a healthy head of long blond hair that rested elegantly on his shoulders; however it was the wings on his back that set him apart from the others. Waiting for a moment to think about his words carefully he politely put his opinion forward

"Forgive the intrusion Mother Gaia. Dexithea, even if your words are true, they are our kin and they will do only as we command. We owe it to them to do all we can to protect them and deliver them from evil, we all know what they mean to the world; They must -"

Dexithea sharply interrupted him

"That, brother Actae, is exactly what concerns me, what with our overzealous warmonger brother, Ormen. We have all been in a very delicate state of peace since our birth, if our kin came to possess our powers I fear they would become arrogant and could easily destroy the peace between us" She barked, without care for the insult it may cause.

Ormen, stood like a solid brick wall, he was a dark character without expression, who had simply stood silently as if not even paying attention to his squabbling family. Without a word he intimidatingly turned to Dexithea and glared angrily at her as if he was about to strike her down, however after a few moments of silence and warring eye contact with Dexithea, he turned back to Gaia, who now stared longingly upon her children, hoping that they would see sense. A sudden crack of thunder shot across the glorious blue sky above them, as they all looked up and watched it slowly turning black, forming thick grey clouds, a sight that Quin was only too familiar with as he stood and recalled the demise of the Kingdom of Alexandria.

After a while of uncomfortable silence, Gaia pulled out three daggers from her dress and used a magic which Quin had never seen before, she controlled the daggers as they floated through the air and left them hovering in front of Dexithea, Actae and Ormen. Reluctantly Dexithea took the blade and stepped down from the pedestal to join her brothers. Actae also reached out to take a dagger. Ormen seemed only too happy to snatch the blade up with a devious grin on his face. With all three Daggers now in hand Gaia urged them to fulfil her wishes

"There is no more time to debate my children, Tartaros has begun and he will soon be upon us. You all know what must be done!"

Gaia held her palms to the sky and began to levitate and slowly lay backwards until she was horizontal in mid-air. Quin watched Lycus as he turned and walked away, unable to witness the events that were about to unfold. The others stepped up onto the pedestal and positioned themselves around her. Actae stood at her head; Ormen stood at her heart and Dexithea stood at her womb as they all lifted their daggers above their heads and looked to the sky. Quin suddenly felt emotionally connected to Lycus as he lowered his head and shut his eyes tight with a single tear falling from his face. Although Quin could feel Lycus' pain, he couldn't help but feel there was some significance to this vision, and so forced himself to watch as the others thrust their daggers into Gaia.

Gaia fell to the ground, lifeless and still, as her sacrificed blood trickled out onto the pedestal and began the ritual. Various shaped spheres of white light appeared from parts of the pedestal touched by Gaia's blood as it slowly flowed through each nook and cranny, and with her final breath a single red orb arose divinely from her lips and hovered patiently above her body.

With a face full of tears Actae turned to Lycus, who now sobbed openly into his palms. With a single flap of his wings, Actae rose into the air and glided over to Lycus, landing a single step behind him. Actae embraced him in his arms and wings as they shared a moment of remorse. Actae gently whispered into Lycus' ear,

"Remember who you are."

Lycus understood the words and bravely lifted his head to see his mother now at rest. Actae took a step to one side and looked into Lycus' drowning eyes and whispered "Go, and reclaim your birth right". Almost unable to control his emotions he slowly walked towards the floating orb, Dexithea and Ormen stood empathetically to one side and watched Lycus' proudly as he embraced his fate with each step. Quin fell to his knees and began to sob uncontrollably as he shared the powerful emotions emanating from Lycus.

He now understood what was happening and surmised he was witnessing a memory of sorts, but with a strong connection to the Telchine Lycus. Wiping the tears from his eyes as much as he could to ensure he saw every moment of the memory that replayed before him, Quin watched as Lycus reached out and touched the orb. As his hand connected, his body was enshrouded with a red glow which lifted him into the air. His arms flung out and he let out a mighty roar of agonising pain as the power of the elements were returned to him.

With a mighty seismic explosion that finalised the merging of Lycus and his power, he suddenly plummeted to the ground and fell flat on his back next to his mother, Actae lunged forward swiftly to assist Lycus but the others grabbed him to halt his progress. Lycus slowly opened his eyes and smiled as the clouds in the sky dispersed and a ray of light shone down upon him. However his happiness was soon interrupted as an after effect of the merging began to shock through his entire body causing him great pain, as he flinched and convulsed Actae attempted to free himself from the grasp of his siblings but they refused to let him interfere. Actae realised there was nothing more he could do as he witnessed the torment of Lycus, his youngest and most beloved brother. Crying out, Actae tried to reach out to him with words,

"Fight it Lycus!" he yelled through his tears, as Lycus suddenly stopped and lay perfectly still.

After a moment of absolute silence, Lycus took a sharp breath and sat up. A few moments passed as Lycus' breathing sounded heavy and strained, but Ormen and Dexithea still refused to release Actae. Eventually he rose to his feet and stood facing his siblings; with his head drooped forward as if he had no control over it. Lycus sharply opened his eyes and glared up at the others with a sinister glowing red gaze and his expression turned to one of undeniable anger. Staring straight forward he barged past them without a single word and as he gained some distance away from his siblings, who now stood in disbelief, including Quin, Ormen scolded him with a deep booming voice that demanded respect

"Where are you going?" He asked.

Lycus halted, dead in his tracks and slowly peered over his left shoulder "To find my kin, I suggest you all do the same!"

Quin watched as Lycus abandoned the others and wondered if his last statement was an offering of advice or a threat.

Suddenly there was another blinding flash of white

light as the memory ended and the scene changed to a cold and blustery hilltop in the dead of night.

Atop the hill were a collection of four tents, each made with thick tree branches used as supports and rawhide leather covering them over for shelter. In the centre lay a burning campfire, which was put together with a neat circle of rocks. Quin watched with fear in his heart, although he did not yet understand why. Actae, Dexithea and Ormen were sitting around the campfire in silence, the atmosphere was most discomforting as the siblings appeared to be ignoring each other. Even though it was just a memory, Quin could feel the tension in the air.

In the distance a familiar whistling sound could be heard, which progressively got louder as it drew closer. The three siblings began to look around in an attempt at pinpointing the sound and as Quin gazed over the side of the hill behind him he noticed a familiar sight, Lycus approached in the form of the winds, travelling towards them. He shot over the top of the hill and passed straight through Quin. With a loud crack he reformed and glared at each of his siblings as he took a seat. Quin immediately noticed that his eyes still retained their sinister red glow. Lycus waited for one of them to speak, but after a few moments of continued silence Lycus' voice commanded respect,

"Why have you summoned me here?"

Actae, being a calm and gentle soul, attempting to keep the situation as pleasant as possible as he began to reveal the purpose of the meeting,

"My dear brother, we have much to discuss."

Lycus grunted loudly and glared at his siblings disapprovingly while folding his arms to show he would most likely not be co-operative with them. Staring blankly at Actae he waited for him to continue, however it was Dexithea who stood and spoke out,

"It is as I predicted my brothers; our kin have been blessed with fragments of our powers." She informed them, yet with a hint of fear in her voice.

Angered by her words and slightly jealous that her kin had gained her magic where his had not, Ormen barked loudly against Dexithea's claims

"I have seen no such evidence of this in my kin! You must have betrayed the sacred oath and blessed them yourself." Ormen followed up by drawing his ginormous great sword that glimmered like the sun on the surface of a freshwater stream. Dexithea seemed unimpressed as she glared angrily at Ormen before continuing.

"You dare accuse me of such a crime that is punishable by death!" She scowled "No, I noticed them using my powers when my kin were attacked by another legion, they only used their powers to defend themselves, but now I see it was an elaborate plot by Ormen, to accuse me of betraying the Sacred Oath and having me put down!" The angered glares between Dexithea and Ormen persisted while Actae stood to contribute with his own experiences,

"My kin were also attacked, although I saw no magic." He stated as he looked at Dexithea "There are only four legions in the lands, I suspected it was Ormen's doing as my assaulters bore the weapons of warriors."
Ormen turned his gaze to Actae; in further discontent of the accusations he spoke directly into Actae's face

"It would be nice to have warriors to send against you Actae, but the attack on my kin cost me a lot of men!"

Dexithea's expression suddenly turned to shock as she realised the elaborate plot they had all become victim of

"We were all attacked… All except for -" she said. Without another word Actae and Ormen broke eye contact and turned to look upon Lycus, who suddenly sat up straight as his face dropped in fear of the accusations now being placed upon him. Standing to his feet and staring threateningly at Dexithea, Lycus growled

"You would dare accuse me of attacking your

pathetic kin? What would I have to gain by attacking any of you?"

Lycus watched his siblings in disbelief as he heard them speak of his apparent treachery against them. He went on to plead his case very carefully

"I have not now, nor have I ever had cause to attack you or your kin and I -" Unable to finish his sentence Dexithea interrupted

"No cause!? When we were forced to sacrifice Gaia you made it very clear that you hated us for it, your discontent was unmistakable. Never before have I seen such anger and loathing so deep within your heart that your eyes could glow with such an evil aura. I have every belief that you have sufficient cause to want us all destroyed-" Dexithea paused for a moment as the revelation in her mind reflected in her expression, "Now I see the truth, you seek to destroy us for our powers, I do not know how you discovered the secret, but it appears you have!"

Fascinated by all things secret, cryptic and above all ironic paradoxes, Actae enquired "What secret would this be?" Dexithea rolled her eyes and looked at Actae as if to say 'Is now really the time for this?' Then she looked back at Lycus and divulged the secret,

"Well if you know then it is justifiable that we all

know. Before Gaia's sacrifice she entrusted me with her knowledge, as the keeper of secrets. It is a fact that when each of us dies, our powers are split and absorbed by each of the remaining Telchines."

Attempting to prove his innocence Lycus proclaimed "Any one of us could have discovered this, why blame me?"

Unimpressed by his words, Dexithea explained "Because all evidence points to you!"

Actae, feeling somewhat clever to have solved her cryptic words, detailed

"You attacked each of us under the banner of the other legions, knowing we would retaliate and destroy each other... Then you would have all our powers!" Dexithea did not react to Actae, but instead went on "The Telchines power will always remain while one survives. As each dies the power will be shared between the remaining, with all our powers combined you would be as powerful as both Gaia and Tartaros." stopping for a moment to look deeper into the meaning of his plot she had a revelation once again "You were charged with guarding the gateway to The Underworld! You were going to free Tartaros, it is YOU!" Dying to know what Dexithea was talking about, Actae could no longer hold his tongue,

"What is he?"

Gazing at each of her brothers in turn with a look of terror in her eyes she went on to reveal a deeper secret.

"I swore never to tell this dark secret, yet these desperate times call for the truth to emerge" She said anxiously "One of us is not the child of Gaia. One Telchine is the child of Tartaros!" She divulged nervously swallowing hard in fear of the sinister power that Tartaros' Telchine could possess.

The Siblings sat in silence, astonished at what they were hearing, all in their own way trying to make sense of the newly revealed secrets, in their own minds.

Lycus was unable to deny the accusations and sat silently staring at the dirt on his shoes with only his thoughts to keep him company as he became the victim to a devious plot. Scared half to death of the truth that he may well be the Child of Tartaros, Lycus knew that it was an accusation he could not deny as he simply did not know if it was true or false.

Quin stood and yelled at Lycus, pleading with him to argue his case for deep down he knew that Lycus was innocent. But Lycus did not say a word, instead he rose to his feet and scoffed with disappointment promptly transforming into the winds.

Quin watched as Lycus left the scene feeling

shocked and disappointed that he had not so much as denied the allegations. Behind him the conversation between the other Telchines continued, as Ormen, now said his piece; words that struck fear deep inside Quin as they were uttered without care or consideration for Lycus and his kin, as if excrement off his boot

"He has gone too far; ready your warriors. We strike at dawn; The Legion of Elements shall be destroyed for its betrayal!"

Quin screamed out "No!" as the scene faded and he suddenly found himself back in the chamber. Unable to make sense of what he had seen and heard and furthermore why it had shown itself to him, Quin now stood gazing at the emblem of the Legion of Elements. Now he knew why his generation had never seen nor heard of them. It suddenly dawned upon him that before the war of the Three Legions, the Legion of Elements was eradicated in an unscrupulous deception. He felt frustrated as he was unable to change the horrific past that seemingly brought him full circle to where he now stood. Left with feelings of anger and hatred toward the Telchines for destroying his former Legion, he was also curious to know what became of his siblings; as demi-gods of power surely they would never age. Falling in battle to some very powerful magic would be the only way they could be destroyed, and if that were the case, surely one Telchine still remained somewhere in the world, and that Telchine would likely possess the magic of all four Telchines and would indeed make them a very dangerous threat, gazing over at the wall that held the image of Ifrit, he began to wonder if Ifrit was, in fact, the last remaining Telchine in disguise. Question after question went through his mind until he stumbled upon a cryptic revelation

"If the powers of the Telchines are taken and shared between the remaining upon death… Why do I still have my powers?"

Before he could even think of a logical explanation, the bounced sound of Ragnar calling out to him echoed through the caverns where he had entered in from. As he walking towards the caverns that would lead him back to the hole in which he fell from, he turned and took one last look at the place he so named "The Chamber of Lives Past", smiling as the lantern flames slowly dimmed. Softly and sincerely he whispered "Thank you Gaia" and promptly returned back to 'the real world'.

"Down here!" He yelled, below the large opening where he had entered the hidden chamber,

"Ragnar?" he called again, but this time louder in the hope that he would be heard, but there was only silence from above. He quickly searched the vicinity for some other means of ascending out of the cavern he was trapped in. Making an attempt to climb the tree roots that protruded from the dirt wall that led directly up to the opening, he was quickly thwarted in his attempts as the roots easily pulled away from the soft wall under his weight and tossed him back to the ground.

"Ragnar!" he yelled again at the top of his lungs, only stopping for a moment to listen to the echoes of his voice slowly dying as they bounced deeper into the caverns. He was almost ready to give up, until he heard a rustling coming from above. Nervous that it could be the apparition again, Quin cautiously backed away and, raised his hands to ready his magic, waiting to see what would emerge. With a crash, a large log tumbled down through the opening and landed vertically on the ground in front of him, acting as a ladder to ascend out of the caverns. Peering over the edge as Quin gazed up Ragnar called out to him

"Quin, are you ok?" with great relief and a smile now on his face Quin rushed forward into the light so that he could be seen and replied

"I am fine" As he took hold of the log, which fortunately had a number of branches that he used as footholds, he began to clamber up as Ragnar disappeared out of the way to give Quin a clear exit out of the chamber. As he neared the top, there came a howl of wind from deep within the chamber and a ghostly voice seemed to whisper

"Lycus..." Quin stopped and looked back at the passage, squinting to see through the darkness. As his vision focused he could see a dark figure walking down the passage towards him. Terrified at the prospect of who or what this figure could be he began to scramble up the log as fast as he could, but in his haste he placed his foot down on a branch too heavily and it snapped under his foot causing him to fall. Too afraid to look back, Quin rallied a second attempt at climbing the log, but faster through sheer terror of the figure drawing closer to him. As he reached the top and grabbed the land outside the opening, he was horrified as something, or someone, took hold of his ankle and attempted to pull him back into the chamber. Kicking out his foot in a blind panic to loosen the grip, Quin couldn't help but wonder what it was and almost like a reflex he glanced back.

There he stood; with a pale, half melted face, dressed in the same clothes he was last seen wearing, now tattered and burnt, gazing up at him with bloodshot eyes. His entire body covered in blood as the smoke permeated from his skin. The vision of Origen groaned without any sense of tone in his voice   "Lycus-" As if merely sent to scare him half to death. Kicked out his foot and shaking it vigorously to free himself from its grip, Quin continued to scramble manically to the surface, with a shriek of terror, diving out of the opening and back into the forest above and scrambling backwards in a blind panic, he attempted to gain as much distance from the horror that was coming for him and hastily raised his hand using his earth magic to crack the mountain wall above the opening, causing the rocks to crumble and cover the hole over, sealing it up. Quin was sure there was no way out now for Origen and his rapid heartbeat began to slow as the panic was over. Suddenly a hand grabbed him by the shoulder; startling him, he flipped round and lashed out at ill-timed Ragnar, who now glared at him in a shock and confusion as he stood rubbing his cheek, where he was struck.

"What are you thinking Quin?" he cried, clearly upset that he had just attacked him.

"I- I am sorry, I saw... It was... never mind." Quin garbled as he attempted to make sense, in his own mind, of what he had just experienced. It was then he recalled having seen a vision of Origen as they sailed away from the Phoenix Garrison. He wondered whether it was just his mind expressing his own guilt over his brother's death causing him to hallucinate and experience horrors that only his own mind could conjure such vivid terror. Although he knew this would not likely be the last time he saw a vision of his murdered brother, all he could do for now was learn to live with it and continue his quest, which would be a lot easier said than done.

"What are you running from Quin?" Ragnar asked, curious as to why he would be so startled to lash out at anything that came near him and collapsing half a mountain over the opening of the cavern. Quin sat for a moment and tried to shake the horrendous memory of his brother's appearance from his mind, while choosing his next words very carefully

"It was nothing, merely a shadow!" he fibbed. He did not want to speak of the visions he had experienced whilst inside the chamber as he feared he may be having delusions of grandeur and anyone he told about the things he saw would most certainly think him crazier than a man spoken of in old legends. This man was famously branded insane for claiming he was sent from the heavens to atone for the sins of mankind. His story is well known all over Gaia. He claimed that Ifrit was the result of our sins and claimed that "We must ask Ifrit for his forgiveness. Once all was forgiven, Ifrit would return to the Underworld." It now dawned upon Quin that, although the world branded this man a fool for going on his adventure only to meet a gruesome end, he may well have been sent from the heavens, or more specifically, from the Skies. Quin surmised that, even though the Legions went to war and seemingly destroyed each other until only the Legion of the Skies remained, the tales that are told all around the lands would most probably have some truth to them, that being the case, it was more than likely that the Telchines were still alive and perhaps hidden in plain sight walking among the people, in the same way that Quin had done throughout his life. However he had to wonder

"If the Legion of the Skies had conquered the others, then where was Actae? And why would he abandon his kin and allow them to be destroyed by Ifrit, when he alone possessed the power to destroy Ifrit with relative ease!" Furthermore, the possibility that Dexithea and Ormen were still alive raised the question "Why have they not stopped Ifrit?" With so many questions that were yet to be answered, Quin almost regretted his discovery in the chamber and felt that perhaps it would have been better if he had simply not known. But no matter how hard he tried he simply could not ignore the knowledge he now possessed and began to question if stopping Ifrit was the right course of action. It seemed blatantly obvious that the Telchines had chosen not to get involved with Ifrit, neither to aid nor thwart him and therefore could it be for the greater good that this monster had been unleashed unto the Lands of Gaia, Ifrit alone bought about the end of Actae's reign by destroying Alexandria therefore removing the final Legion from the world and although it pained Quin to admit it, he knew that there was a distinct possibility that the destruction of Alexandria was for the good of all Gaia. On the other hand, what if he chose to believe this and sat idly by, refusing to assist in ending Ifrit's reign of terror? Maybe Ifrit was simply a freak of nature that happened to get the upper hand on the Legions in the Telchines absence.

Through all these questions, Quin's thoughts kept returning to one absolute, he had been blessed with another chance at life after death. Perhaps by Gaia, or maybe it just wasn't the right moment for him to leave, irrespective, he now believed he was the reincarnation of Lycus and for whatever reason was grateful for his second chance. He swore to himself that his life would not be squandered and he would do whatever it took to ensure he removed the corruption from Gaia's lands, to honour his mother's sacrifice. Although angered by the betrayal and deception he had been a victim of, he now held one simple belief in his heart:

'Everything that has happened to me, starting with my death as Lycus and the loss of my friends and family since my return as Quin, The Telchines' were to be blamed for. It is a result of the actions they have taken and have failed to take that has put the lands in such devastation. Therefore all the pain and anguish I have felt since Ifrit came into my life is their fault!'

With this belief held stubbornly in his heart, Quin now realised his quest was far from over and there was much more for him to accomplish past destroying Ifrit, he vowed to rise up and claim his right to the Legion of the Elements. He alone would pave the way to an end of the war that tarnished the face of Gaia and the Telchines blatant disrespect for their own Mother, Quin swore he would take his revenge and destroy them all.

He rose to his feet with an overwhelming hatred in his heart, and stared off into the distance in a day dream he recalled the reality of his past; who he was and what he was becoming. Deep inside he could feel his power boiling from his gut as it swelled and pulsed through each and every muscle in his body, shaking uncontrollably as the adrenaline coursed through his veins and the overwhelming urge to call out to the heavens and summon the Telchines to come and face him. Tears fell from his eyes as his body could no longer handle the pressure of the hatred in his heart.

"Quin, are you ok?" Ragnar asked concernedly, frightened by his unexpected actions. Quin did not respond to Ragnar's concern, but merely continued to stare into space as his anger had, by now, drowned out all sound around him, his attention focused solidly on the sound of his heart as it thumped rapidly until, finally, Quin's mortal coils could no longer control him. All the mortality that he once had suddenly vanished and gave way to a new mind-set as the anger and hatred he felt, had taken over and diplomacy was no longer an option. Within a matter of a few heartbeats, Quin had become everything that he once despised; the belief of Origen and that which he stood for. He could no longer contain himself or his magic as it freely burst forth from him creating a huge seismic wave that blasted Ragnar away, hurtling him into the forest behind him. Dust, rocks and trees around them were violently lifted and scattered everywhere. As the debris settled and Quin regained control of himself his eyes began to alter to the same sinister red glow that Lycus bore. Quin felt a burning sensation in his eyes, although it gave him comfort and felt oddly compelling. He lifted his hood over his head to cover his eyes and determined that henceforth, only those he deemed *'worthy'* would ever have the honour of seeing his face and witness his true power. With no such words of regret or apology towards Ragnar's potential injuries as he sat up covered in dirt and sawdust gazing upon Quin, startled and somewhat impressed, as he began to walk away. Ragnar now found himself feeling somewhat intimidated by him and was unsure of what to do, cautiously calling out to him,

"Where are you going?" but with no response. Quin continued to walk away without even acknowledging Ragnar, however with a few more steps Quin stopped and peered over his shoulder to reply,

"I am going to finish this!"

As Quin vanished off beyond the trees, venturing further into the forest, Ragnar sat and watched him leave, grinning triumphantly to himself.

"Welcome back Lycus… Fate awaits you!"

Full of anger, hatred, betrayal and regret, Quin was no longer the boy he was when his journey began. Although his feelings of compassion had not been completely lost, he knew that he would likely never feel the same again. As he stomped through the forest of the island, he merely left it to the elements to lead him to his destination, wherever that may be. Realising that his only true allies had been, and always would be the elements, Quin cursed himself for neglecting them for so long. His thoughts revisited memories of his childhood and more specifically, Origen. He now finally understood what Origen was trying to explain to him every day as they were growing up. He felt ashamed of himself for being so callous and thick-headed in denying his true allies instead of embracing their care of him. But he had to wonder if he would have turned out this way had Prince Reaven survived the onslaught from the barbaric Centaurs. Knowing that he could not change the past and save the Prince, Quin shrugged it off as he would never know and so could only accept that this was simply his cruel fate; nevertheless a fate that the Centaurs, Ifrit and the Telchines would now and forever, live to regret as his thoughts turning only to plots of revenge.

Quin continuing on through the forest, the winds guiding his every move, while deep in thought. A shout from Ragnar broke his concentration as he vainly attempted to catch up. But Quin gave the distinct impression that he was purposefully rushing along in order to leave Ragnar behind

"Quin, will you please wait for me" He shouted. But he didn't stop or even slow down to accommodate Ragnar's plea as he pressed on,

"If you fall behind, you are left behind" he shouted back to Ragnar, who was still surprised by the drastic change in Quin's attitude since arriving on the island. Ragnar stopped for a moment to catch his breath and, attempted to regain some small amount of authority as he rebutted Quin for his arrogance and lack of courtesy

"Without me, you cannot hope to finish this. You know you need my knowledge!"

Grinding to a halt, Quin turned sharply to face him. Ragnar instantly tensed up as he feared his power and the prospect of what he could possibly do to him, he subtly attempted to apologise as he continued to speak diplomatically, but also with a sense of authority.

"Quin, please. We must stay together. I understand that I may not have fully earned your trust yet, but we cannot do this unless we work together. The scripts from the book of Necr-" Before Ragnar could even finish the sentence; Quin used his magic to move in the blink of an eye bringing himself nose to nose with Ragnar.

"And where is the book?" He yelled angrily. Ragnar stumbled over his words attempting to explain.

"I had to destroy it. When I heard the Sirens attacking the ship, I had to take steps to avoid the book falling into enemy hands, so I used an incantation to create an explosion to destroy the ship along with the book. I ran to find you so that we might escape the blast and survive, which we did – and please, do not even consider thanking me!" He said sarcastically.

Quin's anger towards Ragnar was almost tangible, yet Ragnar foolishly continued to finish what he was saying in a babble as he cowered away from Quin's wrath,

"Please try to understand that I could not let it fall into another's hands, the book held things that could destroy everything; I had no choice. It was my duty!"

Scoffing loudly at Ragnar's cowardice but with a slight admiration for his sense of duty, Quin took a hold of Ragnar's vest and pulled him in close.

"If you do not have the book, what purpose do you have? You are most certainly of no further use to me!" With that Quin shoved him to the ground and simply turned to walk off once again. Desperate with fear of being left alone on the island and the creatures that might hunt him, Ragnar pleaded his case further

"The book may be gone but I can still help you! I memorised the texts. Therefore, I am the only person qualified to help you now!" Only to be undignified with Quin's departure once again, all he had left was to come clean and reveal the knowledge he had been concealing from him this whole time.

"I know where we are, this Island… I know what it is!" Quin began to wonder as he heard Ragnar's words spilling from his lips and was curious as he pondered the extent of Ragnar's knowledge about the island. More than anything, was he aware of the hidden Chamber, just how much more information was Ragnar hiding from him? Torn between the urge to leave him behind, yet compelled to find out everything he knew, he turned to Ragnar, who was still grovelling pathetically as he scurried along on his knees, covered in dirt. Quin knew he had to obtain the information that Ragnar held, his only concern was that this knowledge could quite easily be a threat to him.

"Speak!" Quin ordered sharply, as Ragnar picked himself up off the floor and dusted off his shame.

"This small island, where we now stand, is just the

tip of the whole land. We are standing on the southern mountain of the very island that we set out to find! The main city is under the ocean." As Quin heard the dreaded name fall from Ragnar's lips, all his senses came alive at once and now, for once he listened intently to his every word "It was within the city that Tartaros created the Underworld" he continued "Tartaros commanded his most trusted kin to protect the entrance to the Underworld and handed him a book with powerful magic to use to protect his land and use against Gaia and her kin. The book I speak of is the same book that I destroyed; the book of Necropoleis. Now do you understand why I had to destroy it?" Quin stood in silence as he listened to Ragnar's story, Although he had to wonder what had become of Tartaros' kin, if such a being was blessed with seemingly endless power how then would he have just vanished and why would he have been so careless with the book to allow it to fall into human hands? Furthermore, if the book held information on how to destroy Gaia, then how many incantations had Ragnar memorised that could also destroy a Telchine and its powers? Meaning, Ragnar was now a potential threat.

"What else do you know about this island?" Quin asked, hinting that there was more to the island than he may know about. Ragnar paused for a moment, wondering what Quin knew that he didn't and suddenly realised how it felt to have mistrust towards another who may be withholding secrets.

"That is all I know, other than… I know where we need to go next!" Gazing upon him in disbelief, Quin was angered at what he had just been told, Ragnar knew where to go the whole time, but rather than just telling him he kept it a secret to use as a bartering tool for later. But his anger was short lived as he realised his journey was almost at an end. Soon he would use his powers to raise the rest of the Island from the depths of the ocean and would finally be reunited with Asha, his friends and his family. However, he was no longer the boy that Asha once knew and even if she loved him, the anger and hatred in his heart may deny him the ability to love her back. Quin was fearful that she may ask him to choose between her and his power, or worse, his revenge which could serve to punish Asha and ultimately destroy her. Once again he found himself faced with another cruel and difficult choice determined by his fate, it became more and more apparent that no matter how powerful he was, his fate would always play a stronger hand in his life and would inevitably bring about the end. For the first time Quin was now unsure of whether he wanted to bring Asha back, with a high possibility it could put her in quite considerable danger. He began to feel the cold stab of anguish as he prepared to accept that Asha could be lost to him forever. Perhaps it was better that she, and all he once held dear stayed dead, for in death they would never be the victims of harm for his actions. He knew that he must finish what he started and not even the memory of Asha would sway him from his path. Unwilling to go back on his word, he could not ignore the torture that Lycus had endured in his life that now continued into the present. He had so many questions that needed answers and he knew that in finding those answers, anyone he dared hold close, would also be affected by what he would find lurking in the darkest corners of his fate. Although for all his doubts he knew he had little choice but to move forward and bring back the fallen to take the fight back at Ifrit, as alone he could never hope to fulfil his objectives.

'I must go on. Revenge is my only fate now' he thought, as if destined to continue and witness the resurrection of his friends and family, to then watch them die before his eyes all over again, a fate so cruel that death itself seemed like a blessing.

The sound of rustling bushes nearby broke his trail of thought, catching his eye he stared into the foliage, watching the branches swaying violently back and forth, being shoved aside by someone or something that was yet to be determined as friend or foe, Quin stood with a flaming ball of fire in his hand, ready to strike down anything that would dare to come at him. Ragnar however, took a different approach to the situation and rushed over to cower behind him for protection. Then, with a stumbled and entirely inelegant entrance, the Siren emerged and fell flat on her face at Quin's feet. Knowing who she was, Quin felt she was no threat. He stared down at the female Siren without any show of compassion in helping her back to her feet. Clearly exhausted from all the running she had been doing, the siren simply lay in the dirt and took a moment to catch her breath, eventually she pushed herself up to look at Quin who was still just standing there, staring at her from behind the shadow of his hood, as she waited for him to help her up, or at least speak to her.

For what seemed to be a long and uncomfortable stretch of time there was complete silence, broken only when the Siren uttered sarcastically, in the hope that she might get some help or attention

"I apologise, am I interrupting something?"

"As a matter of a fact, you are; I was trying to think!" Quin retorted. Shocked at his blatant lack of good will and a little hurt that he didn't even seem to care that she was alive and well, she bit back,

"Well then, by all means, please do not let me interrupt you, after all we are only stranded on a strange island in the middle of - Gaia only knows where! The sun is setting and there is still an extremely dangerous black cloud monster chasing us. So, please, do not let me keep you from your thoughts!"

Quin was quite unimpressed by the Sirens sharp wit and patronising tone as she lay on the ground looking rather pleased with herself for her remarks giving the distinct impression that she lacked any kind of respect for his power.

"Stranded? A very poor choice of words for your kind to use, do you not think?" Quin spat out discourteously at the Siren. Before the Siren could think of a response to his nastiness, Ragnar stepped forward and respectfully bowed his head before Quin as if he was now his servant, in an attempt to calm the situation down and ensure the safety of the beautifully woman that stood before them,

"Quin; perhaps the young lady is right. Night is drawing in and it would be too easy to get lost in the woods at night... Also In the darkness the black cloud would have an advantage over us, it could easily hunt us down. I fear she is correct, we must rest." He reasoned diplomatically. But Quin did not seem convinced and paused to think on Ragnar's words. Loathed to accept that he trusted Ragnar more than the Siren at this point, he accepted that even with his powers he wouldn't want to face the black cloud again until he knew of a way to defeat it. Convinced that the elements would always guide him safely, he now realised that if Ragnar were to come to any serious harm, there would be no way to raise the army against Ifrit and the knowledge obtained from the Book of Necropoleis would die with him. Suddenly Quin found himself, ironically, back where he started, feeling dependent upon Ragnar, although such a feeling sat uncomfortably in his stomach and left a bad taste in his mouth, his own fate lay in the hands of someone else, a position that he had vowed never to find himself in again. He unfortunately found himself with no alternative,

"Very well we should-" cutting his sentence short Quin closed his eyes and listened to the sudden voices of the elements crying out to him, warning him of the danger that was fast approaching,

"-There is a storm heading this way". He warned with a sense of calmness in his voice as if pleased of the threat this would pose to the Siren, he watched her gaze up at the clouds with sheer terror as they gathered above them, darkened and seemingly angry at her betrayal to her Kin. Quin was fully aware that if she was to come in contact with any form of water, her scaly fin would return, however he suddenly realised that the prospect of this prank would seem hilarious to begin with, he was unsure of the consequences of her being in that state whilst outside of the ocean. Knowing that they would never reach the beach in time, Quin removed his cloak and threw it over the Siren to keep her dry for as long as possible while they searched for shelter. Ragnar looked at Quin, confused as he now suddenly seemed to be showing her compassion, after treating her with such ill-repute merely moments before. Ragnar, once again, felt the bitter stab of being left in the dark about certain secrets that he felt he should know. Furthermore, he noticed that Quin's glowing eyes had now returned to their natural colour.

As Quin placed his arm around the Siren, he gently guided her away to a nearby shelter leaving Ragnar frustrated at Quin's inconsistency with his identity and impulsiveness. Without taking his eyes off them he continued to glare as they walked away. Ragnar surmised that this girl would weaken Quin's mind and prevent him from realising his full magical potential. And with a single act of kindness towards her from Quin, Ragnar's previous liking of her was abolished and he knew she would have to go… One way or another!

- Chapter XV -
The Legion of the Seas

As Quin and the Siren entered the rocky shelter provided by a chasm in the mountains wall, the siren removed the cloak from around her shoulders and graciously held it out to him with a coy smile on her face as she struggled to make eye contact through the embarrassment of the obvious crush she had on him, it made her feel like a little girl again, however such feelings reminded her of the day she met her siren mate and she took a moment to reminded herself of why she was on the island. She sat down on a small rock near the back of the shelter and looked out into the forest as the rain began to fall heavily and night settled in, although the rain was potentially deadly to the Siren girl, it had been far too long since she had heard the droplets tapping on the leaves of the trees and slowly, drop by drop, soaking the forest floor changing the once dusty ground to a shimmering scene of sparkles. In the distance she could see Ragnar, who stood glaring back at them both with an expression of discontent.

"No, you keep it; it is going to get cold tonight" Quin said courteously, placing the cloak back around her shoulders. The Siren carefully considered her next words as she fancied her sarcastic attitude, and usually shied away from gratitude by simply dishing out back-handed compliments, but on this occasion she simple said

"Thank you" and curled up inside the cloak to keep warm. Quin smiled and remembered how good it felt to help others and the positive effect it made to their lives, no matter how big or small the gesture.

"It is my pleasure" He humbly replied. Knowing that he assumed she was thanking him for the cloak, she went on to elaborate,

"I mean, for saving my life. You bravely put yourself in harm's way when that – thing came for me. You do not even know my name, yet you risked your life for mine. It is a strange experience. For once in my life, someone selflessly protected me but not because of my association with…" She paused, "Well, never mind." Quin frowned as he looked upon the Siren who had now shyly lowered her head to look at the ground. He knelt before her, curious to know else what she was trying to divulge, but knew she would need some kind of reassurance before she would continue. Reaching out his hand, he placed it on top of hers and spoke sincerely

"You too saved my life, so let us just say we are even" Uncomfortable with the physical contact they now shared, she slowly pulled her hand away and attempted to change the subject

"You never did explain how you came to possess the powers of the Siren." She pointed out. He reached into his pocket and pulled out the lock of hair he had placed there for safety and presented it to her. The Siren took the lock into her own hand and stared. Her expression portrayed her disbelief

"Where did you get this?" she demanded. Before thinking carefully about his answer Quin simply blurted out the whole truth as if he had just been disciplined by an adult.

"It was a gift, given to me by the Barmaid at the Phoenix Garrison. She asked me to use it to find her daughter-" Sighing deeply he went on to disclose his guilt "Deep down, I knew I could not hope to find her daughter, but how could I say no? She was so desperate to see her daughter again and I concluded any hope would be a blessing to her." The Siren too let out a sigh as she muttered a single word

"Ligeia…"

Quin was astounded that the Siren knew where the lock of hair had come from and felt compelled to know what had become of the lost Siren girl.

"You know of her?" He bellowed excitedly, like a

child waiting for a special gift. The Siren gave a small and embarrassed giggle and revealed,

"You might say that Quin - I am Ligeia." She said smugly, feeling like a legend told in stories. "Well, at least I was her; a long time ago." She said sadly, as she came to the realisation that it was merely a name and she was no longer a human, nor the girl she once was when she disappeared

Shocked and a little disturbed by this ironic turn of events, he got up and walked out into the forest as the rain poured down harder and harder, allowing himself to get soaked. Once again he found his mind flooded with questions, yet he felt there was only one that really mattered

"Why did you not return home?" He enquired innocently.

Ligeia paused for a moment and then spoke softly, as if from shame, recalling her past and the actions she took, which changed her life forever.

"The first born Siren kin of the Legion of the Sea was a man named Glaucus. I say *'man'* because he too was once human, much like myself. He would often tell the story of how he served under our goddess, Dexithea, and how he stood by her side through the darkest of situations. The Legion originally lived in peace on the sea shores, until the day that the war of the Legions began and they were forced to leave the lands and live on boats out at sea. The Legion of the Seas was all but doomed as they struggled to find sufficient sustenance to keep them all alive, and they slowly began to die of starvation and various ailments. Then one fateful day Dexithea returned to her people from the bottom of the ocean, she had transformed into the first Siren and told her kin that she had found a magical herb that would give them the power to live in the safety of the ocean free from the reach of the others. She so commanded that all the men were to swim down to the ocean's floor to find and eat the herb to obtain this power. The men blindly followed Dexithea's wishes and they all swam deep into the cold waters. One by one they either drowned or were crushed by the weight of the deep waters, until only Glaucus remained. After much struggle he reached the herb and scoffed it down just before he lost consciousness. When he awoke he was greeted by Dexithea's kiss and found himself transformed into a Siren. It was only then that Dexithea informed him of the curse that came with it,

'As a Siren you now possess a portion of my powers' She said 'You are now a Seer and keeper of secrets. You have been given the gift of eternal life to serve as the leader of our legion. It is your duty to replenish our legion by converting the worth to our cause.'

However Glaucus was baffled by his new powers as they instantly flashed through his mind as undiscovered secrets made themselves known to him, but worst of all, he could see glimpses of the future and gazed in horror as he witnessed the deaths of all those he had ever known in his life and would continue to do so with every person he laid eyes on thereafter. He asked Dexithea why he had been rewarded with the curse of roaming the seas for eternity simply to abduct innocent sailors.

'Our women are unable to become Sirens without a mate, it is your job to find them suitable mates so that they may join us, in our new home' she explained.

For many days Dexithea swam at his side as they both abducted sailors from their ships and dragged them to the ocean's floor where Glaucus would either accept them as a worthy siren or reject them and send them back to the lands, with a warning to never roam the sea again." She explained.

Pausing for a moment to consider if this story was divulging too much, after all she too was a keeper of secrets and had to wonder if this was one that should not be told to others. This in itself was a curse as she had always struggled to see the difference between honesty and secrets. Although having met Quin, Ligeia had already seen his future and foreseen his death. Knowing his demise was only a day away, she continued to tell her story.

"The Siren population grew with every passing day until there were no more women left to pair up with a Siren male, although Glaucus refused to stop capturing men, claiming that it was Dexithea's wish. They soon became too overpopulated with men and Glaucus was forced to reach out to Dexithea for a solution. Answering his plea, she revealed the Siren had another power that allowed them to leave the ocean and return back to their human form upon the lands. This gave the Siren men an opportunity to roam the lands in search of a mate to bring back with them, although we would only have the chance to do this the once. For when they returned to the waters they were bound there, either with their mate or alone, forever. With this new discovery, Glaucus ordered The Siren men out onto the lands to find a mate and with the ritual of *blood melding* two would become one and together return to the ocean and spawn their own kin, which would become the next generation of Sirens. However, the same as any gift of magic, this power came with a curse. When a merged Siren dies, so too does its mate; unless that mate returned to the lands never to feel water's touch again."

Quin interrupted her story, wondering why Ligeia would take the risk of leaving the waters. It seemed to him that she had made an unthinkable sacrifice in leaving the ocean to save a mere human she didn't even know.

"You have a mate? Then why would you leave the ocean for me? This is your one and only chance to be out of the waters... Why would you take such rash actions simply to save me, instead of using your one opportunity to see your mother again?" However Quin's lack of understanding only served to anger Ligeia.

"I believed my mother had the ability to come to me! I gave *her* the lock of hair and pleaded for her to come to me; I had no idea that she had given it to you" Then explained the actual reason why she had left the ocean, "Besides, I do not know what has become of my mate. If he is dead then the moment I touch the water and retake my Siren form, I too will die!"

Hearing her words, Quin empathised with Ligeia's pain as he remembered the reason that he came on this quest to begin with; to find Asha, but maybe for all the wrong reasons. He thought to himself while staring out into the forest

    'I too am taking a great risk and now both Ligeia and I are faced with a choice. This quest to raise an entire island from the depths of the ocean using my powers could easily kill me. Should I take such a risk in the blind hope that Asha could be returned to me? Much like Ligeia, if she seized the opportunity to go back into the ocean! Either way, we both could pay the ultimate price.' Before Quin's trail of thought went any deeper he was struck by the realisation that Ragnar was no longer in sight within the forest which now lay dark and eerily still. He scanned the forest for Ragnar and thought it best to distract Ligeia from noticing Ragnar's disappearance by asking her to continue her story.

    "Was it the blood melding ritual that changed you into a Siren?" Quin subtly asked.

"I was young and impressionable back then and had I known my future I most probably would not have fallen so stupidly in love with him. It was just another beautiful day in the Phoenix Garrison and I was sent out by my mother to do my daily chores of collecting food from the market. I began to tire of the same old Merchants selling me the same old things and greeting the same old people, as I had done for most of my life. I wished so much for something different to happen so that I might break the monotony in my life. And then, as if my hopes had been answered, there he was; a man I had never seen before, he was masculine and handsome, I felt myself going weak at the knees just looking at him as he strolled around the marketplace, greeted any woman who crossed his path with a dashing smile. All I wanted was to be greeted by him and so, having forgotten about my chores, I walked towards him and subtly strolled by gazing at him, and as our eyes met it seemed there was an instant connection. He stopped and stared at me, ignoring all other women. Although I was too afraid to speak to him, I simply walked on by and hid myself behind a wall for a moment to compose myself. As I peered around the wall to take another look at him, he was no longer anywhere to be seen. I have no idea what came over me, but I knew I had to see him again and so I rushed around the market looking for him, eventually I found him at the docks and plucked up the courage to talk to him. From the moment we spoke it was as if magic was in the air and I honestly cannot remember a single word we said to each other that day, it all felt like a dream. Soon the day became night and we were still sat on the docks sharing stories, while watching the waves of the sea, I grew cold and he held me in his massive arms to keep me warm. It felt like love at first sight and I could not help but kiss him, even though most would shun such actions. It was only then that he told me about The Siren. Of course I did not believe him and, to prove his claims he jumped into the sea and swam to a distance away from the docks, calling over to me to join him, stupidly I swam out to him and I had not even realised that he had fins instead of legs until he pointed it out to me, but I remember not being frightened or even shocked, something about it all felt so natural and right. I allowed him to take me further out to sea and that is where he asked me to be his mate. I could not just say *'yes'* straight away so I politely told him that I would have to consider it. He returned me to the safety of the docks and informed me that he could no longer leave the ocean and I would have to go to him. I spent many days out in the ocean meeting him on the surface; until one day he cut a lock of my hair and blessed it with a magic that would allow me to breathe underwater and told me to visit him any time I wanted, naturally it was a lot to take in and so I did not use it for some time thereafter." Quin gazed at the lock of hair still sitting in Ligeia's hand and pointed at it as he proclaimed,

"This is the lock he blessed?"

Ligeia nodded gently and gazed longingly at the lock as she continued her story,

"After a few days he stopped visiting me on the surface, despite waiting most days for him, he never came to the surface, so I decided that I would have to go to him. At the time I did not care if the enchanted hair allowed me to breathe or not; I would have gladly drowned trying to find him. Each day I searched a different part of the ocean hoping to find him or a sign of the siren, but I was unable to find them anywhere. Soon I began to lose hope and instead of searching the ocean I just sat on the docks and gazed out to sea from morning till night, only returning home to eat.

Many a day went by without any sign of him, that is, until one day he suddenly returned, splashing on the surface of the water far out at sea waving to me. Without hesitation I dived into the water and swam to him as fast as I could. As we drifted on the surface he informed me that he had been away with the Siren in search of a magical relic that their enemies sought after, being a keeper of secrets he knew of the relic and its power; a most dangerous weapon that, if in the wrong hands, could turn the tide of any war. They had located the relic and Dexithea had taken it and disappeared without a trace. He feared it was only a matter of time before the other Legions would seek his revenge on the Siren, so told me that he could not take me with him fearing it would only bring death for me; he begged me to forget about him, to find another on land and live a happy and prosperous life. With that he swam away, deep into the ocean, and I foolishly swam down after him, however I had left the enchanted lock at home and it was not long before I began to struggle. Even though I was unable to hold my breath for much longer, I refused to give up and swam deeper and deeper. The weight of the Ocean began to crush me. As my final breath left me, I began to drown and just before my life slipped away from me, he reappeared and unexpectedly kissed me. Blowing air into my lungs he quickly pulled out a dagger from the holster he wore across his shoulder, and promptly sliced the palms of both our hands. He pressed our wounds tightly together and took the sea plant he wore around his wrist and tied it around our joined hands. In an instant I could feel myself gaining the ability to breathe for myself. It was the most peculiar feeling to then experience my legs joining together and forming a tailfin. Within mere moments I had become a Siren, although I soon found out that I had not become just any Siren, it transpired that my mate was actually Glaucus himself and my blood had now merged with his, making me the Princess of the Sirens!"

Quin tried his best to listen to Ligeia's story whilst still gazing out into the forest for signs of Ragnar.

"The Princess of the Siren; now that is most interesting, at least that explains how we arrived here while lying unconscious in the middle of the ocean." Ragnar said as he had entered into the shelter without detection and propped himself up against the wall behind Ligeia listening to her story. Startled by Ragnar's abrupt interruption, Ligeia jumped to her feet and backed towards Quin obviously fearing him. Quin placed his hands on her shoulders to reassure her and more importantly, to stop her walking out of the shelter into the rain. Curiously he began to wonder why Ligeia would be so frightened of Ragnar that she would completely neglect the danger she would face by walking out into the rain. Quin whispered into her ear

"Everything is alright, it is only Ragnar." Ligeia had by now begun to trust Quin, despite his somewhat sinister tendencies. She grabbed the cloak, which was falling from her shoulders and pulled it aggressively over herself, whilst staring daggers at Ragnar, who was now stood with a smug grin on his face, pleased with himself for having discovered Ligeia's little secret.

Quin gently ushered her into a corner and sat her down, speaking in a gentle whisper, so that Ragnar would not hear his words,

"You should rest now. At sunrise I must leave, whether it is raining or not, I have a very important quest that I need Ragnar's help with. I imagine it will hold some untold dangers and quite honestly, I may not return. Just promise you will stay safe and find your way back to your mother." With fear in her eyes, Ligeia attempted to tell Quin of the vision she had seen of his impending death, but was interrupted by Ragnar

"Quin, I would speak with you!" He acknowledged Ragnar's request by nodding his head, but did not take his eyes off Ligeia, who had now decided to say nothing more. She simply smiled at Quin and watched as he left the shelter to join Ragnar in the forest. After he was gone, she collected some dry sticks scattered around the shelter and piled them up, cleverly rubbing two pieces together she created embers that soon grew into a smouldering fire that she curled up next to for warmth.

Ragnar stopped abruptly, turned to Quin and voiced his concerns,

"This Siren is toying with you. She is using her magic to enchant your mind." Although Quin knew that it was impossible for a Siren to enchant another magical person,

"Do not be so ridiculous, I-" He protested, but before he was allowed to finish, Ragnar rudely interrupted him and poked fun at his obvious lust,

"I ask you to look me in the eyes and say with honesty that you do not have feelings for her!" Angered by the accusation, regardless of how true it may have been, Quin's rage quickly built up causing his eyes to flash red as he took hold of Ragnar's throat and stared into his eyes,

"You would not wish me to look you in the eyes Ragnar, for you will fear what you see!" In shock Ragnar raised his hands in a pathetic attempt to shield himself from his gaze and cowered as he attempted to redeem himself,

"Quin, please. She is a Siren and we cannot keep stopping for shelter each time it threatens to rain. What if we need to swim through water or if we face something dangerous? You are far too important to put yourself at risk for her. You must understand she endangers everything we are fighting for!" Ragnar exclaimed. Beginning to doubt himself, Quin knew that Ragnar made a valid point and wondered if Ragnar may have been right all along. He realised that he was at his most powerful when he was enraged, so he could not afford to let feelings of compassion get in his way. He accepted he had come too far to throw it all away for her, yet he also realised that Ligeia's death would only serve to strengthen his resolve even more as death and despair seemed to empower him all the more, although he would never wish death upon her. With all this in mind, Quin knew that he would benefit more by taking Ligeia with them, for while she was around, he had something to protect and furthermore something that he could be angry about especially if she were to die.

"She is coming and therefore is my responsibility" Quin angrily snapped at Ragnar as he shoved him aside to return to Ligeia. Entered the shelter he turned his head away from Ligeia as she curiously watched him walk over to the far wall and slump down with his back to her. Although it felt as if he was giving her the cold shoulder. He was ashamed of the anger and resentment he felt that was reflected in his sinister red eyes and felt that Ligeia would disapprove or fear such a power. Yet in his own mind, he knew that this was now the only way he could continue with his life for the good of everyone. He had to become a selfish monster that would only use his magic for his own personal gain to strike down his enemies with. Although it would be the first time he struck down a member of his family in a blind rage, he knew it would not and could not be the last.

Quin tried to let go of the reality of his situation, having become everything he once despised. He shut his eyes and tried to sleep yet his mind began to wander as he recalled everything Ligeia had said about Dexithea. He couldn't help but wonder if perhaps, as Lycus, he had tried to destroy the other Telchine Legions, knowing how he felt now. He began to think that perhaps he wasn't really following his true emotions, but instead was simply overwhelmed by his powers, which created the great urge to kill and exact his revenge for the injustice that had befallen him as Lycus. He then started to recall the feelings that Lycus had felt in the memory of the Telchines meeting, Quin knew that Lycus was not responsible for the attacks on the other Legions 'So then, who was responsible?' either way, He no longer cared about who was at fault and merely held onto the rage that would fuel his life henceforth.

The night went on and the flames of the fire gradually dithered down. Quin and Ligeia had both drifted off to sleep leaving only Ragnar awake, who sat and watched the rainfall while plotting his next move. He took a moment to look over at Ligeia as she slept peacefully and grinned, as if victorious, and muttered silently

"Well at least we have our royal blood now, fate is on our side master!" He then tip-toed quietly towards Ligeia. On the way he picked up a piece of charred wood from the burnt out campfire and blew gently on the embers and began to draw a strange ritualistic symbol on the wall above her head. Once finished, he quickly slunk back to his rock and held out his hands toward the symbol and began to chant an ancient ritual.

*"**Ligatura sanguinem et animam sanctam vis vitalis, et conciderent hoc vasculum ad munus nostri amet justo**."*

As Ragnar spoke the words, the charcoal symbol on the wall began to glow with a mystical blue light and magical orbs were drawn into Ligeia's body as she slept, unaware of the devious happenings that surrounded her. With the ritual now complete, Ragnar grinned even more congratulating himself for getting one step closer to revealing the truth of his own hidden agenda.

- Chapter XVI -
Burning Bridges

Early morning lurked on the horizon of the small island. A foggy haze quilted the landscape and hung in the air like a bad omen of dangers to come. Ligeia awoke to find she been left alone. She immediately jumped to her feet and called out for Quin, but quickly realised she had lost her voice. In a panic she dashed out of the cave and into the woods, but with no idea where she was going, all she wanted was to find him. Suddenly the ground gave way under her and she plummeted into a dark hole, looking up she could see the sky moving further and further away as she fell deeper and deeper. She landed on the ground in a dark, dank cave and as she cautiously stepped forward into the darkness a torch lit up in front of her. It wasn't long before she noticed that it was being held by the Apparition that had previously chased her through the forest. Strangely the Apparition gently handed her the torch, pointed to a light at the other end of the cave, and then promptly vanished. After a few steps forward she oddly found herself stepping out the other side of the cave and was now standing in the middle of a ruined temple, of sorts. Quin stood in the middle of the ruin along with a tall, dark haired man, who was holding a sword with a flaming blade in one hand and a small dagger in the other. Horrified by this vision, Ligeia quickly recognised the scene as the one of the premonitions she had seen of Quin's death. She tried to call out to him but still no sound came out of her mouth. Quin turned and stared at her with his red gaze, and whispered, "Tartaros", the man then stabbed Quin with the dagger and watched him slump to the ground, all the while keeping eye contact with her, as his life expired.

Ligeia sharply woke to the eerie sound of silence; a silence that left a sense of uncertainty lingering in her mind. It seemed as if the Island was completely uninhabited, there was no chirping of birds or seagulls and the earth lay deadly still, as if even the insects had abandoned the island. She cast off Quin's cloak and rose to her feet to look beyond the shelter at the scene outside. Holding her breath and closing her eyes in an attempt to hear the faintest sound of the ocean's waves far off in the distance. The soft sound reminded her of her life with the Siren and she began to pine for Glaucus 'Are you still alive?' She wondered. Her heart thumped at the very thought of him being alive and desperately searching for her, she could only imagine him yearning for her, and the prospect of losing her. If he still lived he would believe himself to be cursed to continue living his immortal life forever searching for her. The mere prospect of these thoughts bought a tear to her eye before being startled, once again, by Ragnar who had now also awoken and had perversely been watching her,

"Be careful Siren, you would not want your tears to change you back into your true form" He said, with an oddly sarcastic yet gentle tone, as if he actually cared. However, Ligeia still did not trust him. Glared at him she declared,

"My tears will not endanger me!" Quick as a flash Ragnar responded with presumption while reaching into his pocket

"No? Is it not true that a Sirens tears hold magical properties? How unwise it would be to let them fall into the wrong hands!" Ragnar pulled out a piece of folded parchment and held it out to Ligeia, smiling sweetly "Here wipe your tears, we would not want them landing on the ground here, we have no idea what sort of dark magic this island holds" Ligeia gratefully accepted his seemingly kind gesture and took the parchment from Ragnar, albeit remaining defensive as she kept her distance and reached out as far as she could to grab the parchment, without bringing herself too close to him. Having taken it, she politely thanked him and wiped her tears. With the last of her tears wiped away from her face, Ragnar was quick to snatch it out of her hands and promptly unfolded it whilst turning his back on her. Holding it out in front of him, Ragnar smiled as the secret began to reveal itself within the parchments hidden text. Reading the newly revealed texts he exclaimed,

"No! That is not possible!"

His face dropped to a clear expression of shock and horror at what he had just discovered. Ligeia too became curious to know this secret and shuffled closer to him assuming he would share this knowledge with her, but as he spotted her out the corner of his eye, he quickly folded the parchment and stuffed it back into his pocket.

"What was that?" She asked inquisitively.

"It is nothing!" He snapped. Turning to face her he continued in a desperate attempt to redeem himself "It is a page from an old book, the text is written in an ancient language and I needed a tear-"

"You tricked me!" Ligeia exclaimed angrily. Shocked, but not surprised, that Ragnar had deviously lead her on and used her to get at her tears to use for his own heartless benefit "Give it to me this instant, I would see it with my own eyes!" she ordered reaching for Ragnar's pocket, clutching at his cloak to prevent any means of escape, but Ragnar shoved her backwards with great force and yelled,

"I said no!"

Quin was woken by Ragnar's sudden raised voice as the situation was seemingly escalating between Ligeia and Ragnar for no apparent reason. He jumped to his feet and stood in front of Ligeia to defend her and pushed him away.

"Do not dare lay a finger on her Ragnar" Quin bellowed as Ragnar stumbled backwards attempting to stay on his feet. Falling back against the solid cavern wall, Ragnar managed to stabilise himself, suggestively brushing off his cloak where Quin had shoved him as if his very touch was an insult to him.   "I apologise..." He muttered in an unconvincing tone. There was a moment of silence as Quin glared at Ragnar, his eyes burning red emphasised his anger as they all bit their tongues and waited in anticipation of the antagonistic atmosphere to calm. When Quin himself felt calm enough to speak rationally, he felt it prudent to make peace between them   "Ragnar, I understand why you do not want her to come with us, however we both owe her our lives. So we owe it to her to get her home safely. She is coming with us. You need to find a way to deal with that" He then turned and walked away into the forest, leaving Ragnar and Ligeia alone with each other, but with his pride bruised he continued staring Ligeia in the eyes with an expression of distaste. No more was said between them as Ragnar barged past her and left to follow Quin into the forest, leaving Ligeia alone with her thoughts.

"The rain has ceased, it is safe for us to continue." Quin pointed out as he turned to Ragnar "Can you lead the way?" he asked, as he closed his eyes and used his powers to sense the movement of the elements. Ragnar stood in front of Quin and waited for him to open his eyes before talking again

"We must head north to the peak of the mountain." Quin looked at Ragnar, confused by his words,

"We need to find the sunken city, what good will the top of the mountain do us?" Smiling smugly, Ragnar didn't explain and instead, simply turned and began to walk towards the tallest mountain. As Ragnar walked away, Quin looked up through the trees to see a glimmer of the mountain through the thick foliage; it lay directly ahead rising high, as if above and beyond the clouds. Shortly after Ligeia joined him, although she was not interested in the mountain that he gazed upon, but instead focused on Ragnar as he vanished beyond the treeline. As Quin turned his attention to Ligeia, he smiled and secretly admired her beauty; but Ligeia continued to stare out into the forest catching glimpses of Ragnar between the trees and muttered

"He is hiding something. You do not need magic to see that!"

"You do not trust him!" Quin stated assuming that was the cause for her suspicion.

"I am a Siren; a Seer and Keeper of Secrets. I do not trust him because I cannot seen his future." She revealed with a concerned look on her face.

"Perhaps he is immune to your powers in some way!" Quin suggested, trying to ease her worries.

"A person, who has sought out and obtained the power to conceal their future from the Siren, surely has something to hide!" She replied as she walked away. Quin stood and watched her walking away and wondered how much information Ragnar may still be hiding. It seemed that he was being very selective with the information he volunteered and that which he did reveal seemed suspiciously inconsistent. He knew he couldn't afford to put his trust in Ragnar's word; but on the other hand he really had no other choice. Without Ragnar's knowledge of chants from the Book of Necropoleis, he could never obtain the power to destroy Ifrit; then again, he had to question if he really needed an entire army to succeed. Could his powers alone stand up against the might of such a titan?

Either way, the fact remained, he was here to raise an army and take the fight to Ifrit with Ragnar's help, even if the army should fall before they reached Agartha and the awaiting enemy forces. All he knew, for certain was he would have to face this threat head on, with or without an army. Then he would complete his quest to find the Telchines and exact his final revenge!

When Quin had caught up with Ligeia and Ragnar, he was entirely aware that they both contributed to the silence of the island as neither spoke a word and furthermore the atmosphere between the three of them was uncomfortable, to say the least. The silence gave him time to realise that although they were now working together as a team, it would only be a matter of time before they would each go their separate ways, whether dead or alive. The situation at hand was temporary and he figured that any attempt to break the silence in the hope of them becoming civilised was probably pointless. Instead he took advantage of the silence and allowed his thoughts to run away with him to try and make some sense of all that had happened thus far. What better time than now when it was quiet enough to reflect as he marched towards his goal. Although it was not long before they stumbled upon a rickety old rope bridge which spanned over a deep valley with sheer cliffs on either side. He immediately questioned the existence of this obviously man made bridge and knew that Ragnar would have some kind of explanation

"A bridge on an uninhabited Island, now how did that get here Ragnar?" He paused to think for a moment before turning to look at Quin, however he simply flapped his mouth silently and shrugged his shoulders as he attempted to answer, this of course, raised Quin's suspicion that once again Ragnar was keeping secrets. Eventually Ragnar replied;

"Who can say how long this bridge has been here? Apart from us three and that black cloud, I have seen no evidence of anyone else on the island. As far as I am aware this island is completely uninhabited" Ligeia knew that Quin would take her side and, felt this was a perfect opportunity to put Ragnar on the spot and prove that he was hiding something.

"Uninhabited, really? I found this island because I saw a fire on the beach? So who do you suppose lit that fire?" She interrogated. Ragnar turned away to face the bridge so that Quin and Ligeia could not see his face as he grew increasingly aggravated with all the accusations. As if being interrogated, he felt obliged to give any explanation he could think of,

"Uhmm… Perhaps it was some burning debris from the ship that landed on the beach!" he suggested, but he was by now under no illusion that they actually trusted him. He was finding that a challenge in itself, making it difficult to regain his integrity. In truth he had no idea where the fire had come from, or who had built the bridge before him now. He felt he had to attempt to answer their questions if only to gain their confidence. "Like I said *'As far as I am aware'*, I do not possess all the answers you think I have." Sadly for Ragnar his lame explanations only served to raise more suspicions.

However, during this time Quin recalled the sound of the footsteps he heard whilst in the chamber, although he wasn't sure if they were part of the Magic or whether there was, in fact, someone or indeed something else down there with him.   "After you Ragnar" Ligeia smugly offered, hoping that it was some kind of trap that he had set for them, but one that would ultimately end in his own death. Unimpressed with her smugness Ragnar simply tutted out loud and rolled his eyes in disdain at Ligeia, stepping cautiously onto the first plank of the bridge, satisfied it was stable he placed his entire weight down and began to cross. As he foolishly peered over the edge, he could see the ocean waves crashing against the sides of the mountain and then roared as they fell back down. He soon realised that should any of them fall, the impact alone would most certainly kill them, even if they landed in the water as opposed to impaling themselves on the jagged rocks. Terrified with each step he took, the bridge swayed back and forth under his hesitant footsteps and the wind blew against his body with such force that he felt it was going to blow him off. Ragnar decided to turn to face Quin, who watched his progress with Ligeia on land, and called out

"Is there anything you can do about this wind?" Quin started laughing loudly enough so that Ragnar could hear him, who was by now stood a good third of the way along the bridge. Quin raised his hand and focused his magic upon Ragnar's body and created an invisible bubble that forced the wind to go around him rather than hitting him. A little disturbed by this, Ligeia complained;

"Quin, you should not use your magic to help others, you could end up cursing him!" As Quin slowly turned to look at her, but while keeping his spell in sight, being a *'Focus Spell'* Quin knew he needed to stay focused on it, he smirked and sarcastically muttered

"oops!" and they shared a moment of laughter, albeit slightly perverse, as Ragnar continued his way across the swaying bridge.

As soon as Ragnar had reached the half-way point of the bridge, Quin nodded to Ligeia to acknowledge that it was time for her to progress. As she stepped forward onto the bridge Quin raised his other hand intending to place a magical shield around her too, however before he could do so Ligeia cried,

"Stop! Please do not use your magic on me Quin." A little taken aback and confused by her request, Quin responded

"I only mean to protect you!" However she continued to deny his assistance and it seemed that Ligeia had been hiding the fact that, for some reason, she had become fearful of Quin's power

"Just watch me and do not, under any circumstances, use your magic around me, ever!" She heartlessly blurted without any sense of care for his feelings. Naturally, he was hurt by her comment and rejection of his powers; a rejection he thought had been left behind him the day he fled the Alexandrian border, he couldn't help but wonder what it was that Ligeia was so afraid of, after all, she was a magical being herself and therefore she should know that no harm would befall her by accepting his magic to assist her. He soon realised that, although he thought he understood his powers and the danger of using them around others, it now transpired that Ligeia knew more than she was revealing, just like Ragnar. He couldn't shake the feeling that he was completely secluded from his companions and now began to question his trust for both of them.

Regardless, Quin watched Ligeia's every step carefully, whilst attempting to maintain the shield around the more distant Ragnar. He was soon reminded that he was not as powerful as his ego had allowed him to believe as he struggled to focus on the magic at such a distance, which becoming greater with every passing moment. He wondered if perhaps Ligeia his limitations and was concerned that he would eventually succumb to the immense pressure of supporting both her and Ragnar. It eventually became too difficult for him to reach Ragnar with his magic and he could feel the magic slipping away. His every muscle trembled with the strain of focusing the spell, and thus forced him to make a decision to either move forward himself to alleviate the strain and maintain the shield, or put Ragnar in very serious danger by allowing the shield to fail. Quin tried to call out to Ragnar in order to warn him that the shield would soon collapse if he did not slow down. However he was too far away to be heard over the howling winds and roaring ocean waves. Fearing that a sudden blast of wind would certainly throw Ragnar off the bridge, Quin stepped across with haste to close the gap between them, causing the bridge to heavily rock back and forth. Quin was now in a tricky situations as he had to keep a close watch on Ligeia as she wobbled around on the bridge gazing down in terror at the aggressive waves below that broke against the Cliffside sending sprays up towards the bridge. Although the water was not even close to hitting the underside of the bridge, let alone on top of it, Quin could see Ligeia gripping the rope on either side of the bridge tightly, clearly frightened and distressed. He completely understood her fear knowing that every drop of water was like death grabbing out at her, as if the souls of the underworld themselves were jumping up to grab her and drag her into the depths of darkness.

As Ligeia reached halfway she paused for a moment and took a deep breath and reassured herself

"You are almost there Ligeia, you can do this!" Holding her head high. She stepped forward onto the next plank of the bridge, not noticing it was already cracked and obviously weakened. It creaked underfoot as she distributed her weight onto it and with a loud crack the board willingly gave way under the pressure leaving Ligeia treading thin air.

Falling straight through the gap, she screamed in terror. The scene before Quin seemed to slow down, just as it had with the Centaurs back on the Mountain. He immediately released his shield spell on Ragnar and prioritised Ligeia's safety. He shot towards her quickly using his wind form and amazingly managed to catch her just as her body fell through the bridge. Diving onto his front, Quin threw out his arm and grabbed hold of Ligeia's hand. She stared up at Quin with unquestionable terror in her eyes and then gazed down at the water below as it splashed up and tiny drops made contact with her bare feet.

"Pull me up, please, pull me up!" she shrieked in absolute hysterics. Quin attempted to lift her, but found that he was not strong enough after being under so much pressure from his shield spell. Panic ensued as her hand began to slip from his grasp and Quin feared the worst, his eyes began to well up,

"Do not let go" He cried out "hold on!" Not knowing what to do, Quin thought that this would be the end for Ligeia. Just at that moment he lost his grip, but seemingly from out of nowhere, Ragnar emerged over the side of the bridge, diving through the rope, using it to hold his feet. Grabbing onto Ligeia with both arms stretched out Ragnar shouted

"I have you! You must climb up me!" although Ligeia was frozen in shock and simply cried in terror,

"I cannot!" Ragnar looked at Ligeia with hope and care in his eyes, and in an attempt to calm her down he called out,

"Ligeia look at me" With an expression of sorrow on his face, as if the thought of her demise saddened him. Quin watched with a sense of pride and started to believe that Ragnar did actually care, and perhaps he just had difficulty showing his feelings, that is, until death was staring him in the face. "You can do this, I know you can. Climb!" He encouraged. As she began clambering up, Quin reached over and grabbed her, pulling her back to safety on the bridge.

Quin took a moment to examine her to ensure she had not come to any harm. He was at a complete loss for words, his lips fluttered but words failed to come out. A deep feeling of self-blame filled his heart, as he realised he was just mere moments away from watching her die. Although Quin was not entirely certain of Ragnar's intentions and still had a lot of mistrust for him, it was painfully obvious that he had just singlehandedly saved Ligeia's life, despite his blatant dislike of her.

"Forgive me for interrupting; however a little

assistance would be most gratifying". He shouted as the splashes from the sea covered his face and filled his mouth with its salty texture. Ligeia smiled at Quin and grabbed his arm reassuringly with a glimmer in her eye that said *'I am ok, thank you'* and then carefully got onto her knees and held onto Ragnar's foot. Quin joined her and held the other foot and they lifted him back to safety on the bridge. They now all stood in the middle of the bridge, attempting to catch their breath, as they exchanged relieved glances, and began to laugh at Ragnar's soaked face and hair. But that was not the reason for the joy they were feeling, instead it was the victory of saving each other and were finally beginning to work as a team towards their common goal. It seemed that their friendship was forged from that moment on. The moment, however was short lived as a sudden snapping sound echoed through the valley, which originated directly next to them, from the rope that held the bridge together Ragnar's eyes quickly widened with fear, as his head whipped around to see the rope beginning to unravel. He promptly turned to the others and screamed,
"Run!"

Not daring to look back, they dashing across the bridge as fast as they could. Running at the back, Quin's left foot abruptly slipped between two of the planks and stuck fast.

He desperately attempted to free himself by pulling on his leg and wiggling his foot as much as he could, but quickly realised he was tapped. He cried out to his allies,

"My foot is stuck!" Ligeia heard and turned back. She witnessed what had happened and ran back to assist him.

"No. Get off the bridge!" Quin selflessly called out. Reluctantly, Ligeia turned back and continued to run towards the end of the bridge. Before long Ragnar and Ligeia made it to the safety of the land on the other side and turned to see that Quin was still stuck. By now it was too late to do anything about it. The rope gave way under the weight of the bridge and snapped. Both gazed in horror as the bridge crumbled apart and fall into the valley. Within the blink of an eye the bridge was gone. Ligeia rushed to the edge of the valley and gazed over the edge with a steady stream of tears rolling down her face as she screamed hysterically to Quin.

"No, it was not supposed to happen this way. I stopped you from using your magic on me, I changed the vision – It should not have been like this. Not now!"

Ragnar had to hold her back to stop her throwing herself over the edge. Taking her into his embrace as she wept uncontrollably. It seemed a little strange that with easy access to an abundance of her tears Ragnar actually had no interest in them at all, despite the power that they held. Instead he merely gazed over the empty space that formerly held the bridge and last moments of Quin's life, as if stunned with no more meaning to his life. They sat for a moment until Ligeia managed to compose herself and left Ragnar's embrace. After a few steps away she fell to her knees, groaning and sobbing as she tried to hold back her anguish. Holding onto the slightest hope that Quin was perhaps using the remaining planks of the bridge as a ladder to climb up the mountainside, she carefully looked over the edge, but Quin wasn't there. By now Ragnar knew that Quin was gone and was left feeling confused and unsure of what to do next, he suddenly realised that they were not only trapped on the mountains foot with no other way off the Island, but furthermore, his plan could never be accomplished without Quin's power. He turned away to look for a way forward and allow Ligeia a moment to mourned their loss. As he turned he spotted Quin standing in front of him leaning against a tree.

"This is very touching but we really should move on." He said jovially, feeling rather humbled by their reaction to his loss. Ligeia suddenly went quiet, holding her breath while looking around to see where the voice had come from. She spotted Quin as he pushed himself off the tree and smiled as he walked towards them. Ligeia wasted no time in rushing over to him, grabbing Ragnar along the way she flung her arms around them both, and they all shared a moment of relief for Quin's safety. However, after a moment Ligeia looked up at Quin with a confused frown on her face and asked,

"I saw you - how?" To which Quin simply smiled as he thought that perhaps this was just another one of fate's little games that allowed him to prove to Ligeia that his powers were not to be feared

"I am one with the elements! The power of the Wind gives me the ability to move faster than the eye." He subtly explained. Sharing a moment of laughter as Ligeia scoffed at Quin's apparent boast, they turned to gaze at the mountain before them, which they knew they now had to climb, already physically, mentally, and on Ligeia's part emotionally drained they continued onto the mountain together.

- Chapter XVII -
Raising Hope

Reaching over the edge Quin took Ligeia's hand and pulled her up to the top of the mountain where he and Ragnar now stood. Ragnar looked into the distance at the endless waters of the ocean stretching for miles before them. After a few moments sharing lustful glances, Quin and Ligeia joined Ragnar also and gazed out at the sea. Quin found it a very peaceful sight to behold, as the afternoon sun reflected on the surface and shimmered like countless diamonds, whereas Ligeia saw nothing but an old place she called 'home' which relentlessly beckoned her. The wind blew gently around them, there was a calming moment for Quin and he felt the bliss of the freshness of the elements, as if he was returning to a long lost paradise. Although his judgement knew better.

"There is nothing here, why have you bought us here Ragnar?" Quin asked as he looked around at the mountaintop they were stood on a very small flat area overlooking the ocean with no visible means of progressing, Ragnar took a moment to turn to Quin with an undeniable expression of disappointment on his face. Quin immediately began to think that Ragnar had taken them the wrong way and had more than likely doomed them all to die on the mountain top with no way back since the bridge had collapsed. However, Quin was not angered, but instead filled with the disappointment that he would not have the chance to complete the task he set out to accomplish and furthermore would most certainly never see Asha again, in life or death. But no sooner had Quin given up hope and thought that all was lost than Ragnar looked back at the ocean below and pointed out a strangely misplaced pole protruding out of the water that was barely visible, unless you knew it was there. Quin's expression dropped as he followed Ragnar's finger and spotted the pole in the middle of the ocean. Swallowing hard he softly asked

"We made it? The lost city is down there?" but Ragnar remained silent and simply nodded; his eyes still showing his sorrow. Quin couldn't help but wonder what it was that could possibly be so sad about their arrival at the sunken city, but didn't really care to ask as his excitement for being reunited with Asha took over his rationality and he threw out one hand towards the pole. He focused all the powers of the elements and foolishly attempted to raise the island from the depths.

Through the sheer power of Quin's magic the ground began to quake causing Ragnar to look around to see what was happening, to his horror he saw Quin using his magic and called out,

"No! Quin, stop..." but it was too late. Quin had already become so intensely focused within his magic he was now completely unaware of his surroundings, as if in a deep trance. His body began to buckle under the pressure as the intense drain of using his magic and energy barely moved the island out of the water. Although Quin was aware of the lack of effect his magic was fully having and could feel his consciousness slipping away as the ringing in his ears grew louder and blood began to trickle from his nose, he was still unwilling to give up. He raised his other hand, and forced his magic even more. Not caring for the consequences of disrupting Quin's magic while he was so intensely focused, Ragnar had no choice but to lash out and slap Quin across the face as hard as he could. But it had no effect. He remained as solid as a rock. Ragnar continued screaming at him to stop. He grabbed his arms in an attempt to push them down and break the spell, but as he touched Quin his hands were shocked with a bolt of static which instantly burnt and blistered his palms and cast him hurtling backwards. Skidding back to the edge of the mountain, Ligeia quickly jumped forward and grabbed him by the scruff of his neck, preventing him from falling to his death. Without any concern for his injuries, Ragnar spoke to Ligeia

"Stop him, or he will die!" She looked around for some way of which to bash Quin around the head and soon spotting a small rock. Grabbed it, she reluctantly throwing it as hard as she could at Quin. But his magic was so powerful that the stone simply orbited around him and was then release away from him out to sea with ten times the force. Quin soon began buckle but his focus would not falter as he continued to use his magic, oblivious to the fact he was dying. Ligeia ran behind Quin and apologised as she summoned a siren scream that, if used out of water could easily cause one's head to explode. This power was usually used as a means of long distance communication between Siren. Holding his hands over his ears Quin screwed up his face, and screaming in pain through the vibration he now felt stinging in his ears, as if they were about to explode. Confident that Quin had snapped out of his trance she immediately stopped screaming, unfortunately she had neglected to warn Ragnar who shortly thereafter passing out and fell flat on his face. Quin slowly released his ears and opened his eyes. He was rather confused to see Ragnar lying unconscious on the edge of the mountain and as he turned around to see what had happened, he was startled to see Ligeia standing directly behind him. She stepped forward and knelt down in front of Quin, and gazed into his eyes with much concern,

"Are you alright?" She asked. Quin blinked a few times and stuck a finger into his ear attempting to shake off the ringing sound he was experiencing, then wiped the blood from his nose and ask

"What happened?" but before Ligeia could answer Ragnar regained consciousness,

"You almost killed yourself, that is what just happened!" Ragnar scolded angrily as he held out his hands to show Quin the damage he had done. "Would you mind?" he enquired politely hoping that Quin would be generous enough to heal his wounds. Quin was shocked at the sight of Ragnar's hands as they lay before him, sorely blistered and dripping with blood. Without another thought of the consequence of using his magic, Quin placed his hands over the wounds and used his magic to quickly heal them.

Thanking Quin, Ragnar rose to his feet and turning his attention to the ocean. He began by explaining what he needed Quin to do in order to raise the Island, without killing himself.

"Within your mind and out of your body you must travel through the ruins and locate the Ceremonial Stone Circle that lies in the centre of the cities palace. It should resemble a platform with symbols of the ancient language on it, but -" before Ragnar could finish Quin interrupted

"I know what it looks like!" Ragnar seemed surprised by this and wondered how he could possibly know of the Stone Circle, but he thought it best not to ask and went on to hide his curiosity. Instead he would wait and bide his time in order to find out just how much Quin knew. Recalling a similar stone circle in the memories of Lycus. It sounded identical to the platform that Gaia she had used to sacrifice herself to save mankind.

"Very well, once you have located the Ceremonial Circle you can focus your consciousness on the area. All you need to do is reach out with all your magic and you will reactivate the magic within. That will bring the island back to the surface" Ragnar explained, Quin nodded in acknowledgement of what he had to do and felt more than ready to go. However he soon realised that he did not possess the power to take his mind out of his body and had to question what Ragnar meant by this.

"Ragnar; you stated that I must take my mind there. I do not know of anyone with such power. To separate your body and mind, can this be done?" Ragnar smirked as he sat Quin down and asked him to close his eyes. Obligingly Quin crossing his legs, shut his eyes and listened to the sound of Ragnar's voice as he began

"Clear your mind; forget who you are; focus on your breathing and be at peace with the lands; be one with the lands." Quin did as he was told "Now allow your body to fall into a deep sleep, but tell your mind to remain here with me." Ragnar sat opposite Quin with folded legs and also closed his eyes, holding his palms to the sky. All the while Ligeia stood watching with fascinated anticipation. After a while of complete and uninterrupted silence, Ragnar began to breathe heavily and suddenly opened his eyes widely, staring at Quin with an undefined expression that could only be described as slightly creepy. Quin was still sitting peaceably listening to his breathing, remained still, silent and unaware. Ragnar leant in close and softly spoke Quin's name, which startled him causing him to open his eyes and look at Ragnar. He attempted to respond, however he felt rather strange as if losing all control of his body except for his vision which was all he could control. A little afraid of what was happening to him, he attempted to speak but the words would not come out. Ragnar slowly raised his finger and lightly tapped Quin on the forehead. Upon that touch, Quin's mind was unexpectedly swept away in a motion similar to rolling down a mountainside and soon found himself standing just outside the 'Lost City'.

Quin was surprise to find himself watching the city bustling with life in the blazing heat of a glorious sunny day. Children played games and merchants gathered to sell their wares to the passing citizens, and crowds of people greeted each other all around him, gossiping and laughing at one another's tales.

"What is this?" Quin asked himself as he stepped forward and called out to a lady who was standing on her own in the shade, "Pardon me…" He politely approached. The woman turned her head and stared at him with a blank expression. It wasn't long before he noticed that her eyes did not meet with his, she just looked through him and smiled sweetly. Naturally he assumed she was blind but was hoping she could help him find his way anyway and so continued to address her, "Can you tell me how to get to-" But he was unable to finish and was horrified to experience that instead of replying, the lady simply stepped forward and walked straight through him. Quin turned and watched her as she walked away and it transpired that she had actually been looking straight through him in order to meet her friends. Feeing entirely discomforted with his situation Quin surmised; either he was seeing the ghosts of the citizens who died in the city, or he was, in fact, the ghost. Now a little disorientated, he backed himself up against a wall out of the way hoping that no-one else would pass through him.

"Is everything alright Quin?" a familiar voice said as if coming from within his mind. He looked around frantically trying to see where the voice had come from,

"Ragnar? Where are you?" Quin called out, confused and frightened as he gazed upon each of the faces of those who strolled past, none of them even aware of his presence.

"Quin you must remain calm, for whatever it is that you think you are seeing now is not reality. It cannot harm you; you must continue on." Ragnar said, However Quin was in shock and felt he had seen more than enough. He pushed away from the wall and ran down the street, passing directly through children and adults alike, each time making him feel nauseous and somehow violated. It wasn't long before Quin had to push his back against another wall to get away from the ghosts around him, still going about their day as if nothing was out of the ordinary. After composing himself for a moment, he continued to run through street upon street, through tunnels and over bridges, turning left and right; until he was exhausted and couldn't go any further. He collapsed on a set of stairs.

"Ragnar please, let me out; I cannot do this anymore, it is tearing me apart" he begged, but Ragnar did not reply leaving Quin feeling defeated and alone. After a very long period alone he sat up and placed his hands over his eyes, trying to calm down and make sense of this terrifying situation. But his attempts to block out the world fell to naught as he discovered he could see through his own hands and remembered that he was no longer within his human body; dealing with trauma of the mind is much more difficult than dealing with it physically, especially with the healing power of water to assist him in such cases. Moving his hands away from his face Quin scanned the area for any sign of a way to return to his body, but there was no visible way out. But before long his attention was drawn to a familiar character who he noticed walking up the stairs beside him. He quickly jumped up and watched Lycus as he entered through the doors that lay at the top of the stairway, leading down a long passage into a beautiful castle garden with a tall circular building in the centre. Quin glanced around at the amazing view before him and began to calm as the bustle of the town had now been left behind. After realising Lycus had progressed some distance from him, Quin rushed to catch up, as Lycus marched on with purpose and an angered expression, complimented by his glowing red eyes. He burst through the set of doors that lead into the circular building. The guards took one look at Lycus and promptly stepped aside, laying down their arms and fleeing the room at the mere sight of his arrival. Inside, the walls rose high bearing a flawless glass roof. But the scenery was not Quin's main focus as he watched Lycus march up to an overweight man who was sat upon an ornately decorated throne on the opposite side of the room.

"Lycus; what do I owe for the honour of your presence?" the man said buoyantly, while smiling and battering his eyelashes as if he had some sort of strange adulation for him. However it quickly became obvious that Lycus was in no mood for pleasantries. Grabbing the fat blob of a man and dragged him by his hair from the throne and into the centre of the room. Quin watched intently and a revelation hit him when he noticed the dethroned man was now grovelled on the Stone Circle that made up the majority of the floor within the room. The man crawled on his hands and knees, pleading with Lycus for mercy. Although Quin knew that his task was simply to locate the Stone Circle and use it to raise the island, he felt compelled to see how this scene played out, and pondered the possibility of being inside another memory of his former life and if that were the case, then it was obviously important. Lycus stomped over to the fat tub of a man and grabbing him by the throat lifting him off the ground and holding him in the air with little effort.

"You dared to tamper with my magic and thought it would go unnoticed you pathetic human!" Lycus scorned.

"I know not of what you speak my dear Lycus, my loyalties lie entirely with you!" He rasped as his face proceeded to turn red. In a wild rage, Lycus roared as he tossed him away like piece a discarded parchment causing him to rebound off the wall and fall flat on his rotund face.

"Your reign here is at an end, I see now that I can trust only my Kin and as my brother will not allow my kin on his land; I am left with no alternative…" Lycus declared. Uncaring of the lives he would be taking with his forthcoming actions. It seemed obvious to Quin that Lycus was ruthlessly cold hearted when it came to the lives of others and a mortal life meant nothing to a Telchine.

Lycus slowly paced towards the injured man as he raised his head and looked up at him, terrified of his intentions. Lycus turned and cast an incredibly powerful spell; the likes of which Quin had never seen. A glowing white aura manifested like smoke, emanating from his hand and gently flowed down, covering the stone circle in the middle of the room. As his magic merged with the circle's, it gracefully absorbed the power and began to shine. After a few moments of watching the magic swirl around the Stone circle, Quin's fixation was disrupted as the ground began to quake violently and the walls began to crack and crumble. In retaliation knowing he had nothing more to lose, the fat man rose to his feet and pulled a concealed dagger from his boot, thrusting it into Lycus' back. The cold sharp blade slid into his body. Quin also felt the stab and cried out in pain, whilst Lycus staggered away as if mortally wounded. The man grinned greedily and shoved Lycus. He stumbled backwards into the centre of the stone circle,

"I tried everything, but in the end it was your blood that I needed Lycus!" He spluttered joyously, bouncing up and down clapping his hands with glee of his victory. However, Lycus reached round and pulled the dagger from his back. Gazing at the blade now coated in his blood, he was a little disappointed that he had fallen for such an obvious deception. Quin, who now stood behind Lycus watching in anticipation, noticed the wound had instantly healed after the dagger was removed.

"My blood?" Lycus said with a sarcastic tone "All you need do is ask!" He said still gazing at his blood on the blade, "Take it!" He snapped as he tossed the dagger forward sending it shooting across the room, faster than any man could possibly throw. Quin could only watch in awe as it collided with the fat man's forehead and carried him along with it. It emerged through the back of his skull and soon thereafter buried itself deep into the wall and decorating the room with his lifeless corpse.

Quin was somewhat ashamed at his reaction as he let out an uncontrollable laugh, connecting once again with the feelings from Lycus and his triumph that day, while the building continued to crumble around him. As Lycus walked out of the room he paused for a moment next to the dead body and muttered

"Never again will anyone see this place; I condemn you all to the bottom of the ocean for your treachery!" and left the room without any signs of regret or compassion, leaving Quin alone in the crumbling room to witness the end of a civilisation. He stood emotionless and confused as he, listened to the citizen's terrified screams from the city outside. Having discovered how the island came to be at the bottom of the ocean, he had to question 'why would he now be working to undo all he had done as Lycus?' Quin had no doubt that Lycus had done many evil deeds, but he had to believe that his second chance was a gift to redeem himself for his former actions and right the wrongs that had befallen the world because of his actions as Lycus. Once again Quin found he was straying from his path and becoming increasingly frustrated as each discovery of his past turned his entire meaning upside down. He could no longer comprehend what he was supposed to do. Fate reared its ugly head once more to taunt him. He now found himself more lost than ever and had no choice but to follow Ragnar in the hope that he would eventually lead him back to his own path.

Quin looked up at the sky through the shattered glass roof above him and called out to Ragnar,

"I have found it Ragnar, what now?" But there was no reply. He panicked as he found himself trapped in the memory. The city crumbled around him and slowly submerged into the ocean. Quin soon noticed that Lycus' magic was still flowing within the stone circle. He watched the glow spiralling around the intricate patterns with an overwhelming compulsion to reach out and touch it. He placed his hand down inside a groove and began to absorb the power from it. Startled, Quin jumped back and attempted to shake off the magic, but in vain. It clung to him and seeped into his body through his skin and glowed through his veins. The mist began to float out of the circle and engulfed Quin in a searing pain. He cried out in agony as it felt like it was ripping him apart from the inside outwards. Quin quickly felt a whimsical jar of irony as the spell that he cast in a previous life would be the one to destroy him in the next. Suddenly Quin heard Ragnar call out his name and was immediately returned to his body. Opening his eyes just in time to see Ragnar slapping him round the face. Quin found himself quaking from the shock in a cold sweat and out of breath. He appeared to be back upon the mountain top. As he tried to compose himself, Quin's attention was drawn away from his personal anguish as he felt the ground shaking right under him.

Ligeia stared out at the ocean and calling out to Ragnar and Quin. Picking themselves up, they followed her gaze and witnessed the ocean seemingly becoming land as the Island arose from the depths. Ragnar laughed joyously while putting his arm around his comrades and exclaimed

"See that was simple, was it not?" But Quin was unimpressed,

"Speak for yourself Ragnar, I feel like I have just travelled through the underworld and back!"

Finally, land was in sight with a mere river separating them from the island. As they stood and looked over at the landscape, the danger they were about to face was clear to see as building after building crumbled and collapsed. The ground looked unsteady and everything was covered in a mass of thick sludge and seaweed.

"So how do we get over there?" Ligeia asked, anxious to get the quest over with,

"I regret to ask, but I may need to ask another favour of you." Ragnar said turning to Quin, who still gazed at the island. But he had already figured out a way to get across to the island, so did not require Ragnar to say anymore. Quin raised his hand and cast his magic on the masses of rocks and debris below, dislodging them from the land to float upwards. He eventually managed to line them up in mid-air to form a walkway for them to cross. Quin focused his concentration hard on the rocks ahead as the three adventurers proceeded to walk across. As they reached the Island and all stepped onto solid ground Ragnar made an observation

"You have that much power, so why have you never used it before now Quin?" He enquired, wondering why they had been through so much trouble when Quin had such powers and probably many more that might have saved them a lot of time and trouble.

"Perhaps I do not know my own strength Ragnar!" Quin said, smirking to himself as they stood gazing at the pillars that once formed the entrance to the city before them, "One thing is certain; before this day is done I believe I will discover the true limits of my strength!" He announced with a heavy heart, much to Ragnar's delight, seeing evidence of Quin's apparent weakness. Ligeia, on the other hand, simply screwed up her face and interjected sarcastically

"And we will all probably end up dead as a result!" However her comment seemed to fall on deaf ears as Quin set off in silence towards the palace where Ragnar would finally recite the incantation from the book of Necropoleis to raise an undead army powerful enough to destroy Ifrit.

It was now that Quin had come to realise he had finally made it half way through his quest. Believing this, he again began to reflect on everything that had happened since the day he left Alexandria and feared that the path ahead could conceal terrors and traumas far worse than any he had faced thus far. Taking a deep breath he preparing himself for what lay ahead. With a single motivation.

'Fate, I am coming for you, ready or not-'

- Chapter XVIII -
Behind the Facade

"We have much to accomplish and not very long to do so" said Ragnar, as he dashed ahead with a single goal in mind.

"What do you mean?" Ligeia enquired innocently, to which Ragnar turned round and glared at her angrily

"What part of *'not very long'* did you not understand? I could stand here and explain, wasting what few moments we have before the island submerges back into the ocean, or you can trust in me and keep up. Or is it that perhaps you would prefer to die?" Ligeia and Quin were completely taken aback by Ragnar's sudden agitation but could not respond quickly enough as he simply continued to walk away with haste. As they rushed after Ragnar, Quin had to wonder what had suddenly rattled him to such an extent that he would snap at those who he would call his friends. Albeit a little sceptical about trusting him at all, Quin knew that he had not really done anything to show he was unworthy of his trust. Yet, a nagging mistrust persisted in the back of his mind, screamed out the danger that Ragnar posed, even if it was unjustified.

As Quin caught up with him, he felt he had the right to know exactly what Ragnar was planning and where he was leading them, considering Quin's recollection of the city's layout proved that they were in fact moving away from the very place where they needed to be which was the Palace.

"So where exactly are we going?" Quin asked. However Ragnar did not speak and simply continued onwards. Quin soon noted his solemn expression, almost as if holding back tears of remorse, which initiated many questions.

'Is it possible that Ragnar has been here before? Perhaps he knows something important that he is neglecting to tell us! Something is clearly upsetting him, but he is too ashamed to speak of it.
I have felt the gritting reality of such feelings myself and know from experience that anyone who would attempt to pry into my personal feelings would have been shot down immediately in a flame of rage and turned away. I want nothing more than to forget everything that plagues my mind. Therefore it would stand to reason that Ragnar does too!'

With the revelation, Quin felt it wise not to pry into what was taunting him. However, he still had to know where they were going.

"Ragnar, the Palace is the other way, yet we still travel away, do you not think we should-" Quin started, but before he could finish the sentence Ragnar exploded in an almighty rage

"Have I not just said *'we must hurry'*? If we survive this I will tell you everything you need to know, but until then we must keep going and cease this constant questioning of my judgement; it is becoming increasingly insulting!" And with that, almost as if reciprocating Ragnar's anger, the ground began to quake and the Island prepared to submerge again. Grinding to a halt, Ragnar stared in horror as the ruins beginning to crumble and collapse around them.

"No! This is too soon..." Ragnar cried scanning frantically to ensure Ligeia and Quin were not in harm's way. His heart sank as debris began to fall over blocking the cavern passage that they needed to go through. Ragnar knew that if the path ahead became blocked before they made it through, they would be cut off for good.

"Run!" He screamed at the top of his voice and promptly darted towards the opening. Quin and Ligeia followed promptly behind him. Quin raised his hand and attempted to use his magic to hold the debris in place a little longer to allow them secure passage through, but as he tried to do so he was stunned to find that his magic was no longer with him and he was unable to cast any form of spells. Suddenly a large rock dislodged and began to fall towards the travellers. Quin dived through the opening just in time, as the rock slammed to the ground behind him sealing the entrance to the cavern.

Inside the small cavern Quin frantically shuffled back on his back side as the debris continued to fall inwards towards him, before Ligeia grabbed him and pulled him to his feet, then turned to run onwards again, the cavern roof began to crack with a deafening snap. Forced to dodge left and right the large rocks fell, one landing directly in front of Ligeia, who was close behind Ragnar. Tripping over it, she landed face first onto the floor, but luckily Quin lifted her and dragged her towards the exit through which Ragnar had just escaped. The way out began to collapse and selflessly Quin threw Ligeia forward, out of the cave just in time as the roof caved in. Raising her head she looked back and was mortified to witness the cave coming down on top of Quin. She screamed out to Quin, which grabbed Ragnar's attention. He stopped his ascent and rushed back to Ligeia, who was now beside herself with grief.

Ragnar reached the cave and raised his hands, focusing on the rocks that had caved in. Roaring as he thrust his arm out, he instantly cleared the rocks that blocked Quin's exit. As the dust settled there seemed to be no sign of Quin. However, Ligeia's continued to call out to him, tears streamed down her face as she thought he must be dead. But it was only a few moments before he began to emerge from the debris, limping, cut, bruised, and bleeding and covered in dust, but alive! Ligeia jumping to her feet ran to him and put his arm over her shoulder to aid him. Ragnar had by now disappeared down a set of stairs and out of sight.

"What just happened?" Quin asked Ligeia, referring to the blast that freed him, confused at how he managed to escape.

"It was Ragnar! He has magic; powerful magic. He is unlike you; I have always been able to sense your magic, but never with Ragnar. Quin, what is happening?" he couldn't believe what Ligeia was saying, but at least he now had an infallible reason not to trust Ragnar; he had lied to him from the very start about his magic limitations. He claimed his only skill was the ability to conjure spells from ancient scrolls and tomes, but had actually possessed a lot more power than he had previously let on, which posed a threat to him.

Quin suddenly felt a bitter taste of irony as he remembered the Prince. After he discovered Quin was one with magic he too was angered and felt betrayal and mistrust towards him. On that day, Quin could not understand why the Prince was so hostile towards him and his powers, but now it was all too clear as the tables had turned and Quin felt the same towards Ragnar, He felt foolish for ever trusting him and began to wonder what else Ragnar was hiding from him. Although Quin had questioned this before, he never really had a good reason to suspect he was hiding such powers, there again Quin never thought that Ragnar had real magic. But now that Quin had undeniable proof, he knew it was time to stop playing mind games and would make it his personal goal to find out everything that Ragnar knew and would make it very clear that, should he suspect Ragnar was withholding even the smallest detail, he would readily strike him down.

When they reached the top of the staircase that Ragnar had by now run all the way down, Quin watched him as he stood on a platform below staring at a fissure in the ground, which overlooked the southern edge of the island. He now witnessed the reason why Ragnar was in such a hurry, for the ocean had begun to engulf the island once again, such that it gradually began to submerge back unto the watery depths. Quin gently removed his arm from around Ligeia's shoulders and supported his own weight, then looked at Ligeia and smiled kindly, in the hope it would give her confidence for his safe return after dealing with Ragnar. Although he was in a great deal of pain from the injury he had sustained to his ankle, Quin progressed as fast as he could down the steps.

The sea splashed manically as the land submerged, as if angered by its continuous intrusion sweeping away almost everything in its path as the tsunami's height continued to rise ever closer, spelling out certain death to anyone foolish enough to step into its path. Quin eventually reached Ragnar, who stood with his eyes closed facing the fissure, as he recited an ancient ritual from memory. Before Quin could enact his anger for Ragnar's blatant betrayal, Ragnar had completed the ritual. The fissure exploded with incredible rays of light in a multitude of colours, as if it were the origin of the mystic rainbows that were rarely seen in the skies. Quin strangely found he was unable to stay angered as he took in the beauty of the aura, but more than that, he couldn't think of anything and merely gazed upon the tranquil beauty of the fissures light, becoming enslaved to the overwhelming urge to reach out and touch it.

Quin reached out with his hand, holding it above the fissure as the blinding light subsided and as he glanced around he found himself alone on the Island. However, there was an unmistakable difference.

There were no signs of a civilisation or in fact anyone ever setting foot on the Island. The ocean stretching out for miles ahead and behind him lay a land that was ripe and fertile with an abundance of greenery that had only been disturbed by the natural animals that seemed to inhabit the forests that could be heard chirping, singing and galloping in the distance, their presence known but not seen. Before him lay the fissure, with water that gently rippled and gave out an ambient white glow of its own. Quin smiled and took in the glorious beauty around him, feeling like he had found a secret paradise. The winds blew up and a single leaf fell from the nearby Leuka tree. Gracefully twisting down, the perfectly formed green leaf with its white underbelly danced graciously in the wind and eventually landed, gently kissing the water of the fissure. After a few moments the glow of water reacted to the Leuka leaf and appeared to be absorbed by it before strangely sinking into the Fissure. Then the land began to shake and the water of the fissure began to erupt and spill out onto the ground. Quin stepped back and watched the water curiously as it seemed to defy all usual characteristics and soon realised that it was not water at all. To his baffled amazement a hand slowly began to form and appear from the liquid inside the Fissure and before long a full bodied young boy emerged standing atop of it. Strangely, he began to move and raised one hand in front of his face and appearing to examine himself before stepping out onto the land, shortly followed by another figure, but this time it was a young girl. As each of them made physical contact with the land they appeared to take on the form of a human and began to transform into flesh and bone, which Quin was finding quite disturbing and felt he had seen enough. However, he was quickly drawn back to the youngsters as the reaction from the earth seemed to differ between each of them. The young girl's presence seemed to work in harmony with the land around her as it began to flourish and sprout new life, encouraging the growth of a bed of White Galanthus Flowers. Whereas the young boy's presence had the opposite effect and seemed to be destroying the land, as the grass withered and died beneath his feet, leaving behind a black mass of dead plants and dry cracked earth.

As they both stood naked they gazed upon one another, seemingly confused at what they were looking at, before long the girl looked the boy in the eyes and asked

"What are you?"

The boy took a moment to look around at the Island before

recognising the fissure he had come from and walked over to it. He looked down and stared at his reflection in the water while touching his face, yet he still did not speak and simply gasped at his own reflection. It was obvious to Quin that both children had no idea who or what they were. Eventually the boy managed to tear himself away from his own reflection and returned his attention back to the girl.

"I am unsure!" He exclaimed with a confused expression on his face, the girl smiling cheekily at him,

"Well what should I call you?" She asked before continuing to lead by example "You should call me…" She paused to think for a moment "… Gaia" and promptly followed up with an excited and slightly embarrassed giggle. The boy smiled and pondered for a while, but Quin had lost all interest in the boy as he got on his knees and gazed at the young girl that was his mother, amazed at the way she was created.

"Then you should call me…" The young boy said, but Quin was not really paying attention as he muttered to the young girl

"You are my mother, Gaia. So then he is-" as the Boy then finished both, his own and Quin's sentences

"Tartaros." Quin glared at the boy in utter horror as he revealed who he was. Backing away from the boy he tripped backwards. Suddenly he found himself gazing back at the fissure on the rotten island with Ragnar standing over him with a look of confusion on his face as he had just witnessed Quin's seemingly causeless panic.

By now the water had receded back into the ocean and the island seemed to have stabilised. Apparently Ragnar's ritual was successful. However, Quin was still in shock at the vision he had just experienced and panicked as he glanced around to see the land, which was once filled with life and had since become little more than a desolate graveyard. He guiltily realised it was all the result Lycus' actions. Quin couldn't help but question his motives, he was so reckless and selfish and because of his callous heart he single handily destroyed the land that was the beginning of all life; Gaia, Tartaros and the Telchines, and indirectly, the entire human race! Quin knew he could not hope to understand the world as much as Lycus did, but he had to wonder if destroying the island and all life upon it was the wisest thing to have done. Knowing that his mother and siblings were born and most likely grew up there, the Island probably held some incredible powers that could have been, and probably were, used for both good and evil. Still he could not help but question 'Was Lycus so utterly heartless, that he would destroy the ultimate symbol of sentimentality?' by submerging the Island he not only erased the memories of his own childhood but also the memories of all who once lived there, causing countless deaths in the process.'

As the ocean was now far enough away for her safety, Ligeia caught up with Quin and Ragnar and gently helped Quin to his feet, putting his arm on her shoulders again to support him as he continued to limp due to the damage to his ankle. Ragnar however, paid no attention to them and simply gazed out at the ocean and the sun setting giving a sigh of relief before stating,

"We made it; the island is secure, for now." Quin was in no mood to celebrate this victory and lashed out at Ragnar in a blind rage punched him in the head, then grabbing him by his throat and slamming him against the fissure he screamed in his face

"You dared to deceive me? You have magic!" Naturally Ragnar was shocked and intimidated by Quin's reaction. All he could do was fumble over his words as he attempted to regain some dignity

"well, I… Yes Quin, I told you that!" Still enraged, Quin continued his rant

"You told me you only had the power to unleash the rituals written on scroll and tomes, yet you freed me from a collapsed cave by blowing a gaping hole in it without breathing a word." Ragnar now knew he had been caught out, but still attempted to lie his way out of the situation by using Quin's ignorance to his own advantage

"I do not need to speak to summon forth the power of a ritual; I can say them within my mind…" Quin had heard enough and threw him to the ground as Ligeia knelt to comfort him

"Why do you have magic here, when I do not?" Quin foolishly blurted out, revealing his weakness to Ragnar. There was a sudden silence between them as they each contemplated their next words very carefully. Through his thoughts, Ragnar could only stare fearfully into Quin's glowing eyes, as Quin demanded the truth, "What else do you know Ragnar? I will have no more lies, no more secrets. You will tell me everything you know, right now!" Truly shaken by Quin's anger and too scared of the consequences of standing up for to him, Ragnar knew that his knowledge was probably the only thing keeping him alive and as such, could use that to bargain for his life.

"I know everything Quin… I have all the answers to your questions, but we cannot do this now. If we survive this, I will tell you everything… Who you are, where you came from and more importantly, where you can find your siblings" Quin's rage erupted from inside of him as Ragnar admitted he had been hiding behind a facade of lies and deception, while the whole time he tortured himself, discovering Piece by heart wrenching piece, the truth of his past. It wasn't enough to let Ragnar go on for a moment longer holding back his knowledge and as Ragnar stumbled back to his feet, Quin demanded

"You will tell me now!" Ragnar too, had become aggravated with Quin's aggressive attitude and finally plucked up the courage, if only through the frustration of being pushed around, to put Quin in his place and held the high ground. He realised that as long as he withheld his knowledge he would be safe from Quin's wrath, or whatever he had left as Ragnar now knew that he was powerless. Ragnar retained his powers which finally put him in command, although he knew that Quin would not easily fall into line and he would have to assert his dominance over him before he would step down

"If I refuse to tell you, what then Quin? Will you strike me down with your magic?" Ragnar taunted "Now you know what it means to be powerless, I am the one in control now so you will do as I say! You will show me respect or perhaps I will have to threaten you with my magic. Maybe then you will understand how you have made us feel and how it feels to be afraid!" Before the argument escalated any further, Ligeia forced herself between them and attempted to control the situation

"Both of you stop! What has become of you?" Flicking her head back and forth between them with a look of disappointment in her face "We are a team. Now please let us finish this and then we can discuss the exchange of our knowledge or go our separate ways if we must, but killing each other will get us nowhere!" With that Ragnar and Quin merely exchanged angered glances. Quin and Ligeia began to climb back up the stairs; towards the palace in the centre of the Island, to which Ragnar advised Quin in a civilised manner

"We cannot go that way now; the passage is blocked. We will need to go around." However Quin, not feeling quite as civil as Ragnar replied sarcastically,

"You could use your magic to clear the way!" Ragnar was unwilling to even dignify Quin with a response, he knew anything he said would not have been pleasant and would have caused yet another heated discussion. Instead he took Ligeia's hand and walked away with her along the beach which seemed to take them along the eastern side of the island leading north. Quin glared at Ragnar with anger in his heart as he saw the 'happy couple' sauntering along the beach in the sunset. But before he left to catch up with them he gave himself for a moment to look upon the Fissure that now stood glowing as he gazed into its calming water and he heard a voice in his head

"and from the Primordial, life was given to all…"
he was unsure of why or when in his life he had heard this voice before, but he somehow knew that it was the voice of Gaia. Although having little time to think more about it, he had to catch up with the others. Limping off, he looked ahead to see where they had gone and quickly spotted them further up the beach standing atop a manmade stone bank complete with a set of steps. For a moment Quin assumed they were waiting for him, but as he limped closer he realised they were staring at the ground, seemingly inspecting something they had found.

When Quin finally reached them, he saw exactly what they were looking at, the pitch black hole before them was incredibly wide and even deeper than that, it wasn't until Quin gazed into the depths of the darkness himself that he heard various moans and whispers echoing within. The hole seemed so deep that they wouldn't know what was really down there unless they dared to venture down themselves. But whatever it was filled Quin with a fear that gave him no desire to enter such a place in order to find out.

"The Pit of Despair" Ragnar declared, snapping Quin out of his fixation. Ligeia looked up at Ragnar with a confused expression on her face and proclaimed

"Pit? It is just a large hole full of water!" much to Quin's confusion as he squinted while gazing down the hole to see the water that Ligeia was referring to. Ragnar began to explain as Quin's fixation fell back to the depths as the sounds grew louder in his mind

"That is what you see Ligeia; this pit holds that which you fear the most. It is said that Tartaros created this pit to test his own kin and only those who were truly strong would make it through, not merely in body but in mind too. He cursed this pit with dark magic; it brings all your worst fears to life. The torment one would endure in such a place was also known as 'The walk of death'. Many went in, and of those who made it out, most went on to end their own lives!" Ligeia swallowed hard and fearfully stepped away from the edge of the pit

"Can we leave now?" A little shaken by what she had just heard, as Ragnar looked up at Quin and watched as he continued staring into the pit

"of course, we have much to complete Ligeia" he replied suggestively, "The eastern gates should be over to the north of here. That will lead us into the city. From there it is just a short walk to the centre of the Island where we can begin the ritual". Ligeia excitedly rushed off and climbed on top of a rubble pile, looking north to see the gate, Ragnar walked past Quin and glared at him loathingly as he followed Ligeia. After a few moments Ragnar caught up with Ligeia and tightly grabbed her wrist startling her. She attempted to pull away assuming that he was joking but his grip grew tighter the more she struggled. She looked him in the eye only to see him grinning psychotically, she knew that something was about to happen and began to scream in fear for her life. Little did she know that it was not her life that was in danger; as Quin turned round to see what was happening, Ligeia attempted to get free of Ragnar's grip and looked at him in desperation for his help. Quin dashed towards them ready to kill him for his treachery but Ragnar raised his other hand as Quin got near, releasing a forceful blast of magic that sent Quin hurtling backwards. He shut his eyes tight and braced himself for a hard landing, but as he re-opened them he flapped around in desperation, as he discovered he had fallen into the Pit of Despair. Screaming out in sheer terror, Quin's descent into the pit was accompanied by the screams of Ligeia, as she was promptly dragged away by

Ragnar. Persisting in a struggle to free herself, Ragnar smashed his fist against her head, rendering her unconscious. He flung her over his shoulder and carried her towards the palace muttering,

"Do not fret Princess; it will all be over soon!"

- Chapter XIX -
The Pit of Despair

Quin could feel the uneven ground digging into his back and strained to open his eyes as the sunlight shone into them. He sat up to find himself in the lush green meadow just outside of Alexandria's Kingdom, which now stood before him in all its former glory. For a moment Quin felt complete relief, as the horrors he had faced now seemed to have been nothing more than a terrible nightmare. He was instantly filled with joy at the prospect of finally being able to walk back into Alexandria again. It almost seemed too much to comprehend. Realising that he would have the chance to see Asha alive and well, he was ready to return back to his simple life as the Royal Blacksmith. Smiling ecstatically, he began to run towards the Kingdom gates. But as he neared, the sky suddenly began to darken. Skidding to a halt he raising his head to the skies and watched in horror as giant balls of fire rained down upon the Kingdom, just as it had before.

Suddenly, from out of nowhere, a hand grabbed his shoulder and span him around. Staring up at the giant that stood towering over him he could not believe his eyes as his farther looked down at him. Placing his arm around Quin, he turned him around to show him an army of noblemen. A scene that Quin remembered from his childhood. However the army was a mass of undead, mindless men. This sight was entirely confusing as horrifying for Quin to behold. Then, his father began to talk,

"My Son, when you are older and stronger than I. You must be the saviour of the damned. You will defeat the monsters in the night and all the unbelievers. For one day I will be gone, so you will lead the Condemned Army." With that he joined the army and charged off into the distance and vanished into the thick shroud of fog.

From behind him there was an almighty explosions. He turned just as the Kingdom began to collapse. Falling to his knees, with his dreams shattered once more he tortured himself by watching as the Kingdom went up in flames and the walls crumbled. Hearing the screams of the citizens slowly turning to a deathly silence as each of their lives were extinguished.

Experiencing his anguish all over again, he recalled the loss of his mother, Origen, Asha and everyone he cared for. Crying out at the vision that before him, he turned away, unable to watch it happen all over again. The anguish he had learnt to shut out returned to rear its ugly head and tears rolled down his face. All that could be heard for miles around was the cracking of the fires that torched his home, the clashes of steel blades as the remaining knights fought for their very lives, against the merciless Ifryte. Shuddered as this once mighty Kingdom fell to the ground, shaking the land and filling the air with the stench of death and burning flesh. The offending senses only served to paint a vivid picture in his mind, tormenting him further and forcing him to cover his ears and curl up into a ball to shut it all out. With only his fear to keep him company, he cried out as loud as he could. Then there was silence!

Confused, heart broke and terrified by the vision of his past Quin slowly released his ears and began to open his eyes. Looking up he expected to see the remains of the Kingdom, but to his surprise he found himself at the foot of Asha's special tree where they would sit. Over to one side of the tree stood Asha who was gazing out into the distance in her tattered blue dress which blew gently in the breeze. He was overwhelmed with the joy that he had finally found her. He rose to his feet and walked towards her, reaching out his hand to rest gently upon her shoulder to let her know that he was there. Blubbering and sobbing uncontrollably he softly whispered her name.

Asha hauntingly turning to look at him, covered from head to toe in horrific burns, cuts and bruises. Shocked at the very sight Quin gasped and stumbled backwards, as the woman he loved unconditionally had been so severely injured. Knowing that he had no magic to help her, he had to come to terms with the fact there was no way to ease her pain and prevent her death. He could only state his sorrow,

"No, oh please no... Asha!" He blubbered.

"Where were you Quin? I needed you"

"Asha, I am so sorry... I should have been there for you, I should have saved you" She turned away and gazed back out at the fields ahead that were ablaze and dying with each passing moment

"You forgot about me Quin! You found another to take my place in your heart. I hope your love does not ultimately end her too." Her words punched holes into his heart, while he tried to explain what had happened, seeking only to be forgiven   "I tried to find you Asha, but Origen - he was in danger too, I had to stop him and save my mother..." Unable to continue with his excuses he was abruptly interrupted by his mother's voice speaking from behind him

"But you did not save me child!" snapping his head around he gazed upon his mother standing before him.

"I tried mother... But Origen-" snapping back at Quin his mother was angered by his excuses,

"Do not blame the brother whom you murdered boy. He was doing that which you were never strong enough to do! He believed in his magic and tried so many times to teach you. But you arrogantly ignored him. You were always jealous of his power, he was stronger than you could ever hope to be. Your father would be ashamed of you! With all your power, you still refused to stop Origen and as a consequence you allowed me die. If you had just stayed away, my beloved son would be alive this day, safe in my arms. You would bless the world with your death!" With more and more excuses and reasoning entering Quin's mind he found it hard to redeem his actions

"Surely you do not mean that mother. You know that I tried to stop him to save you. You must know that?" enraged by his words she scolded him once more with utter detestation

"Do not call me mother, you pretender. You are a Telchine, a child of Gaia! You claim that you could not stop your brother, yet there is no stronger power than yours! I have grown weary of your excuses. Go, leave us. Leave us to our graves, which you so graciously bestowed upon us." Reaching out to his mother, he fell down flat on his face and suddenly found himself inside a dark cave. Looking up he could see the hole from where he entered which was now no more than a flicker of light that lay miles out of reach.

Attempting to see what lay down the dark, mist filled cavern he found the path ahead was clouded over with a thick and eerie fog. It was blatantly obvious that climbing out of the pit was impossible, so he had no alternative but to blindly follow the pathway and enter the fog to face the horrors that would certainly lie in waiting between him and his only chance of escape.

Suffering from the injury to his ankle, he limped into the mist. With each step the visibility became more and more obscured as the fog thickened. The path seemed to be never ending as he hobbled along the seeming endless path, using the wall to help support his advances as the pain increased. Yet he tried to ignore his injury and press on regardless of the pain, while clinging onto the hope that he would soon be free to save Ligeia. Sudden a blast of icy cold air blew in from behind him. He turned to see where it had come from and as he stared into the fog he noticed that it was beginning to clear. Scanning the area for a moment as the fog slowly turned into a shower of snowflakes, he found himself standing on the peaks of the Centaur Mountain. To his surprise it appeared that the camps had long since been destroyed and abandoned, there were no signs of any Centaur in the area, nor any other creature for that matter. There was nothing more than a few ruined structures that the Centaur once called their homes. Quin started to think that this could be a vision of what was yet to come for the Centaur Mountains. As he trudged through the thick snow, which engulfed his legs up to his knees, he concluded that the land had not been walked on for many days. However, he was all too happy to bear witness to the destruction of the barbaric Centaur tribe and although he did not want to think himself heartless and sinister, deep down he wanted to believe it was his actions that would eventually lead to their extinction as an exaction of his revenge. Suddenly stumbling, he yelping in pain as he fell and twisted his injured ankle even more on a block of ice, concealed beneath a foot of snow. Falling to the ground, he grabbed his leg and squeezed it to relieve some of the pain, he soon thumped the block of ice in a blind fury. During his flailing and pummelling he had inadvertently uncovered a small area of the ice, which allowed him to see into the crystal clear block. He quickly discovered where he was as he found himself looking down upon Prince Reaven's body encased within. Having only recently managed to calm down from the torment of Alexandria's demise he now faced yet another sorrow. He gazed down at the Prince's body, resting peacefully below, proudly clutching the magical sword that he had given him back in the day that Alexandria was still a mighty Kingdom. Despite all the pain he had been through, he felt comforted that at least he was able to give the Prince a somewhat honourable burial, given the circumstances. But Quin still held himself accountable for what happened and punished himself for his feeble attempt to redeem his actions that day, with a poor excuse for a burial ceremony, no more fit for a peasant than a prince. Quin quietly begged his forgiveness and while he spoke quietly into the Block of ice, Reaven's eyes suddenly opened wide and stared at Quin in a spine chilling look of horror. The Prince began to struggle whilst screaming out in, as Quin scrambled away crying with terror.

Breathless and stricken with panic, Quin closed his eyes tight, jabbering and desperately trying to compose himself. Reaffirming to himself that it was not real he begged to Gaia for a way out of the nightmare. However, it seemed the nightmare was far from over as a short while later, he opened his eyes to see Sir Leander and the Knights of

Alexandria standing over the Prince's icy grave, their heads bowed down muttering various sentimental and nostalgic words over their Prince.

Quin believed that his prayers had been answered and with a sigh of relief he joined the Knights circle around the grave. Too afraid to look at the Prince again, he simply shut his eyes and bowed his head.

As Sir Leander finished reminiscing there was a long period of silence as Quin waited patiently for someone else to speak. However after a little while, he thought that perhaps no-one else had anything to say, so he raised his head with the intension of contributing a few words.

As he opened his eyes and lifted his head, he discovered the Knights were now standing in a circle around him. All were staring at him with an angered expression. Quin searched each of their faces, hoping to find as much as a glimmer of compassion towards him. But he soon recognised that even Sir David, the most compassionate of the Knights, showed no such signs of forgiveness. The situation grew all the more intimidating with each passing moment, Quin was now unsure of what he could say or do to gain some kind of redemption and it wasn't long before he realised that, in their eyes he was beyond redemption. Suddenly, without warning Sir Leander lashed out, grabbing Quin by the arm and spat him his face to make his feelings known,

"How dare you show your face here traitor!?" He cursed reaching for his sword. Quin stepped back to get some distance between him and Sir Leander's Sword. But his withdrawal was obstructed by Sir Shimri, who promptly shoved him back. Quin turned to Sir Shimri in frustration of being pushed around but noticed that he had also reached for his sword, and before he could say anything Sir David and Sir Daniel joined in drawing their swords. The sound of the metal grinding as they pulled them from their scabbards sent a chill down Quin's spine, and now gave him good reason to fear for his life. Sir Shimri likewise spoke aggressively towards Quin,

"You have bought shame and dishonour to the memory of your father and Alexandria, Deserter! You abandoned your Prince for a few pathetic peasants!" before Quin could even respond to this charge the other Knights began making their own accusations, all shouting over each other,

"You used your magic around us and cursed us!" Sir Daniel yelled.

"You could have saved me with your magic, but you obviously wanted us dead. I dare say you were pleased to see me go, miscreant!" Sir Benjamin accused.

"You saved only yourself with your cowardice, running to safety without caring that you left us behind to fight for your freedom. We died at the hands of the Centaur for you." Sir David Criticized.

Then, in complete unison, there was silence. Sir Leander suddenly gasped and wheezed from behind him, which caught Quin's attention. He knew that something terrible lingered behind him as he fearfully turned and glanced from the corner of his eye. The vision that Quin had previously witnessed at the Phoenix Garrison presented itself to him in no delicate way. Sir Leander lay beneath him his body bloodied with wounds from the Centaur's attack, which bled out uncontrollably.

"You left me to die at the hand of a physician and abandoned all hope for our survival to go on a little adventure. You could have saved us Quin…" he muttered, coughing and wheezing, struggling for one final breath.

Quin stood in shock, aggrieved to have watched Sir Leander's death. The guilt began to boil over inside him as the harsh reality of his words confirmed only that which Quin had always believed deep down, which had now been revealed for him to face, alone. He knew he had to come to terms with the truth but also realised that sometimes things are easier to cope with if he simply turned a blind eye and buried them deep down, but now discovered that they would always return with a vengeance.

Having given up, Quin slumped into the snow and allowed his thoughts and feelings to consume him. Hoping the other Knights would end his suffering and give him his just reward by striking him down. He was stricken all the more to see Sir Shimri and Sir Daniel lying dead and frozen in the snow and with his final words Sir David cursed Quin,

"You ran away from danger to save yourself. All Telchines are the same, you despise them, yet you are no different. No, you are the worst of them!" and with that Sir David shut his eyes with his face in the snow and became still.

The Knights lay dead around him, each with a bloody wound that freely flowed onto the snowy white fields, which now ran red with the blood of the fallen. The cold winds soon picked up and swiftly blew the surface snow into the air and off into the distance like a swarm of bees, revealing the frozen, desecrated bodies of humans and Centaur alike littering the mountain as far as the eye could see. Quin's only thoughts now dwelled on it having all been his fault, despite his distasteful hopes not just a few moments before, now witnessing the devastation first hand, he soon realised that the death around him was the direct result of a war that he had caused in his attempt to aid the refugees of Alexandria.

Quin reached out his hand and held Sir Leander's foot, shaking it in the hopes that he would awaken. But there was no sign of life from him or any of the other Knights. Once again his heart break got the better of him and he broke down in tears. But this time for of the loss of his allies and indeed those he would call his only true friends, which now lay dead because of him. It was all too clear that they blamed him for what had happened, and for good reason, it was entirely his fault and he openly admitted it to himself.

With tear filled eyes he glancing around at all the bodies that were scattered on the ground. He realised that all life is sacred with equal value. Killing each other only served to weaken the unity of the planet that Gaia had spent her life creating and ultimately gave it for.

"The damage is done, you cannot change it now. It is typical for a human to simply give up when things get tough, how did I ever let myself become you!?" A familiar voice said. But, Quin had by now lost all interest and didn't care which ghost of the past was next to come and torment him, as long as it was one with the intension of ending his misery. He lifted his tear filled face to look upon his conqueror and noticed that he was no longer on top of the Centaur Mountain, but inside the Chamber of memories. A dark figure stood almost invisibly within the shadows of the entrance of the cavern, which provided the one way in or out of the chamber.

"Lycus!" Quin exclaimed dully, not really surprised and without real care. Lycus stepping out of the darkness of the cave and into the light of the chamber, slowly pacing around the room, while examining the scripture engraved into the walls and pillars.

"Look at how pathetic you have become. Powerless and weak. Tell me; do you believe that you honour me with your actions?" Lycus interrogated as if he did not care for the answer and was more of a rhetorical insult. Quin was, of course, in no kind of mood to play games, especially with Lycus of whom he had lost all respect for and grown to despise him for all had done, which had now been left for Quin to rectify. Without a care for the consequences, Quin relished the opportunity to speak his mind and reveal his true feelings towards Lycus, almost in the hope that, in retaliation Lycus would end it all.

"Your life was nothing more than a stampede of lies, deceit and destruction. You deviously plotted against your siblings, manipulated and cheated your own kin. But not before you murdered thousands of innocents and destroyed the Island and the lands that gave birth to Gaia herself, after you stood idly by and watched the Telchines sacrifice her for your greedy lust for power! You sought only to please yourself. Scheming your way through life until it got you killed. And now you have the tenacity to ask me if *I* have honoured *your* life? Your life had no honour to begin with!" Lycus was amused at Quin's lack of understanding and went on to taunt him and laugh in his face,

"Oh yes, of course. I forgot that you had experienced a few memories and from those you have everything figured out!? You truly believe everything you have seen and take it all on face value? You know nothing!" Lycus blurted, sarcastically taunting Quin with every passing moment, which only served to frustrate and anger. He glared at Lycus, wanting him to simply strike him dead rather than continue playing blaming games.

"I know enough, lest you forget, I *am* you!" Quin stated, believing that there was no denying the point. Lycus stopped and became silent for a moment, as if completely baffled, but after a few moments he let out a big sigh

"You are me!" He stated as if astonished at the

revelation, before changing his tone to make it obvious he was being sarcastic yet again, "So by that you mean to say that you know yourself?" The seemingly simple question raised many questions within Quin's mind as he quickly reflect on his life and who he was. Although he would never admit it to anyone else, especially Lycus, it dawned on him that Lycus was correct and Quin actually had no idea who he was.

After a life as the son of a Blacksmith in the Kingdom Alexandria, the only battle he had ever faced was for Asha's hand and heart, his only burden was living each day pretending he was a mere human. By the standards of how he now lived, he was a spoiled brat and deserved to have it all turned on its head with the destruction of his home, friends and family, which was the harsh wake-up call he needed to bring him back to reality. It was only after the devastation that he stopped hiding and began to embrace his powers, although not proudly to begin with. The use of his magic set him on the road to understanding his power and the realisation of who he was. Throughout his journey he had faced and overcome many of the obstacles in his path. He had witnessed fragments of his life as Lycus and although he did not fully understand what it all meant and feeling that he had only scratched the surface of discovering who Lycus was, he finally understood that it had all happened because fate had planned it that way. Quin had put so much effort into avoiding fate and loathed it for leading him into the Pit of Despair, yet he now understood that this was meant to happen, for without it he would have never discovered who he is now and who he was meant to become.

Lycus, having left Quin to his thoughts, continued to pace around the room until Quin asked,

"Why me?" Lycus stopped dead in his tracks and turned to meet Quin's gaze as their red eyes met and reflected off of each other; a paradox of sorts. Lycus smiled triumphantly and only confirmed that which he already knew but perhaps needed to hear from someone else in order for him to believe it,

"Only you can decide who you are and it is something you must discover for yourself. Find your own truths and your own mind. Live your life as you need it to be and not what it was when you were me." And with that Lycus was gone.

Quin now swore that if he made it out of the pit of despair he would hunt Ragnar down and kill him for his betrayal. Sitting there winding himself up into frenzy, he realised that killing Ragnar would crush any hope of ever seeing

Asha again. However in this though he wasn't sure if he could find the motivation to continue his fight without the motivation of finally being reunited with Asha.

Quin was now faced with one simple choice 'Fight and live or surrender and die?' Although he felt that the world was by now too far beyond redemption, he also felt that if he wasn't willing to try then he may as well destroy the lands himself. Unwilling to go on, yet filled with the guilt of doing nothing, which could potentially result in the pain and suffering for the entire world. He was torn between wanting to at least try to make a difference or surrendering to the futility of his efforts. Before he could come to a conclusion he was interrupted by the sound of footsteps which could be heard echoing in the distance of the cave. He remained still and stared in anticipation as the footsteps gradually grew louder and closer until the figure emerged from the darkness causing his heart to sink as he was forced to face it head on,

"It is time Quin!" Prince Reaven said calmly but with a subtle look of sorrow on his face, like he was about to put his pet down. He drew his sword, which spouted flames from the blade and tossed his gauntlet down at Quin's feet and ordered him "Pick it up".

Quin gazed at the gleaming silver gauntlet, scared half to death of the consequences he would face if he was to accept the challenge. However, it was not a request and he knew that if he wanted to make it out of the Pit, he had very little choice but to battle with the memory of his best friend.

"I have challenged you Quin! Now pick it up!" Reaven yelled with anger and authority. Quin rose to his feet, staring Reaven in the eyes and answered the challenge,

"No, I will not fight you!" Reaven's face dropped and his lips screwed up as if sucking on a sour lemon and bellowed

"Pick it up!"

"I have already been the cause of your death once. Do you really wish for it again?" Quin retaliated, knowing there was nothing the Prince's apparition could do about it, for the Prince was bound by 'The Knights Code of Honour' and therefore could not attack until the challenge was accepted by ways of picking up the Gauntlet. Quin folded his arms and stood with a stern expression on his face. However, Quin quickly discovered that he had a weakness.

"You are an abomination. It is all too clear that without your pathetic magic you are no more worth of Asha than she is of living. Cower if you wish, I have eternity to wait for you to accept my challenge and when you do, I will slay you with ease - you pathetic little rat!" Reaven taunted.

I was not long before Quin's anger boiled over. Memories flashed through his mind of Prince Reaven's reaction towards him and his magic when they were at the Legion Halls, being threatened with his life by a man who claimed he was his most trusted friend and ally, yet contradicted himself when he discovered his magic and branded him a traitor and cast him out as if he were contagiously sick, no longer worthy of a life. Quin was no longer willing to allow the human's to look down on him and he allowed his anger to take over as he hatefully retrieved the gauntlet and tossing it back at Reaven's feet.

"Very well then."

Reaven kicked the Gauntlet aside and did not hesitate to begin his attack. Without taking his wide staring eyes off Quin, he slowly circled around the room.

"You sentenced me to death with your cursed magical sword and now I shall return the gesture!" Prince Reaven growled as he lunged forward, swinging his blade at Quin. Tactfully dodging the blade Quin dashed to the opposite side of the room and turned to face Reaven again, but instead found himself face to face with Sir Leander,

"Die for us Quin!" he said stepping to one side pointing at Ceremonial Circle in the middle of the floor. Quin looked around the now darkened room and was faced with those he had lost on his journey, all taking a place around the edge of the circle, speaking in unison.

"Die for us. Die for us" Reaven stepped forward from the shadows and waited in the centre of the platform.

"Step forward and do what you were fated to do, sacrifice yourself for them Quin. You can save them all! Is that not what you wanted from the beginning?" Quin gazed around the room and identified each of the faces pausing only to wonder if he was willing to give his life for them. Eventually he spotted Asha. Realising his entire journey was solely meant to bring Asha back, Quin's mind was made up, and he knew that he would give his life for Asha alone.

"Very well, I shall concede!"

Quin bravely stepped onto the centre circle and began his ascent to the centre of the room, not once taking his eyes away from Asha. She smiled sweetly at him with the same bashful expression he remembered so well. As he reached the centre Quin took the few more moments to look around at all those whom he would sacrifice himself for, before extending his final sentiments to them all.

"Father, I am sorry that I was unable to make you proud of me. You wanted our family to achieve the noble status, yet I was too weak to live up to your legacy, you bravely gave your life for that dream. When I came to face battle - I froze; a coward, unworthy of being a noble… Unworthy of your pride!" He began, plagued by the thought that he had failed them all. "Nobel Knights of Alexandria I failed to use my magic when it really mattered. I was simply too scared to use my magic to protect you, had I done what needed to be done, you would all be alive today and I would have been discovered for my magic, I should have embraced my execution as my reward for being a hero, but because of my cowardice you died in my stead." He continued, pausing only to turn to the next person. "Asha I truly loved you, but I was too much of a child to tell you, I was immature. It is amusing now, to think that of all the fears I have faced, I am still be more afraid of telling you how I feel. Even as death awaits me." He explained, beating himself up for being so pathetic. Quin took another look around and noticed his Mother. He was about to speak to her however he suddenly realised that one face was missing from the crowd; Origen. Distracted by this revelation Quin began to ponder the situation and finally turning to Reaven, it seemed appropriate to leave his final words for him. "Reaven, you were my dearest friend and I did as you commanded. I abandoned you when you truly needed me. Please know that for all my mistakes, I wish it had been me. You should have lived on. I thank you on behalf of all those who died that day, and although your life was always more important than mine, I have to wonder how many would have died if I had not been there at all. Would you have died either way? I suppose we shall never know. What I do know is that Origen would have been proud of me for trying and embracing my magic, and if I am to be punished for doing what I thought was right, then so be it!" he finished.

Falling to his knees and closing his eyes, Quin awaited his punishment.

Time stood still and Lycus' voice echoing through his mind,

"How did I become you? You would freely give your life and take responsibility for these people? They had their chance and with or without you their fate remains the same. Your love and compassion for their kind makes you weak. Without these emotions I was able to preserve this world; I protected it for as long as I lived and as such created a world that gave them life. Your sacrifice may give them their lives back, but for what? So that they may corrupt the world further. To die another day at the hands of another enemy? One has to wonder who they would blame then. It seems that everyone else is at fault for the poor choices they make for themselves!" Quin finally understood Lycus' perspective, but only had one thing left to say,

"I am not you Lycus!" and with that Reaven prepared to strike him down

"Your fate is sealed!" he muttered as he raised his sword above his head and prepared to strike Quin down. However, his words troubled Quin. His life instantaneously flashed before him and he immediately realised that his ultimate fear was never anything that the world held. It was not the deaths of those around him including his own. It wasn't even facing his past mistakes once again within the pit. Quin's sudden shock was the revelation that fate was his darkest fear and it was about to win their lifelong battle.

"No!" He shouted as he opened his eyes and glared at Reaven, who had begun to swing his blade towards him. He swiftly dodged aside and was shocked at the near miss of the blade as it clanged loudly on the floor beside him. No longer full of fear, remorse or sorrow, Quin was now enraged at Fate, who blamed for planning this deception from the very start, in an elaborate attempt to conquer him and his magic. Quin's rage empowered him to such an extent that his magic tore out of him in a huge wave of fire, overpowering the illusionary appearance of the room and causing it to evaporate, and Quin found himself back inside the Pit of despair. Directly in front of him, a mere few steps away, was the opening that led out of the pit and as Quin rushed towards it, believing he had conquered the pit, his escape was soon hindered as Prince Reaven stepped out of the shadows and stood in the entrance holding out his sword in Quin's throat.

"You have condemned us all with your selfishness. You are a coward and a frightened child just as Lycus was. You would run away from your responsibility?" Reaven bellowed. But Quin was no longer afraid of Reaven or sorry for the other apparitions of his past,

"I owe you nothing! Much like myself and Lycus, you were all the masters of your own fate, with or without me your fate was sealed due to your own actions, my only guilt is doing what I could to help you stave off you fate just a little longer. Tell me why I should hold responsibility for your mistakes, you have only yourselves to blame, nothing I could ever do will change that. All I can do now is let you rest in peace and attempt to right the wrongs that were done to you. I cannot take back what happened, but that is my burden to bear and I will live with it, and allow it to strengthen my resolve. Only my forthcoming actions can make amends for the many wrongs done. I swear to you I will do all I can to put right the injustice that has befallen you. Sacrificing my life for you would only place my burdens unto you and *that* would be an act of cowardice. For those who have witnessed the passing of a friend knows that death is a burden on those left behind! Your burdens are mine to bear, but my love and fondness for you and your memory makes me strong. It gives me something to fight for. It gives me the will to go forth and find a resolution to the burdens that you would hold onto, even in death. That is what I will do!" To which, the Prince gave Quin a simple verdict,

"Not good enough!" Quin now knew that there was no reasoning with him. If his heartfelt and sincere words were not enough to convince Prince Reaven, then it was blatantly obvious that nothing would be. It seemed Reaven would settle for no less than Quin's death and Quin knew it was time to put an end to this nightmare and angrily lashed out and grasped Reaven's blade.

Throughout his life Quin had always put up with the frustration of knowing that he had the power to strike any foe down with a mere flick of his wrist and could use his magic to rise to power and command his own army. If he had listened to Origen, they both could have conquered Alexandria themselves and could have claimed the crown. However, compassion was more than enough reason not to use his magic to harm another, regardless of the situation at hand; a moral that Lycus did not share with Quin. At that very moment Quin had unknowingly annulled his moral standing and had taken a step closer to becoming no better than Ifrit himself. By using his powers to destroy anyone who stood in his path, without remorse or feeling. Perhaps this was something that Quin had to become in order to achieve all that he had set out to do, but in doing so he would cross a fine line and find a new way of dealing with a clash of opinions.

"You dare use my own sword against me!? If you will not accept my sentiments and persist in your efforts to stand against me then you will be destroyed!" Quin snarled as his eyes regained their red glow. Still grasping the blade, he contently activated the hidden magic concealed within the weapon, forcing it backfire. The apparition of Prince Reaven burst into flames. Reaven immediately released the hilt of the sword and flailed around manically and let out a very familiar roar. Within moments Reaven transforming into the black cloud that had been plaguing him ever since his arrival on the island, and it quickly retreated.

Quin finally stepped out of the cave, after what seemed like many days. He watched the black cloud flying off into the sky over the Island as it gradually dispersed, and began to wonder about it. He now knew without a shadow of a doubt that it had been following him ever since he left the Phoenix Garrison, which was coincidentally the moment that he was seemingly no longer in control of his own fate as Ragnar took control of everything he would do thereafter. The revelation seemed all too obvious and had been staring him in the face the whole time. The Black Cloud was the physical manifestation of his fate, which had now caught up with him and had almost killed him within the Pit of Despair. He knew it was that moment that he had to take back control of his life.

"No longer will I be hunted by my own fate!" He swore to himself before gazing up into the sky "I know what you are now, for I have seen you with my own sinister eyes! You can be seen and therefore can be touched and killed. We will meet again and when that day comes, I will destroy you!" He declared.

A clap of thunder and lightning pulled Quin's attention to a dome-like building in the distance. Regardless of how natural thunder and lightning was, he could sense a strange power emanating from it. It soon became apparent that this storm was being summoned with dark magic. The clouds above the dome began to change to a dark grey and spiralled around the building like a vortex. He could only assume that this was the result of Ragnar's magic and if that were the case, then Ligeia was with him beneath the forming clouds, which looked ready to drop a heavy rainstorm. Quin could only guess that Ragnar was trying to use his magic to make Ligeia change back into her siren form. If that were to happen she would assuredly die. Fearing for her life Quin hurried towards the impending storm in the hope that he would get there before it was too late. However, Quin was quickly reminded that his ankle was still injured and in his current state he could not hope make it in time.

It was not long before Quin came across an old decayed pillar that had a small pool of crystal clear water gathered in the middle of it. Placing his hand into the fresh water, he used his magic to absorb the water's healing properties and mended his broken ankle. With a large and uncomfortable crunch his bones slotted back into place allowing him to walk normally once again, although not fully healed, it was good enough for him to continue. In a moment of reflection he stared in curiosity at the sword he still held in his hand and had to wonder how it was possible that he was still holding Prince Reaven's sword, as he quite clearly remembered burying it with the Prince back on the Centaur Mountain, miles away from the Island. Sliding the sword through a gap in the side of his belt, he took a deep breath, closed his eyes and transformed into his wind form. He immediately took off towards the dome-like building which lay in the centre of the city, which was the palace he had seen in his meditated vision. There he would find the Sacrificial Circle and more than likely, Ragnar and Ligeia too. Ready to face off with Ragnar, Quin's anger boiled over as he swore this would be the moment that he would put an end to him and his deceit.

- Chapter XX -
Love and Hate

Standing before the Sacrificial Platform, Ragnar used his magic to imprison Ligeia, who was now suspended over the centre of the circle, as he recited the texts of the Book of Necropoleis from memory.

"Custodite et audite vocem meam coeli. Emitte quia de tua substantia et bene vivendi liquoris potestate. Reformabit hoc ens, et offerre illi sanguinem nostrum rituali"

He chanted as Ligeia slowly regained consciousness. Due to Ragnar's magic she was unable to move her body and could only use her eyes to look around in order to see where she was. The old building was nothing more than ruins, with walls that had disintegrated and turned to rubble over the large span of time at the bottom of the ocean. She was frightened and felt completely alone and helpless as she glanced down at Ragnar and pleaded with him,

"Why are you doing this Ragnar? How could you kill Quin?" She cried. But Ragnar ignored her plea and simply continued his chant.

"Et aperire portas inferi clamavi festum sanguine dives vita eius. Et consumet eam, et devoret ammerge iterum in regno hominum potentiam."

Ligeia gazed in horror as a clap of thunder and flash of lightning prompted her to glare up at the sky. The clouds began to release drops of rain and as each drop missed her and landed on the ground her heart skipped a beat. She realised that she would very soon turn back into her siren form and would thereafter be sacrificed in the name of Ragnar's evil scheme. A single droplet of rain landed on her cheek and gently rolled down her face as if comforting her, before it began to glimmer and her legs began to tingle as the skin proceeded to transform into scales. Knowing that a mere few drops would be enough to make the transformation irreversible, Ligeia began to cry hysterically, begging for her life.

"Ragnar, please do not do this, I will do anything you ask of me, just stop!" Nonetheless Ragnar was persistent and unsympathetic towards her emotional cries. He stepped forward onto the outer ring of the platform and slowly drew a concealed dagger from his cloak which was excessively decorated with glimmering jewels and inscriptions of an ancient language. He presented it to the skies and used the same levitation magic to push it into the air, incanting manically at the top of his lungs so that he could be heard over the now uncontrollable thunder that struck the land and ruins all over the island.

"Dimittam te ad magica ferrum, et meam perficere opus tuum da mihi potestatem"

With these words uttered, a mighty flash of lightning struck the blade and travelled through it connecting with Ragnar as well. Ligeia smiled as she witnessed his most unfortunately ironic Situation. However, much to her dismay, Ragnar continued his ritual without as much as flinching and held out his hands as the dagger gradually sank back into his palm. He gently grasped the hilt of the blade, which was now glowing. Then took a deep breath and finally made eye contact with Ligeia.

"You will thank me for this when we meet again in the Underworld! Please do not be afraid, your sacrifice is necessary for the greater good." And with that Ragnar aimed the dagger at the sky above and released an almighty bolt of magic that struck the clouds causing them to release a torrent rainfall.

As the rain descended towards Ligeia, she closed her eyes and prepared to meet her end bravely. However, after a few moments she wondered what had happened as she had neither felt nor heard a single droplet hit the ground or her body. Shyly opening her eyes and looking upwards she gazed in utter disbelief as she saw countless raindrops motionless and floating in mid-air above her. Understandably frustrated with the assumption that Ragnar was playing a torturing game with her, she looked down at him and scowled angrily. It was then that she discovered Ragnar gazing up with a perplexed expression. Appearing from a darkened hallway behind him, Quin emerged with a hand held up to the rain, using his magic and control over the elements to halt its descent. In a moment Ligeia's expression turned to one of great relief and joy as Quin metaphorically walked back into her life. However, as Ragnar searched for some explanation to the enigma, he soon noticed Ligeia's gaze fixated behind him. Frowning and pursing his lips in a rapidly escalating rage. Against all odds, Quin had survived the Pit of Despair and now infringed on his carefully executed plot. He turned to face Quin, with the dagger held tightly in a clenched fist.

"How did you survive? I was assured you would be dead." He growled, infuriated at his presence. But Quin stood deathly silent, glaring angrily at Ragnar with a spark of fire in his eyes as he reached for his sword. "It seems you have circumvented your fate once again, but you are oblivious to the ramifications of your actions. Leave now or you will doom us all Telchine!" he argued with a tremble in his voice before lunging at Quin with his dagger, "You must die!"

Forced to drop his hand to defend himself Quin used the power of the winds to swiftly blast Ragnar away, sending him hurtling over to the other side of the platform and into a wall, which consequently collapsed and buried him under the rubble, but in doing this Quin had momentarily released his magical hold over the rainfall and the drops began to creep towards Ligeia once again. Quickly shifted his focus back to the rain, he reached out with his hand and this time pushed it back up to the sky, although it was a huge strain on his energy, he had to do everything he could to protect Ligeia, who had by now regained some control over her body and was able to move a little more. She frantically began struggling to free herself from the spell that was still holding her,

"Quin, get me down!" She begged, but he was too focused on pushing the rain back to hear her. However, she was confident that he would eventually get around to breaking the spell and freeing her. That is, until she heard the sudden tapping of rocks, and turned round to witness the rubble that concealed Ragnar had begun to stir. Her heart sank in fear.

Using his magic to blast himself free, Ragnar burst through the rubble, sending rocks and dust of all sizes hurtling back into the room and rushed at Quin with the dagger pointed at his heart,

"Quin, look out!" She screamed. Although he did not heard Ligeia's warning, he sensed Ragnar's magic and promptly opening his eyes and glared at Ragnar. He forcefully cast the rain he controlled around Ligeia and towards his enemy. As the masses of droplets splashed into his face and eyes Ragnar was forced to raise his arms to shield his face. Quin continued to take advantage of the storm by bending it to his advantage.

"Quin stop, you do not know what you are doing!" Ragnar called out, pleading over the roaring sound of the gushing rainfall. But Quin was no longer willing to listen to his web of lies and deceit. "Quin, listen to me, I am only doing what must be done. We came here to put an end to Ifrit and we can still do that; we can still save the world, together!"

"Not like this, not this way!" Quin called back, dismissing Ragnar without as much as hearing him out.

"This is the only way!" Ragnar cried "Ifrit can only

be destroyed with a power greater than his own!" At this point Quin's interest peaked. It appeared that he had finally pushed him far enough to get the answers he desired. Quin flicked his palm back and stopped pummelling Ragnar with the rain but continued to hold it away from Ligeia.

"You have my attention but make your words count, for if I do not like what I hear, I will finish you!" Quin threatened as Ligeia's hopes of freedom began to dwindle, knowing that Ragnar was sly enough to cheat his way out of his deserved punishment.

"Do not listen to him Quin!" She pleaded, but to no avail. His frustration had gotten the better of him, now that he was on the verge of discovering all that he wanted to know. His determination to obtain all the information that Ragnar knew suddenly became a priority,

"Silence!" Quin growled at Ligeia, his aggravation reflecting through his magic, causing the clouds to thunder angrily.

"What do you know of Ifrit?" He asked.

"All you need to know is that you can trust me; the Siren's life is a necessary sacrifice for the greater good; kill one in order to save the rest!" Ragnar began to explain. "A blood sacrifice is required to open the gateway to the

Underworld. But not just any mere mortal blood, it must be Telchine blood, or the blood of a direct descendant of a Telchine!" Ragnar divulged pointing at Ligeia.

"To raise an army from the underworld, Ligeia has to die?" Quin reiterated.

"No Quin. Not an army, an individual; the resurrection of a being with infinite power; one who could smite Ifrit by merely willing it." Names flew through Quin's mind as he attempted to guess who this individual might be. He surmised that it was most likely one of his Telchine siblings, as they obviously held the most power in the lands. Only one name came to mind; the war monger of the Telchines; he who could manipulate the minds of his kin and control them in battle.

"Ormen" Quin declared.

Ragnar burst out laughing uncontrollably as he derided Quin's lack of knowledge of his own heritage.

"Of all the beings in Gaia, you believe the Telchines are the most powerful? Your ignorance, let alone arrogance, amuses me Quin." Ragnar taunted, before turning deadly serious and instantly angered at the mere mention of the Telchines. "You know nothing of the Telchines! It is because of them that the lands of Gaia are in this mess! They selfishly battled for dominance over the lands, which were evenly split between them to begin with. They created nothing but pain and suffering for their kin, rather than fighting their own battles. They are at fault for the creation of Ifrit! It was you Quin - or should I call you 'Lycus'? You and your juvenile siblings have done nothing but destroy the planet, because you just would not let go! Your refusal to die when you were supposed to has condemned the lands to eternal suffering. The Telchines were blessed with gifts of magic and charged with a single task, to nurture mankind until such time that they can sustain themselves. Instead you abused both your magic and kin alike to create frivolous wars amongst yourselves. The Telchines are monsters who have overstayed their welcome in this world!" Ragnar scorned, as if reciting a script from memory that he had been passionately waiting to get off his chest his whole life. Meanwhile Quin was silently taking in all the information he was spilling out through his verbal attacks of hatred and loathing for him and the Telchines. It was not long before the area between Ragnar's ranting and Quin's knowledge finally began to come together. Although for the most part Quin urged to strike Ragnar down for his insolence, he wanted to see how much he could learn, so he allowed him to continue. "No Lycus, even if the Telchines were dead I would never burden the lands with their presence again. My goal has always remained the same; to bring back the only being who can fix this world. He alone can undo all the damage caused by the Telchines; He will come and destroy Ifrit and the Telchine Plague along with it!" He continued as he quickly swiped his dagger forward and slashed Ligeia's wrist. Quin could only watch in horror as the blood trickled down her hand and fell from her fingertips onto the Sacrificial Circle. "Come forth Tartaros - Lord of the Underworld!" Ragnar summoned triumphantly, giddy with the prospect of success.

The circle began to glow with a shadowy haze as dark magic flowed through it awaiting more power from the blood sacrifice. Quin's attention was drawn to the power that was being emitted from the circle, giving Ragnar the perfect opportunity to strike at him unawares with a wave of magic that was strengthened by his dagger. The sheer force of the blast sent him hurtling backwards. Having caught him by surprise he carelessly lost grip of his sword leaving it to freefall to the ground with a disdained clang. Much to Ragnar's annoyance, Quin had collided with Ligeia, which broke the levitation spell and allowed her to fall freely to the ground, shortly followed by Quin, who landed hard on his back and bumping his head on the solid stone floor. He took a moment to allow his head to stop spinning before realising that he no longer had control over the rainfall and watched as it began to fall towards him and, more to the point, Ligeia. Quickly throwing both hands up, he regained control of the rainfall and held it in place to allow Ligeia enough time to escape.

Ragnar had now become aggravated by Quin's interruptions and roared furiously as he pounced on top of him, aiming his dagger directly at his heart. Quin had no option but to grab Ragnar's wrists and attempt to push him away, as he placed all his weight onto the dagger. Quin could not afford to focus on anything else as his strength buckled under the pressure and the dagger drew ever closer to his body. Although, Quin's concern for Ligeia's safety was more important to him,

"Ligeia, find some shelter." He cried. She scarpered under a nearby ruined hallway and shuddered as she stood helplessly by as Ragnar's dagger drew ever closer to Quin.

Quin desperately trying to think of a spell he could use to free himself from his ever deteriorating situation. But in his panic he came up empty handed and the dagger made contact with his clothing, slowly breaking through to his skin and penetrating into his chest. The burning sensation of the daggers magic flowed through his entire body, which far outweighed the pain of the sharp blade slicing through his flesh cartilage, but for all his efforts to break free, he was simply left to struggle and scream out as both pain and fear became one, with the acceptance that he couldn't hold on any longer. His thoughts turned to those he cared for and he prepared to extend his final sentiments.

"I am sorry Asha, I have failed!" He muttered. His eyes changing from their empowered red glow, back into the eyes of a frightened boy on the edge of his demise. Ragnar grinned sinisterly and stared into his very soul.

Preparing for a fatal push, Ragnar's body lifted as he shifted all his strength into his shoulders. Suddenly Prince Reaven's sword burst through Ragnar's chest. For this Quin was both startled and confused wondering what had just happened, as Ragnar's blood spurted out and dripped down the long blade that now protruded from his body! Gawping down at his chest, he struggled for breath at the shock of discovering his mortal wound. Feebly rising to his feet and dropping the dagger to the floor as he stumbled round to discover Ligeia standing behind him with a burning hatred in her eyes. Her soft skin gently absorbed the rain that now soaked her. Bearing witness to this triumph, Ragnar could only smile knowing that in mere moments, he will have successfully released Tartaros, even if he had ultimately paid with his life.

Now doused in sparkling raindrops, changing her once flawless skin back into scales, Ligeia had begun the irreversible transformation back into a siren. Gradually losing the ability to stand as her legs merged together to become a single tailfin. She sank to the floor, all the time glaring angrily at Ragnar, who now stumbled around grasping Reaven's Sword, and eventually fell to his knees.

"My Lord Tartaros will revive me, you have already lost." he gasped with blood spurting from his mouth with each word, before finally flopping to the ground, bashing his head on the solid stone floor.

Quin desperately clambered to his feet and rushed over to Ligeia,

"Ligeia, why?" he asked as he gently lifted her head and rested it in his lap, with a tremble in his voice. He knew that each moment she spent out of water was killing her.

"Others would have given much more for the opportunity to save the life of a Telchine!" She proclaimed modestly as she bravely prepared for death with honour and dignity.

"No, I will not let you die. Not for me! You must tell me how to save you!" He begged, experiencing a remorse that felt like another old friend returning to haunt him, in the same way that fate had revealed so many times before. Quin couldn't help but think that this was his fault; the result of avoiding his own fate and in so doing, disrupting the balance of life and death. He imagined that for each time he avoided his own death, fate would act to balance it out again and punish him in the process, by twisting events to cause the deaths of those he cared for.

"Do you happen to have a tankard of ale with you?" She joked, if only to lighten the mood in an attempting to avoid acceptance of the situation.

"Put your arms around me, I shall carry you back to the ocean! That will save you, yes?" Quin suggested, hoping that it would be that simple, but Ligeia gazed lovingly into Quin's eyes,

"Either way, returning to the ocean or remaining here, I will die!"
But Quin refused to give up on her and desperately searched for a way to save her as he gently stroked her hair away from her face. Before any more could be said, he watched her eyes suddenly widen as she stared over his shoulder with a look of horror on her face. Quin slowly

turned, following her gaze to see what she was looking at and was both astonished and infuriated to see Ragnar rising to his feet with Reaven's Sword in hand.

He was floating in mid-air with his arms extended outwards and his head tilted up to the sky. He then sharply opened his eyes wide and let out an almighty roar that felt like it was shaking the entire island. After a few moments he snapped his head forward and glared at Quin with solid black eyeballs, which appeared to be the prison for an unnerving abyss of tormented souls. Gradually descending back to the ground he began to speak in a booming, strange voice, which clearly did not belong to Ragnar.

"Lycus! What a pleasure it is to see you again. Although I sense something different about you. Can it be that you have chosen the life of a mortal once again?" He said inquisitively, yet with a subtle taunting patronisation as if with no fear of Quin's power. Neither Quin nor Ligeia said a word and simply waited to hear what he would say next,

"Do you not remember me boy? Surely I have not been forgotten?" He asked, but still Quin said nothing and continued to glare angrily "Perhaps when you became human you forgot your heritage!? If that is the case, I should reintroduce myself. I am Tartaros, your father!" He uttered. Quin's heart jumped into his throat and he immediately felt the intimidation of the infinitely superior power before him. One that could easily tear his entire body to shreds with a single spell. He suddenly feared for his life but nonetheless, prepared to face the being that was only equalled by Gaia herself. Much to Quin's dismay, he knew that even with the full power of all four Telchines, Tartaros' power made them look like novices in comparison.

Still unsure of Tartaros intensions, Quin recalled the memory that dubbed Lycus as the son of Tartaros. If that were true then striking first would be rather foolish as he would most certain die. On the other hand, if it was all a part of an elaborate deception slyly arranged by the other Telchines, then Tartaros held no allegiance to him and would strike him down regardless. Either way, he knew he could not make the first move and simply remained still, staring at Tartaros with an unthinkable fear in his heart. Tartaros soon realised that Quin was not going to do much more than continue staring at him like a startled squirrel and decided to get straight to the point,

"Bring me the girl and I shall reward you with the one thing your heart truly desires; the restoration of your immortality! I need a few more drops of her blood to fully regain my powers and leave this circular prison and then together we will destroy our common enemies." He bartered, albeit foolishly as Quin now realised that he was currently in a weakened state which gave Quin a slight advantage and may stand a chance at defeating him, but at what cost?

"I vowed that no more would die as a result of my actions. I intend to stay true to my word!" Quin growled through gritted teeth.

"That is most noble of you! But tell me, was it your siblings that made you mortal? Naturally you can never get revenge on them unless you have greater power than them! Bring the Siren to me and I will bless you with more power than you could possibly imagine and make you my own Telchine! I will give you all the knowledge you desire. Together we can crush them and create the most powerful legion ever seen, together we rule everything including the Underworld and the Heavens!"

Quin took a moment to seriously consider his offer; after all, it would give him everything he wanted. But as he glanced back into Ligeia's eyes she whispered

"Do not trust him Quin!" He nodded and smiled at Ligeia as he gently placed her head on the ground and rose to his feet. Walking over to the circle where Tartaros remained trapped, he stopped just beyond the perimeter and retorted angrily.

"You created the Underworld, return back to the fate you created for yourself. If there is but one lesson I have learnt from your Pit of Despair, it is that I am not here to take responsibility for another's choices. You had your chance, do not expect me to help you rectify your mistakes. I may not know everything, but I know that Gaia sacrificed herself to undo your evil, a fate that you created for her. During my life as a mortal I have learned many things, the most valued lesson is that there is no stronger power than hope and love. On my path I have lost many of my friends to the underworld and I shall give you no more. Return to the Underworld where you belong!" Condemning Tartaros to remain trapped in the world he created for himself. This was not what Tartaros wanted to hear and he lashed out, beyond the circles perimeter in a blind rage, grabbing Quin by the throat. However the skin on his arm quickly began to boil and melt as it extended outside the circle, where he could not exist. He viciously pulling Quin inside the circle and cast him to the ground. Now face to face with the most powerful being to have ever existed, he picked himself up and faced Tartaros, who now grossly licked his wounded arm, while maintaining eye contact, in the form of a sinister

Glare.

"Your compassion for others makes you weak Lycus! Still, nevertheless I shall reopen the gateway to the Underworld, I shall just have to use your blood to instead." Tartaros exclaimed with a glint in his eye. Quin couldn't help but taunt him for his ignorance,

"I am not Lycus! I am Quin, the son of a peasant. I have no royal blood running through my veins!" Tartaros was quick to counter his argument.

"The key does not come from the bloodline... It comes from the density of the magic within the blood - which you have an abundance of!" And with that Tartaros threw himself towards Quin swinging the sword overhead. Suddenly everything almost immediately came to a standstill and Quin's mind was abruptly dragged from his body.

Quin took a moment to walk around the vision before him and couldn't make sense of why this was happening, however he took full advantage of it and gave himself a moment to assess the situation. Then he was startled by a woman's voice

"My darling Lycus" she said with a soft and calming voice. Quin turned to find Gaia floating over

Ligeia outside the perimeter of the circle, glowing with a glorious white misty aura which was a strangely soothing and a comforting sight to behold.

"Mother?" Quin stated, rather surprised to see her.

"You have walked the path of an unthinkable ordeal and experienced torments no mortal should ever endure. Yet here you are at the end. An end which was unforeseen even by myself" she explained sadly, looking upon him with great pride.

"Have you come to take me away?" Quin asked. But Gaia's expression dropped, saddened to hear such words leave his lips,

"You are not within my reach here. This sacrificial stone is the gateway to the underworld; a place where I cannot reach. If you die here, you will be dragged into the underworld for all eternity. Therefore you must not give up hope, you must stay strong just a little longer to win this battle!" She explained, with a hint of desperation in her voice. He paused for a moment and looked over to where Ligeia lay and realised he was not ready to die until he had at least saved her.

"Can you save Ligeia?" He asked hopefully.

"I cannot interfere with the fate of others. My

position is to welcome those who have already met their fate and congratulate them on leading a full and prosperous life. Her fate is in your hands now Lycus. If you truly wish for her to live, you must make your own sacrifices and do what you feel is necessary." She explained. Quin now knew what must be done and his only concern was to defeat Tartaros, for her sake.

"But how can I beat him? He is more powerful than anyone, I dare say even more powerful than you!" Gaia smiled sweetly and glided gently towards the edge of the platform and held out her hand to Quin. He walked towards her and stepped off the platform, placing his hand in hers. She gracefully leant in and kissed him on his head before holding him in her warm embrace.

"You are stronger than you know. All you need do is become one with the power within you. Open your mind and let go of all that you think you know, trust in your instincts and allow the elements to guide you. Believe in your power." With that she slowly released Quin and began to float away, gradually dispersing into orbs of light that gently flickered and vanished. The area became brighter and brighter as Quin's mind returned to his body. Gaia's last gift to Quin was to allow him a few more moments to react as she allowed time to slowly return back to its normal flow.

Quin took the extra moments to listen to the elements and much to his surprise his head was suddenly filled with the voices of the elements all speaking to him at once. However, one voice spoke above the rest. Transforming into the winds, he magically split himself in two and flew around either side of Tartaros, joining back together behind him. Reaven's Sword clashed on the ground where Quin formerly stood and Tartaros growled in frustration as he swung the sword round and landed an almighty blow to Quin's arm. Tartaros was astonished to witness Quin's potential power as his arm had immediately transformed into solid rock. Even Quin was surprised and recalled the sensation he was now feeling being identical to his encounter with the Centaur's on top of the Mountain. His intuition had now taken over and he had become one with his magic. He felt like he was dreaming, watching his actions from behind his own eyes. He now knew that this was his true calling and this was who he was destined to become. Allowing his mind to slip into this state of concentration, he was able to cast away his fear and let the magic take control. Lifting his other hand, Quin thrust it forward and cast a scorching ball of fire into Tartaros' face forcing him to stumble backwards clawing at the burns and screeching in pain. He had by now discovered that the seemingly weak human before him appeared to have retained many of his Telchine powers. Tartaros furiously released his smouldering face, which had partially melted, crying tears of blood. However this was the least of his worries as he now faced a horrifying revelation. Quin's eyes regained their empowered red glow and stared at him menacingly.

"The Chaos!?" Tartaros proclaimed, cryptically.

By now it was obvious that Quin would not be satisfied until Tartaros was expelled from Ragnar's corpse and sent back to the underworld. He began to focus on the stone magic in his arm and slowly pushed it all down into his palm, eventually forming a large rock which he promptly cast hurtling at Tartaros with great speed. The rock smashed into Tartaros with a loud thump followed by the sound of crunching bones as the rock caved his chest inwards and catapulted him out of the circle, which added to his pain and suffering as he desperately clawing his way back, all the while his skin was fizzing and melting.

Tartaros picked himself up and promptly used his magic to heal his collapsed chest and promptly went berserk, flinging the blade around manically at Quin as he ducked and dodged around, avoiding each vain attempt. After a few moments of this Quin figured that the most effective way to defeat Tartaros was to simply stand outside the circle and use his magic to finish him off. However, as he attempted to leave the platform he bashed into some kind of invisible wall that lay around the perimeter. Quin stumbled back and surmised that, for whatever reason he was no longer able to leave. He knew he had no time to think about it as Tartaros swooped in to strike at him again, but he quickly avoided the attack by rolling to one side. Tartaros stopped for a moment simply to taunt him for being unable to leave the platform.

"All magic comes at a cost Lycus! That which makes you most powerful will ultimately be your undoing!" Quin aggressively flung out his hand, casting a powerful gust of air towards Tartaros, which caught him off balance and sent him stumbling backwards for a few moments before he shielded his face with both arms. Quin realised that he would need some kind of weapon if he wanted to defend himself effectively.

He focused his magic on Reaven's Sword, summoning forth the power of the blade creating a rapid heatwave from within the hilt, almost to melting point which scolded

Tartaros' hand, forcing him to once again roar out in pain. However, rather than dropping the sword, he tactically threw it outside of the circle where he knew Quin could not get to it.

Tartaros held his ground and smiled smugly as he swapped the dagger to his other hand and threw his arm up to the sky, roaring loudly in an attempt to intimidate Quin. But he was not intimidated in the slightest and took this opportunity to strike back at Tartaros. He glared into Tartaros' eyes as he raised his hand to the sky and summoned a devastatingly powerful lightning bolt down from the enchanted clouds above, which struck the blade. The sheer power of the bolt flowed freely through Tartaros' body, causing him to jolt and spasm uncontrollably as the spell appeared to be cooking him from the inside out. Although, after only a few moments Tartaros countered this magic by blocking the spell which consequently created an explosive wave that cast both of them hurting backwards to opposite sides of the platform.

Tartaros had now sustained more than one fatal wound, but Quin was also drained of energy and the fall from the blast had caused him to bash his face on the hard floor. His nose began to bleed heavily. He now knew that if he continued to stretch the use of his magic he would most certainly perish. Tartaros, on the other hand, had accepted that he could not win and death was inevitable unless he could finish the ritual to empower and release himself, as the scorched and tattered remains of Ragnar's body vastly deteriorated. However he took solace in the knowledge that at the very least he could kill Quin and drag his soul into the underworld, where he could torture him for eternity, all he had to do was simply hold on a little longer.

Tartaros dragged himself to his feet and stormed over to Quin, who still lay on the ground struggling to move. He grabbed him by his throat and threw him across the ground to other side of platform. Quin was emphatically aware that with every passing moment, more of his blood dripped out over the Circle, which glowed more vibrantly with every drop and thus providing Tartaros with more power to heal his wounds. He attempted to pick himself up while all the time soaking up his blood with his clothing. But was barely able to blink before Tartaros approached and kicked him in the chest, cracking his ribs.

Quin lay on the ground, curled up to protect himself, and took a moment to look up at Ligeia, who had been crawling towards him dragging her fin behind her. She gazed sorrowfully into his eyes after being forced to watch the whole ordeal, while Tartaros, who had begun to enjoy pummelling him, continued to kick and stamp on his weakening body,

"Quin, you must get up and fight back." Ligeia pleaded as Tartaros kicked him again. But Quin simply gazed back at her with defeat in his eyes "Please Quin, I need you…" she begged, as Quin slowly began to shut his eyes. "I- I love you!" She whispered, whilst sobbing for him.

Strangely, it was witnessing Ligeia's desperation and the realisation that he was failing her which filled him with a new level of rage that made him remember his vow. Even if it ultimately meant death for himself, it was a sacrifice he was always willingly make in memory of Asha, his fallen friends and family, and most importantly the continued survival of Ligeia.

Quin roared in a blind rage and without care of the consequences of the danger of further using his magic. He transformed his fist into rock and swung it at Tartaros with all his strength. As it collided with his leg, it seemingly flowed through him like he was made of mere water. With an anguishing crunch, Quin's fist shattered Tartaros' bones causing shards of it to burst through his flesh. Quin picked himself up and stared ferociously at Tartaros as he squirmed around on the ground before him, screaming and clutching at the very bones that had splintered through his shin, but that wasn't enough to quench Quin's thirst for revenge. He allowed the hatred to consume him and lost all sight of benevolence and mercy, just as Lycus had. With the soul intent of blithely taking a life, he lunged down and grabbed Tartaros' entire head within his giant rocky fist and lifted him effortlessly off the ground. Dragged him over to the centre of the room, he held him up in the air, and nefariously took pleasure in watching Tartaros flap around like a fish on a rod. His muffled screams reverberated into the stone fist grasped tightly around his skull. The overwhelming lust to seal his act of revenge was far too great for Quin to ignore. In the name of everyone he had lost and had been dragged into the Underworld after meeting an unjust death, He could now gain a glimmer of justice and take a single step closer to completing his goal, but more than that, he would give Tartaros plenty to think about in the underworld, for all eternity.

"I banish you from these lands! Know this; if you ever discover another way to return, you had better destroy it, for I shall be waiting for you, always!" Quin threatened, and with that said he began to clench his fist tighter and tighter around Tartaros' skull. His hysterical screams satisfying Quin's lust, which all came to a final climax as his skull caved in and squished between his rocky fingers like a hand full of grapes.

He then promptly plunged the body down to the ground with all his strength. As his fist collided with the ground, the sheer force cracked the Ceremonial Circle into fragments. The soul of Tartaros was expelled from Ragnar's battered corpse, screaming and clawing at the ground as he was sucked back into the Underworld through the cracked stone, ironically by his own magic. But before he vanished into the ground he threw his hand forth and released a bolt of dark matter, which flew past Quin and out of the ruins, quickly vanishing out of sight.

"You will not leave this Island alive; your soul will be mine!" His voice echoed.

The dark matter ignited in the distance and created a blast that made the entire island tremble, which disturbed the fragile wall above Ligeia forcing it to crack and collapse overhead. Quin promptly transformed into the winds and flew over, and moved her out of harm's way, just before it came crashed to the ground, and consequently covered the Ceremonial Circle, never be tampered with again. Debilitated from his long and heinous adventure, Quin fell to his knees and stared off into space as the rain slowed and eventually stopped, the clouds above dispersed allowing the sun to shine through and illuminated the spot where Ligeia now lay completely still and seemingly lifeless.

Rushing through the ruined city with Ligeia in his arms, Quin desperately headed towards the ocean. She was slumped in his arms barely breathing, leaving him with no alternative but to struggle onwards. Having next to no strength left after the battle with Tartaros, he couldn't even muster enough energy to use his magic to aid them.

Forced to dodge and weave around the rubble still falling in his path, every step counted, yet Quin began to lose hope for Ligeia's survival as the ocean felt to be moving further and further away as his remaining stamina evaporated.

Finally reaching the top of Pit of Despair, Quin gazed out at the ocean, which lay no more than fifty paces away. But it may as well have been fifty miles away. His knees buckled beneath him and he fell to the floor, physically unable to go any further.

Gently laying her head down on the ground, he could only look at her peaceful face,

"I am sorry that I got you involved in this Ligeia" he sobbed as she lay gasping for air, suffocating before his eyes. However, it appeared that his troubles were far from over as the ground began to vibrate and the sound of stomping feet surrounded the area. Turning back to see what was happening Quin looked in horror as he realised that Ragnar's enchantment wasn't a complete failure and Tartaros' dark matter was obviously the catalyst it needed. An army of citizens and soldiers, once buried beneath the ground, now arose from their inappropriately named 'Eternal Rest', charging towards them from all directions. Quin realised now that if either of them were to die on that island, they would suffer a fate far worse than death. Instead they would be cursed to wander mindlessly around the island for all eternity as the undead. However as the hordes drew closer, Quin felt something snap inside, as if a slumbering power had awoken just in time to make itself known. Having no control over this power Quin gazed at himself in amazement as his entire body began to glow a white aura which quickly grew and extended further and further out of him. As the undead entered the aura they instantaneously turned to dust and their souls were consumed by the power and fed into Quin, charging him with incredible amounts of power. However it was not long before the power became too much for Quin's mortal body to handle and as it swelled inside him he felt like he was about to burst. Sure enough, there was a sudden silence as Quin fell into a brief trance which allowed him to expel the power he held.

The following explosion of aura pulsed out of him and engulfed the entire island, blasting the undead to dust, expelling them from the land forever. After a few moments the power was gone, although Quin could still feel its presence within him and presumed that this dormant power needed extreme circumstances before it would awaken. However, without the ability to control the power it gave him, he was now back to where he started. Left without any strength, sitting over Ligeia's pale skinned body, watching her die!

With no-one around to help him now, Quin looked down into the Pit of Despair for a moment before realising that there was still one last thing he could do. His only chance of saving her, was to ask for help. He turned his head to the skies,

"I know you can hear me, I am certain you have taken great pleasure in witnessing my undoing! Well now I call upon you to show yourself, come and claim your prize. You have won… Fate!" he yelled, and within the blink of an eye the Black Cloud burst from the pit of despair and formed into a human silhouette before him, waiting to be begged for mercy. "Save her!" Quin pleaded, glancing out the corner of his eye, unwilling to look directly at the monster before him, as a matter of pride. Although he was well aware of the price he would have to pay for a favour, he realised it was Ligeia's only chance of survival and now for the first time Quin saw his fate as his only hope.

"It is you that shall determine her fate Telchine! Why would you have me interfere? Have you not caused enough pain and destruction by selfishly eluding your own fate?" It said, speaking out for the first time, his voice scratchy and ethereal.

"I will do whatever you ask, give you anything you desire, just please save her!" Quin bartered. Pausing for a moment, Fate appeared to ponder all that he could ask of Quin and eventually made his offer,

"I cannot help her, but I can give you the strength required to get her back to the ocean. Her fate must remain in your hands!" He explained. "For this I require just one thing…" It said, as Quin held onto Ligeia's hand, watching her slipping away. Unwilling to waste another moment making deals he hurried the process along,

"Name it!" He barked, no longer concerned with the consequences of his actions now that may drastically alter his future.

"When I am ready, you will owe me a single favour and whenever that is, you will do whatever I ask of you!"

of course, Quin realised this could be anything, even death itself, yet he knew he had no other choice "Do we have an accord?" it asked, offering out its hand to bind the deal with a hand shake. Quin, reluctantly clasped fate's hand and was instantly blessed with the strength he needed to carry Ligeia back to the ocean. However, with the joining of hands; Quin had all but sealed his fate. With that, Fate burst back into a mass of black smoke and withdrew back into the Pit of Despair.

Quin didn't waste a moment in taking Ligeia back into his arms and ran for the ocean, sparing no effort. As he arrived at the shore, he was unwilling to leave anything to chance and continued to run deeper and deeper until the backward force of the waves caused him to topple forward, dropping Ligeia beneath the water. Quin staggered back to his feet and, panic-stricken, searched for Ligeia, calling out her name. It was not long before he spotted her on the seabed and noticed that she remained motionless and seemingly without any breath. Fearing the worst he dived into the water and bought her up to the surface.

Her eyes were shut and it appeared she was not breathing as Quin placed his ear to her chest and listened for signs of a heartbeat which could be heard, but it was getting fainter as her life ebbed away. He paused for a moment to think that perhaps this was all just another plot; after all it was quite possible that Glaucus had previously perished and therefore the ocean's touch would have only served to kill Ligeia too.

"Did you know? Was this your plan all along?" Quin yelled to the sky, as if Fate was listening and watching his vain attempt to save her. "You used my feelings for her to force my hand! You deceived me for your own personal gain?" He continued "I would like to say I am surprised, but I am not… Well not this day, I will never give in to you! If she dies then our deal is annulled. Do you hear me?" He yelled, looking to the sky. Mustering the remnants of energy he had left, he used his magic to bless the water with healing magic. But to no avail. Ligeia remained still and without breath. He gently began to shake her by the shoulders, the haunting truth that she was gone was too much for him to handle and a single tear rolled down his cheek as he begged her to come back to him. After a moment of gazing at her face, Quin's heart began to pound in his chest as emotions erupted inside him

"Ligeia listen to me. You cannot die now, we made it!" He whispered, gently stroking her silky hair "We won Ligeia! So you see that is why you cannot die; for if you die… we have lost. No, I have lost! Lost everything" he sobbed into her shoulder as she lay still as if sleeping peacefully, "This journey Ligeia - I could not have done it without you. Do you not see? Through it all, there was one consistency that kept me strong. The strength to defeat anything, even Tartaros, but without it - without *you* – I have lost that strength." Quin explained to Ligeia as she remained lifeless in his arms. He leant in to whisper in her ear "I love you too!" Preparing to say his final good-byes. He trembled as he kissed her lips. He then gazed out to the ocean ahead and released her from his arms, pining for her as she gently drifted away. "Good-bye Ligeia and thank you." He sobbed as he turned and walked back to shore.

Reaching the sandy beach, he stood and gazed over the island before him, clearly in shock as he slumped to his knees and burst into floods of tears, running his fingers deep into the soggy sand, grabbing piles at a time and bashing at the shore with each fistful. He placed his face into his sand covered hands and lay his head down, beside himself with grief. He didn't have any idea of what he should do next; the realisation that his life no longer had any direction without Ligeia and Ragnar to guide him. So he decided to simply lie on the beach until the tide came in to sweep him away, just as it had with Ligeia. He rolled over onto his back and stared at the sky, watching the seagulls swooping overhead, with their loud cackles, as they did when he first arrived on the Island. He could swear that they were calling out his name, over and over again. He listened closely but as he sat up and scanned the area, no-one was there.

Suddenly he noticed something emerging out of the ocean. His heart skipped in his chest and within moments his jaw quite literally dropped in amazement as Ligeia slowly rose to the surface. Jumping to his feet, he giddily laughed and rushed into the ocean to swim out to her. Upon reaching her he couldn't help but throw his arms around her to hold her close to his body in a joyous embrace.

"Do not ever scare me like that again, Siren!" Quin exclaimed, relieved that she was alive.

"I did not realise fear was a Telchine trait - Lycus!" she replied mockingly, as she released him and gazed proudly into his eyes, while bowing her head as a mark of respect. Quin gazed back at her and gently lifting her chin with his hand and moved in to kiss her. But before their lips met there was a call in the distance. Glancing over Ligeia's shoulder, Quin could see a man further out to sea waving at them.

Ligeia's face dropped as the revelation struck her; that she was also alive while in the ocean; which meant that

Glaucus was alive. A little disappointed, she turned to her Siren mate and felt her heart sink as she knew what she had to do.

"I presume this is good-bye then!" Quin uttered sadly, accepting the reality that Ligeia would never be able to return to land again and therefore would have no choice but to return to the ocean depths with Glaucus. Smiling sweetly, she laughed, yet with great sadness in her voice, she replied

"It is never good-bye. We will see each other again someday; I know it in my heart." Taking his hand, she placed it on her chest so that he may feel it beating for him, revealing her true feelings for him. Gently pulling his hand away Quin looked Ligeia in the eyes and spoke honestly,

"We are of different worlds Ligeia, you cannot step onto the lands and I cannot breathe within the water." Reaching into the water Ligeia took the enchanted lock of hair from her tattered dress pocket and handed it to Quin, pressing it into his palm and closing his fist around it.

"As long as I live, its magic will work and you will always be able to find me." She explained "The magic calls to me. That is how I found you before. I will always answer its call." She promised, even though she knew that things would never be the same between them. Quin had to question Ligeia's loyalty

"And Glaucus?" He asked uncomfortably. Turning her head to gaze at Glaucus, who waited patiently for her to return, she explained "Siren mates share everything, but if Glaucus ever discovered my feelings for you, his jealousy for our love would enrage him. I will inform him of all that we have been through together but he will never understand our - feelings!" Pausing for a moment, she suddenly felt that she had said too much and was only making the situation worse, so quickly changed the subject "He would want me to extend his deepest gratitude to you for saving my life, but would certainly try to kill you for being a Telchine."

"Well at the very least, we are now even!" Quin replied, still forcing a smile, as she began to swim back to join Glaucus. Both were unwilling to turn away until they were completely out of sight and as Quin slowly drifted back to shore, Ligeia called out

"When you have prepared, call upon the Siren and together we will fight against the enemies of Gaia." With that Ligeia sank beneath the waves and reunited herself with Glaucus and they held each other in a loving embrace, before they journeyed back to the Sirens home. She glanced back one last time with sorrow clearly visible on her face as she was now left with no choice but to turn away and return home with her Siren mate.

Quin stepped back onto the sandy shore and looked around at the land as it continued to crumble and reflected on his time with Ligeia and realised that for the first time since his journey began he had fond memories to hold in his heart. Now left with nothing but endless amounts of time, Quin began to question his direction:

"After this whole ordeal, I have been taken further away from destroying Ifrit than I was back in Alexandria. The motivation that kept me going, which I held closely in my heart, was simply to be reunited with Asha. Only now I realise that this journey was never about finding her. For I have now learned that love can be found in the strangest of situations. But can come and go just as easily. Was all this simply a journey to discover myself?

Granted, I absconded fate and declared it as my darkest enemy. But, perhaps I never really eluded it at all, and in some twisted way, it was in control and guiding me from the beginning, all the way to this point right now, so that I might learn the importance of my past, and to guide me towards my fated future.

I now know all too well that, until I discover the real truth of my life as Lycus, I shall never have the knowledge to create a safe and sustainable world for the kin of Gaia. However, I am no longer a Telchine, that much is certain, and as a human I will age, I will become old and feeble. I will wither and I will inevitably die.

So then, I have to wonder if this mortal life is sufficient to uncover the whole story of my past as a Telchine; a life that may have spanned over many generations. Perhaps I will be simply wasting the gift of this second chance of life, by dwelling on the actions of the person I once was. But in order to correct the injustice done to the world, I must first understand the wrongs that were done to begin with.

While Ifrit lives, the people of Gaia will suffer and die at his hand. Therefore, I cannot continue on the path that led me here in the hope that certain events will trigger another shrouded memory to show me the way.

I know with all certainty, I must find the answers to the many questions that have plagued my mind since the day I stumbled into the Chamber of Memories.

'Who am I? Why was I reborn? Where are the other Telchines? And why have they not stopped Ifrit?'

I feel, with every fibre of my being, that the

discovery of this knowledge will also provide the solution to destroying Ifrit. Like my father once asked of me.

I will lead the Condemned Army and destroy Ifrit and the Telchines' and nothing will get in my way!

From this moment forth, I make my own fate. For Fate is my darkest enemy!

12219456R00220

Printed in Great Britain
by Amazon.co.uk, Ltd.,
Marston Gate.